TRICK OR HOMICIDE

More firecr███ ███ ███ ███ Tres jumped. An█ ███ ███ ███ ███ ur-gently, "To█ ███ ███ ███ ███ the way. I can't ███ ███ ███.

"What dun███ ███ ███.

"The Hallo███ ███ ███y you guys set up in the bathroom to scare people. It's pretty neat," she said to me, grinning. "That guy almost looks real. And he really looks dead."

I closed my eyes tightly, wishing that every-thing—the cafe, Halloween, Munchkin cos-tumes, and especially dead old men lying on the bathroom floor—would disappear.

"We're having some fun now," Del said, blowing smoke out of the corner of her mouth.

....

"Set in South Dakota's equivalent to Lake Woebegon, Taylor's characters are hip, sexy and sometimes overwhelmed by life. Gallop along with their smalltown doings and you'll fall in love with Delphi, South Dakota, as well as Tory Bauer."
Mystery Times

Other Tory Bauer Mysteries by
Kathleen Taylor
from Avon Twilight

FUNERAL FOOD
THE HOTEL SOUTH DAKOTA
SEX AND SALMONELLA

KATHLEEN TAYLOR

MOURNING SHIFT

A TORY BAUER MYSTERY

AVON
TWILIGHT

AVON BOOKS, INC.
1350 Avenue of the Americas
New York, New York 10019

Copyright © 1998 by Kathleen Taylor
Published by arrangement with the author
Visit our website at **http://www.AvonBooks.com/Twilight**
Library of Congress Catalog Card Number: 98-92773
ISBN: 0-380-79943-X

First Avon Twilight Printing: October 1998

AVON TWILIGHT TRADEMARK REG. U.S. PAT. OFF. AND IN OTHER COUN-
TRIES, MARCA REGISTRADA, HECHO EN U.S.A.

Printed in the U.S.A.

WCD 10 9 8 7 6 5 4 3

When I first started writing fiction, I had the complete and total support of my friends and family. But it was Jody Weisflock, after having read my half-completed first manuscript, who asked the most wonderful question a new writer can hear: Where's the rest of the damn book?

Jody, this one is for you.

ACKNOWLEDGMENTS

I dimly remember writing three entire novels before discovering the Internet. Indeed, a few of the original cheerleading crew (including my mom, Diane, and Dave) are still poor WWW-less creatures. But everyone else is online. My agent, my editor, Shirley, Melanie, Carole, Jerry, Curtis, Matthew, Genevieve, Jane, Kris, Lorah, and Betty are all there at the end of the *send* button. They are all charged with the unenviable burden of keeping me on-task and relatively functional, for which they have my undying gratitude.

My wonderful husband of twenty-seven years, whose enduring support is accessible without a modem, has gently suggested that I might write faster without the cyber distraction of DorothyL, James Taylor Online, The Republic of Pemberley, and Sue's Barbie Chat, but I have no intention of putting his thesis to a test.

Prologue

No one has ever accused me of being a physicist. Or a philosopher. I'm just an overweight, middle-aged, widowed waitress, with time on my hands and a library across the street from my trailer house.

Like everyone else, I read the Stephen Hawking book that explained the origins of the universe in terms that even a simple layman could grasp. Or at least I tried to. Unfortunately it took very few pages to realize that Dr. Hawking's generic layman was not the kind of simpleton who never quite understood the ending of *2001: A Space Odyssey*.

Still, I plowed through the whole book, hoping, but failing, to catch the underlying sense, the basic theory.

That happens to me a lot.

Though I can usually spot the obvious, especially when it blows up in my face, the flash of insight needed to go beneath the surface, to tie the threads together, to see what has been in plain sight all along, is an increasingly rare phenomenon.

The commotion, sadness, and hard-won insights of the last few days have reminded me that the only portion of Dr. Hawking's book I truly understood was the theory that all the components needed to form the universe were present right from the beginning. They just needed the proper combination and concentration to reach critical mass. To set off an explosion.

It has belatedly occurred to me that when your universe revolves around what happens in and around Delphi, South Dakota, the Big Bang Theory can, with very little moderation, apply equally as well to murder.

1

·····························

Day Shift of the Living Dead

SATURDAY OCTOBER 31, EARLY AFTERNOON

I hate Halloween.

Not because November signals the last gasp of autumn. In northeastern South Dakota, we know better than to expect fall to be any more than a brief transition between the only seasons with any clout. Our five-day stretch of glorious yellow foliage and fluffy white clouds has been and gone, and we are already raking yards full of sodden brown leaves into large, wet piles under a slate-gray sky.

I don't hate Halloween because harvest is over and bored farmers spend most of their afternoons drinking coffee and taking up table space, undertipping overworked waitresses.

Or because winter is surely on its way—I am perhaps the only person in the state who gratefully observes the shortening of the days, and welcomes the snow and cold.

I hate Halloween because several years ago, the Delphi chamber of commerce, with no evidence to support the notion, decided that unbridled juvenile enthusiasm would be minimized if our collective youth were kept so busy that they would have little time, and no energy, for pumpkin smashing, egg throwing, or setting fire to the few remaining outhouses.

Pursuant to that end, the school did its best to keep the youth of our community busy during the evening. That left the businesses and churches to provide a full day of entertainment replete with treats, games, and the opportunity to decide which local establishment best represented this year's theme, "Let's Go to the Movies!"

It's hard to tell what the confusion level in the cafe would have been without these civic diversions. But in addition to our regular Saturday crowd, we had been deluged with young costumed trick-or-treaters, and older folks oohing and aahing at the little ones.

The older adolescents, at whom this concerted effort was aimed, ignored us completely and spent most of the day tearing around the streets of Delphi, honking and throwing leftover Fourth of July firecrackers at one another.

And those teenagers not yet old enough to drive let their fingers do the walking. We'd already fielded giggling telephone requests to page "Harry Butz" and "Al Coholic."

But we'd put on our costumes and makeup in order to divert juvenile delinquency. And by damn, we were gonna see it through. At least until the end of the shift.

"I feel like an idiot," I said for the fortieth time, trying to readjust my shorts and striped tights discreetly while leaning against the stainless-steel counter that divided the kitchen from the cafe. I frowned down at the clunky, borrowed oxfords I was wearing, cursing the day that Aphrodite Ferguson joined the chamber of commerce.

"Why?" Rhonda Saunders asked, flipping her newly (and we hoped temporarily) dyed brown braids over her shoulder. Wearing a blue-and-white gingham dress, she cheerfully distributed candy from a napkin-draped wicker basket looped over one arm, to several noisy, costumed children who demanded treats just inside the cafe doorway. "You look adorable, Tory. What's wrong with that?"

"At least *she* can move." Del smoothed down her tight floor-length black dress. Even with a pointy hat, green face, and applied warts, Del managed to look more like Elvira than the Wicked Witch of Anywhere.

We stood, cafe bustling behind us, hungry patrons impatient, waiting for Aphrodite to light another generic cigarette and dish up our noon specials.

We waited awhile.

Norman Oberle, the bread man, was in the kitchen, finishing up a nonregulation Saturday delivery of buns and loaves. Smiling, he said something low, and then with a courtly flourish, handed Aphrodite an invoice, which she accepted with a snort that sounded very much like a giggle.

Del and I looked at each other. Short, taciturn, solitary, and well past a certain age, the owner of the Delphi Cafe rarely smiled. And she never giggled.

Norman said something else, and Aphrodite laughed out loud.

"What's going on in there?" Rhonda whispered, peeking over our shoulders. "It's not Norman's day to be here."

No one besides Del and I had witnessed the exchange between Norman and Aphrodite, since the kitchen was only partially visible from the main portion of the cafe.

I'd heard rumors that Norman's company was cutting back on routes and forcing retirement on some of the drivers. Perhaps there was a financial reason behind his newly found enthusiasm for weekend work.

"Well, he lives in town here, and the cafe is handy," Rhonda said, doubtfully eyeing the pair. "Maybe he's just doing Aphrodite a favor."

"He's doing her a favor all right," Del whispered back with a wicked grin. "Looks like Saturday is now Aphrodite's day to get bread."

Aphrodite, usually engrossed in her cooking chores, rarely looked up or out. She was not aware that we were watching her and Norman.

Del cleared her throat loudly.

Aphrodite jumped and blushed. Quickly she dished up our orders and slid them out, avoiding eye contact.

Del raised an eyebrow.

"Isn't she, like, sorta old for the boyfriend stuff?" Rhonda, a college freshman who worked at the cafe when not in school, and who was barely twenty, asked under her breath.

"No such thing," Del declared. A little more than double Rhonda's age, my late husband's first cousin, Delphine Bauer, had never been too young. And she would more than likely never be too old.

A year younger than Del myself, but feeling decades older, I picked up my two orders and stepped carefully around the newest crop of goblins, to a window booth along the south wall, and set one of the specials in front of a dapper little out-of-towner, who grimaced uncertainly at his Tomato Ghoul-ash, Cheese Sand-Witch, and Boo-Berry Cobbler.

The other order went to a fidgety Ron Adler, owner of Adler's Garage. Small and trim, with an undershot jaw, he had a facial tic that caused him to blink wildly every third word, especially when Del was in the vicinity. It was in high gear today. But I suspected the fidgets were actually triggered by pasty makeup, a disheveled gray wig, and a full-length blue lab coat.

I didn't know if he was aiming for Moses or Bill Nye the Science Guy, but considering the movie theme, I guessed the former.

"Tough sermon on the Mount?" I asked him.

"Huh?" Ron frowned down at his plate, blinking as Del slunk by. "No, no. We're supposed to be The Three Stooges. I'm Larry."

"With gray hair?" I asked.

"Those were black-and-white movies." Ron blinked patiently. "Who'd know if they were all gray?"

"Besides, he doesn't have to wear a wig to look like a Stooge," Del, who was eavesdropping, said to the ceiling.

The very married Ron's long-term unrequited crush on Del had been recently "requited," to the intense and opposite dissatisfaction of both. They'd discovered that getting what they wanted wasn't the same as getting what they'd expected, and neither was happy about it. If there had been any other establishment in Delphi that served food, Ron would have avoided the cafe completely.

As it was, he came in only reluctantly. During his visits, he and Del sniped at each other, and frequently took their embarrassment, guilt, and general displeasure out on the rest of us.

"I can see that Rhonda is Dorothy. And Del is *always* a witch. But what in the hell are you supposed to be?" He blinked at me.

"I represent the Lollipop Guild," I said crabbily, counting the minutes until two when I could go home. "And if you even hint that I'm too big to be a Munchkin, I'll whack you on the head with my sucker."

I may have been a rounder than average Munchkin, but I was a Munchkin with an attitude. Or more likely PMS. Either way, after nearly eight hours spent wearing too-tight suspendered shorts and a big felt beanie, not to mention the requisite scowl, I was in no mood to be trifled with. Ron, lucky for him, sensed this.

"So what kind of get-up is Stu wearing?" he asked, changing the subject.

"Yeah, we haven't seen him yet today," Rhonda chimed in, refilling coffee cups here and there, tippy-tapping in her glittery red heels.

I did not need Rhonda to remind me. I was minutely aware of Stuart McKee's absence. Also his presence. Also his estranged wife, who was, for the moment anyway, living in her native Minnesota with their five-year-old son.

"He's not wearing a costume," I said quietly. Stu and I hadn't talked much lately, but that much I knew. "He drove to the state border this morning to meet Renee halfway, and bring Walton back for the weekend. The two of them were supposed to stop in for lunch.'' I shrugged. ''But maybe they ate at home, and then went hunting.''

''He's taking that little boy out with guns and every-thing?'' Rhonda asked, aghast. ''How terrible.''

''Nonsense,'' Del said. ''Walton's plenty old enough to go out in the field with his dad. Every boy in South Dakota has been hunting by the age of five.''

''Yeah,'' Ron said, and then realized he was agreeing with Del. He blinked down at his plate, and then jumped as another string of firecrackers went off somewhere out-side.

Whatever weekend activities Stu had planned with his young son, they evidently did not include checking in with me. Or spending time at the Feed and Seed Store that he ran with his own elderly father. The store's lo-cation, across the street from the cafe, made it relatively easy for me to keep track of him, and Stu's burgundy Chevy pickup had not been parked there all day.

''Miss?'' I heard from behind me. The Halloween Special in the booth next to Ron's said softly, ''Could you get me some more water?''

''Sure,'' I said, clomping over to the counter for a pitcher, wishing I'd opted for Auntie Em instead. She might have been old, but at least she wore sensible shoes.

The man sitting in the booth, now visibly pale, was sixty if he were a day, neat and balding, with his re-maining hair a uniform fringe of Grecian Formula Brown. As I refilled his glass, he shakily reached into a jacket pocket and pulled out a small metal tube, from which he removed a tiny white pill.

''Are you all right?'' I asked as he screwed the halves of the tube back together.

His skin was pasty and beads of sweat dotted his fore-head.

''I'll be fine in a minute,'' he said with a small smile, carefully placing the pill under his tongue. ''Could I trouble you for the key to the men's room?''

"It's unlocked," I said, pointing to the dingy room just off the entryway. "It's unisex, and not very fancy," I apologized.

"It'll be fine," he said, standing up slowly. "Thank you."

I watched him make his way to the bathroom, troubled.

"Is something wrong with that guy?" Ron asked. "He sure didn't look good."

I nodded in agreement, but had no time to chat, because a Zombie Girl Scout Troop, led by my pregnant cousin, Junior Deibert, came in and, unasked, serenaded us with Halloween carols. The girls were dressed in an imaginative mixture of standard uniforms, prosthetic limbs, artificial blood, and dangling eyeballs.

"I never knew there were so damn many ghost songs," Del bitched fifteen minutes later, trying to sidle past the singers, carrying a tray of dirty dishes overhead.

Me neither.

After gamely applauding a couple of numbers, Ron tried to work his way up to the till, first by going around, and then by gently pushing through the girls. But the warblers, including Junior's eight-year-old daughter, solidly stood their ground.

Rhonda came to our rescue by loudly announcing, in a brief respite between songs, that the serenaders had won first place in the Delphi Cafe singing contest. The prize was free milkshakes for all.

Amid the cheering, I shot a look at Aphrodite, who frowned on all freebies, and was astonished to see her cheerfully dancing by herself in the kitchen, oblivious to everything going on in the cafe.

"If I'd known a little flirting was gonna put her in such a good mood, I'da hired someone a long time ago," Del said to me, scooping ice cream into metal shake cups.

Even with me pouring, and both of us mixing assembly-line fashion, it took some time to whip up fifteen milkshakes.

The pay phone by the till rang, and Rhonda answered it. "Dick Hertz?" she said loudly to the cafe in general. "Phone call for Dick Hertz."

Finding no takers, she said something polite into the phone and hung up.

"You wanna tell her or should I?" Del asked me.

"I suppose someone should," I said, sighing.

Rhonda actually blushed when she realized that no one in the history of Delphi had *ever* been named Dick Hertz. Or I. P. Freely. Or Ben Dover.

In the interim, the mangled Scouts amused themselves by laughing, shouting, and blowing paper straw covers at one another, and generally causing a wild rumpus. Even Junior, who could silence the rowdiest youth with her patented Minister's Wife Glare, had her hands full with this group.

I set down a tray at a table full of bloodsoaked, dirty little girls. Like starving prisoners, they lunged for the tray, spilling two of the glasses.

"But I wanted strawberry," one of them whined.

"Jennifer got more than I did," another pointed out, using a large unattached finger as a pointer.

"I don't like malts. Can I have French fries instead?"

"Girls, *girls*," Junior said loudly and sharply over the complaints, "these ladies here were kind enough to provide treats for you. What do you say?"

"Thaaank youuuu," fifteen chastised ghouls chorused.

The phone rang again. Rhonda, who was closest, answered.

"Tory," Rhonda said with a grin, "it's for you."

"Can you take a message?" I asked over my shoulder, carrying another tray. I was in no mood to explain to a young prankster that our refrigerator was, indeed, running.

"Nope, he says it's important," Rhonda said out loud. *It's Stu*, she mouthed.

Rhonda took over efficiently where I left off, scooping and mixing and pouring. And placating disgruntled dismembered entertainers. I picked up the phone.

"Yeah?" I said warily.

Things between Stu and me had been strained lately, and I didn't know why. Perhaps it was because out of bed, we really didn't know each other. Perhaps it was the stress of being subjected to Delphi's microscopic observation whenever we were together (out of bed, that is).

Or perhaps it was because he was not only still married, but in the five months since his wife had packed up and left, he'd not yet shown an inclination to get unmarried.

On the other hand, since our relationship began more than six months ago with no promises or declarations, it was a little late for me to draw such fine distinctions.

"Listen, Tory," Stu said quickly, "I wanted to call you earlier, but this is the first chance I had to get to a phone."

Another group of kids came in clamoring for candy. Since Rhonda and Del were still busy with the milkshakes, I tucked the phone between my chin and shoulder, grabbed the bowl, and distributed handfuls of Tootsie Rolls into outstretched sacks, waiting for Stu to continue.

"I wanted to tell you," Stu said, "before . . ."

The noise level in the cafe ratcheted up another notch, and I missed the rest of his sentence. From across the cafe, one of the Girl Scouts shouted at the new batch of trick-or-treaters, "We got milkshakes. For free. Ha ha!"

"Yeah, losers," a few others sing-songed.

The kids at the door erupted into outraged protests over the inequality.

Phone still clenched to my shoulder, I turned to glare at the Girl Scouts. Junior was horrified at the public rudeness of her charges. Always delighted to see my prim and proper control-freak cousin thwarted, I squashed a grin and dished more candy into the sacks of the whiners.

Junior gained control, and the girls settled down again. Sort of.

We all jumped as, outside, more fireworks exploded. Cherry bombs this time, by the sound. Several of them.

"Listen, Stu," I said, barely registering the fact that he sounded deadly serious, "things are wild in here. Can I call you back when it's a little calmer?"

"No, I need to tell you this now," he said.

"Tory." A small hand pulled on my shorts. "*Tory?*"

"Just a second," I said into the phone. "What?" I asked sharply.

"I gotta go to the bathroom," my small cousin Tres Deibert said, dancing up and down in her zombie suit. "Really bad."

"Well go. You know where it is," I said to her. "Okay, Stu, what?"

Before he had a chance to say anything, Tres interrupted again. Insistently.

"Jesus, Tres, *what* is the matter?"

"The bathroom door is locked. It's been locked ever since we came in here." Even through the makeup and gore, I could see that Tres was near tears. "Please, open the door. Quick."

Blowing my cheeks out, wondering why I didn't have some low-stress job, like bank robber or brain surgeon, I put the phone down on the counter and knocked loudly on the bathroom door.

There was no answer.

"Anyone in there?" I called. And then knocked again.

There was no sound from inside.

"Last person in there must have left the knob locked," I said to Tres.

It happened occasionally. The bathroom doorknob was notoriously touchy. The locals knew to wiggle the handle before pulling the door shut. But the last guy I remembered going in there had been an out-of-towner, who'd probably locked the door without knowing it.

Del and Rhonda were still busy with Scouts and milk-shakes, and a few customers who were actually paying for their food. "I'll get the key from the kitchen," I said over my shoulder, in a hurry because Tres looked as though she were going to have an accident any second.

Aphrodite raised an eyebrow as I grabbed the key, which was attached to a section of yardstick hanging from the nail on the wall near the grill.

"Some idiot locked the door again," I said in explanation on the way out. "Here you go, kiddo," I said to Tres. I turned the key in the knob, and swung the door in with one hand and grabbed the phone with the other, ready to finish my conversation with Stu.

"It won't open all the way," Tres said, peeking around the door.

"Okay, Stu, I'm back," I said into the phone.

More firecrackers went off outside. Tres jumped. And then she turned to me and said urgently, "Tory, the dummy's on the floor in the way. I can't get the door open."

"What dummy?" I asked, frowning, phone and Stu both instantly forgotten.

"The Halloween dummy you guys set up in the bathroom to scare people." In her amusement, Tres forgot how badly she had to go. "It's pretty neat," she said to me, grinning. "That guy almost looks real. And he really looks dead."

2

....

Tory Bauer and the Terrible, Horrible, No Good, Very Bad Day

Though I haven't seen any definitive studies on the subject, I would venture to guess that a considerable percentage of South Dakota's citizenry is of the elderly persuasion. An accurate but unscientific poll could be taken just by walking the streets of Delphi and counting the gray heads (or the heads that would be gray if not for the help of Revlon and Clairol).

Not that an older population base is a bad thing in and of itself. As a group, our older folks can be counted on to be fairly neat, and seldom will you hear Lawrence Welk blasted from speakers in the back window of a 1973 Buick Riviera.

Actually, outside of a near-universal tendency to vote Republican, and to think that a 5 percent tip is sufficient (damn that Depression), the only real drawback to having so many old folks around is that they tend to die on you.

Though as a rule, they don't die on the bathroom floor at the cafe.

I shot a glance at Junior, who was still occupied with shushing the rest of the Scout troop . I didn't want to bring her into this until absolutely necessary. "Why don't you run over and use the bathroom at your grandpa's office?" I said quietly to Tres. Tres's grandfather, my Uncle Albert, worked from an independent insurance agency in the same block as the cafe. "I'm sure he'd get a kick out of your costume."

Tres hesitated, peering warily around the bathroom door, and then back at me. And then over her shoulder at her mother.

"Go," I said. "He'll be thrilled to see you."

Nature got the better of her curiosity. And her usual inability to think for herself when her mother was in the same room. She scooted out the door.

I caught Del's eye and motioned her over, and then remembered the dangling phone. And Stu.

"Are you still there?" I asked him.

"Yeah," he said quickly, but before he could continue, I interrupted him.

"Listen, we got a problem here. I have to go. I'll explain later." I rubbed my forehead and hung up the phone.

"Does Loverboy want you to babysit?" Del asked over my shoulder. Her minimal maternal instincts were overset by the task of raising her thirteen-year-old son, Presley. She was highly suspicious of anyone else's parental urges, and flat-out denied that Stu had any.

I closed my eyes tightly, wishing that everything— the cafe, Halloween, Munchkin costumes, and especially dead old men lying on the bathroom floor—would disappear.

"Take a peek." I tilted my head toward the bathroom, inhaling deeply.

"Oh shit," Del said quietly.

"No kidding," I said.

"Maybe he's not really dead," Del said hopefully.

"He's been in there for going on twenty minutes," I pointed out. "And he hasn't moved since I opened up the door."

So far no one in the noisy cafe had noticed our conference, but it was only a matter of time before Junior's radar registered this new blip.

"Any idea who he is?" Del asked, squinting at the body.

"Never saw him before. He sat alone, ordered a noon special, took a pill, and then locked himself in," I said.

And then he died, I thought.

"I suppose you better go in and check," Del said softly. "Just to make sure."

"*Me*? Why me?"

"Because you're the one with the dead body experience," she said, grimly.

"No, I'm the one with the bad luck and terrible timing," I muttered, kneeling down to look at the guy, hoping the button on the waistband of my shorts wouldn't pop.

I'm not an EMT. Or a forensic expert. But a careful pressure against both the wrist and the neck of the man revealed no pulse and a body temp that seemed to be falling rapidly. I shook my head at Del.

"What's up, guys?" Rhonda leaned over the till and asked.

"I believe we got us a situation here," Del said, explaining quietly.

"Shouldn't someone be doing CPR?" Rhonda asked, paling. "Shouldn't we call an ambulance? Shouldn't we do *something*?" Her voice rose with each question.

I stood up and sighed. "I think he's pretty well past help. But yes, we need to call an ambulance." I looked around the nearly full cafe. "And we need to clear out the kids, and anyone else we can get rid of quietly."

Things were going to get busy, and the fewer people we had gawking from inside the cafe, the better.

"I'll tell Aphrodite," Del said, with an automatic smile for the couple who came up to the till with their ticket. "Why don't you take care of these nice people, Rhonda?" she said, swinging the bathroom door closed again.

The couple smiled in response, unaware they'd shared their Boo-Berry Cobbler with the recently deceased.

"I'll deal with Junior," I said, with another sigh.

"*What*?" Junior asked sharply a minute later. "Are you sure?"

As near as we could calculate, Junior was just about five months' pregnant. To our collective annoyance, she'd pointedly refused to reveal her due date, or any other pertinent details which we felt we had a right to know, since her last visit to the maternity ward had resulted in triplets. Any other woman with four children (three of them only three years old), and God knows how many more on the way, would have spent her days with feet propped up on a cushion.

Not Junior. Pregnancy energized her. And sharpened her ambition to be Ruler of Delphi.

"As sure as we can be without an expert opinion," I answered.

She tried to push me aside. "Well I'd better check. I know CPR."

"So does Rhonda," I said softly. "So do I, as a matter of fact. But he was in there for at least twenty minutes before I had to unlock the door. For Tres."

Whatever complaining I do about Junior, and believe me, I do plenty, she's a genuinely overprotective mother. I knew that bringing Tres into the conversation would divert her from demanding that we allow her to perform useless CPR on our unfortunate patron.

"Tres?" Junior asked, looking around frantically. "Where is she?"

"I sent her over to your dad's. The rest of the troop should meet her outside. There's no need for you to allow these impressionable girls to be here when the ambulance arrives."

That was unfair—none of this was Junior's fault, and the girls would hear all the gory details sooner or later (most likely sooner). But we both knew that getting them quickly out of the cafe was a good idea. And I knew the combination of maternal instinct and community responsibility would override Junior's innate need to control every situation.

She closed her jaws with an annoyed snap, and then nodded. Any triumph I might have felt in getting rid of her was swallowed by the realization that the day, which had started out badly, was deteriorating rapidly.

I heard a mumbled one-syllable epithet. Aphrodite, cigarette in mouth, eyebrows furiously knit, trundled out of the kitchen wiping her hands on a dishtowel. With Del trailing behind, she opened the bathroom door and peered in and then jumped back, so startled that the cigarette fell from her mouth and rolled across the floor. She said something sharp that caused Del and Rhonda to exchange bewildered glances, turned on one heel and stalked back to the kitchen.

I gingerly picked up the rolling cigarette, trying not to touch either the end that was burning or the one caked with red lipstick. Not knowing what else to do, I carefully stubbed it out in the ashtray on the counter.

As Junior ushered the assorted ghouls out the door as quickly as any group of dismembered prepubescents could move, the phone rang again.

Del pointedly started picking up empty milkshake cups and damp, wadded napkins. Rhonda was ringing out another couple, so I answered the phone.

"I have a very important call for Peter Akin," a male voice purposefully deepened, though not enough to mask the undertone of giggle, said. "Do you have a Peter Akin?"

I could deal with dead bodies. Or I could deal with crank calls. But I apparently could not deal with both.

"No, I certainly don't," I said sharply. "But *you're* going to in about two seconds. We have Caller ID, you know."

I heard a gasp, and then a click, and then a dial tone. We should have thought of lying sooner.

"So what do we do now?" Rhonda asked, surveying the cafe, which had cleared out almost entirely.

"I suppose we better call the sheriff," I said, sighing, fishing in my pocket for a quarter. "Let the authorities take it from here."

I made the call, quietly and with as few embellishments as possible. The cafe, fortunately, was nearly empty. Dinner rush was over, the trick-or-treaters had got their fill. I'd evidently startled the prank callers into trying another number. Even the firecracker throwers had found another venue, or pasture, in which to practice their art.

I poured myself a Diet Coke and sat at the counter wearily, enjoying the brief quiet spell, waiting for the ambulance to drive the fifteen miles from Redfield.

Aphrodite slammed things around in the kitchen. She liked her days to run smoothly—with mediocre food going into the customers, and fair amounts of money coming back. Dead bodies on the premises messed up the cash flow.

Del sat on a stool beside me, lighting up a cigarette and inhaling deeply.

"We're having some fun now," she said, blowing smoke out of the corner of her mouth. "What do you think killed him?"

I shrugged. "Heart maybe. I think the little pills they put under their tongues are nitroglycerin tablets. I saw him do that just before he went into the bathroom."

Del tapped a long finger of ash into the tray. "You suppose he called for help or anything?"

I had thought of that myself. Or rather, I was trying not to think about a poor old man whose cries for help might have gone unheard because a troop of little girls was singing an off-key version of "Casper, the Friendly Ghost."

Rhonda was cleaning up the booths by the windows. "Oh look, there's Stu," she said excitedly. "And he's got his little boy with him. And . . ." Her voice trailed off.

She turned quickly, rolled the dirty dish trolley over by the swinging half-door that divided the kitchen from the cafe. "I'm going to load these into the dishwasher

while we have a free minute,'' she said nonchalantly,
with false cheer. ''Why don't you come and keep me
company, Tory?''

She stared hard at Del, flicked her eyes toward the
window, then back, and sharpened her stare even more.

''Tory needs to take a break, *doesn't* she?'' Rhonda
asked Del, abandoning the dish trolley and grabbing my
arm. ''In the *kitchen*.''

Del looked out the window, tightened her jaw, and
nodded grimly.

''Yup, in the kitchen with you,'' she said tonelessly,
grabbing my other arm.

I could hear the faint wailing of a siren in the distance.
The EMTs, who couldn't afford to take our assessment
of the condition of the man on the floor, had evidently
broken a land speed record to get to Delphi.

Del and Rhonda pulled. I resisted. They had seen
something outside the window that had upset them even
more than an unexpectedly dead body nearby. At least
part of my brain told me to play along, already certain
that this whole performance had to do with Stu. A small,
sensible interior voice assured me that whatever it was,
I really didn't want to know.

Unfortunately, I never listen to my sensible interior
voice.

The ambulance drove up front and braked sharply in
a spray of gravel. The uniformed attendants, a skinny
guy and a stocky woman, jumped out, instrument bags
in hand.

''In there.'' Del pointed at the bathroom door.

The EMTs knelt by the prone man, checking for a
pulse, listening for heartbeats, unrolling a blood pressure
cuff in swift, practiced motions.

Del and Rhonda, engrossed by this display of medical
efficiency, loosened their hold on my arms.

I pulled free just in time to look out the window and
see what Rhonda and Del had tried to keep me from
seeing.

I saw a street full of people gaping openmouthed at
the ambulance in front of the cafe.

A street full of people that included an uncomfortable-looking Stuart McKee.

And his costumed son.

And his smiling wife.

3

....

Be Careful What You Wish For

Even here in rural South Dakota, where glamorous jobs are few and far between, waitresses get no respect.

Neil Pascoe says it's because we have no servants to mistreat. He may have a point. The closest we come to hired help are harried day-care providers, and taciturn part-time house cleaners, who know perfectly well how to swab out a toilet without advice from anyone, especially the person writing the check.

And even *they* tend to snap at us if their toast is cold, or we top off a cup of regular with a decaf refill.

The general consensus is that no one who is not putting herself through school or temporarily filling time between other, better, opportunities, would voluntarily spend her days hauling bad food to owly patrons for minimum wage plus tips.

For the most part, that's true. Because I was a widow of little means and no formal education beyond high school, and was living in a town without an overweight middle-aged career track, waiting tables was pretty well

22

my only option—both before and after Nicky died.

That said, the job does have its benefits. It's steady, and, beyond constantly aching feet, not too taxing. The hours are regular, and I get unlimited access to the Diet Coke dispenser. Despite a lack of generous tippers, I make enough money to pay my portion of the rent on the trailer I share with Del and Presley. I have plenty of time to read and to browse in Neil's library, with sufficient leftover energy to carry on a dalliance with the local married seed and feed dealer.

And when things go wrong, as they did this morning, waitresses tend to close in around each other protectively, like a cocoon.

The ambulance had driven off silently, the consensus being that the still unidentified guy inside was, indeed, dead, though the diagnosis would not be official until a doctor declared him so. His seemed an inopportune but unsuspicious death, the kind of thing that would fuel talk for a few days, and then die down when the next juicy story circulated through Delphi's gossip machine.

We hadn't been told to close the cafe, so we were theoretically open, but so far no one had ventured in. Aphrodite was pale and agitated, wandering around the kitchen aimlessly, patting her red beehive, untying and retying her apron, rhythmically tapping a spatula on the empty grill.

She lit another cigarette and pushed through the half-door into the cafe.

"You're off now," she said to me.

"I know," I said, sitting dejectedly in a window booth, chin in hand, scuffing the toe of my oversize oxford, studiously not looking at the burgundy Chevy pickup parked across the street. I couldn't work up the ambition to walk the three blocks home.

"I need to go for a sec," she said, looking mostly at the floor. "Will you run the grill while I'm gone?"

I wasn't ready to venture out anyway—the notion of accidentally meeting Stu and his wife on the sidewalk, while wearing my Munchkin suit, was too much to bear. I opted for cowardice.

"Sure," I said tonelessly. Maybe I'd just set up a cot in the storage room and never leave the cafe again.

"You all right?" Aphrodite asked, squinting at me sternly.

"I'm fine," I said, making an effort to smile. "Go, do whatever you have to. We'll take care of everything."

She peered at me another minute, then nodded, grunted, left by the front door, and turned down the street on foot.

It was unusual for us to be alone in the cafe, but with Del and Rhonda to watch the tables, I could handle whatever rudimentary cooking was required in Aphrodite's absence.

In the meantime, I sat.

Rhonda slid into the booth opposite me. "I know what you're thinking," she said.

That would have been a good trick, since I had no real idea myself.

She talked, expertly rebraiding her temporarily dyed hair. "You're thinking that Stu must be some kind of skunk."

"No," said green-faced Del, who had perched herself on a table nearby. "She's thinking he's a real dickhead."

"I'm not thinking anything," I said, which was almost true.

Del snorted. "Well you oughta be."

"No she shouldn't," Rhonda said sharply to Del. "Stu tried to call, but things got weird. I'm sure he has a perfectly rational explanation for . . ." She hesitated, looking at me closely. ". . . whatever."

"Yeah." Del dug in a pocket for her lighter, lit one up, returned the lighter, and then continued. "The explanation is that he is cheating on his girlfriend by fucking his wife."

"You don't know that," Rhonda said sternly, though without conviction.

Considering that Stu had had little compunction about seeing me while his wife was still in residence, I didn't suppose that the opposite would bother his conscience all that much.

I had pegged Stu as a basically decent guy, and settled for whatever enjoyment I could find, content to let the infidelity fall where it may. It seemed that I was going to have to sort out my feelings in pretty short order.

That realization made me wish for the good old days when Stu and I were sneaking around. The complications would have been the same in either case, but at least we would have been out of the public eye.

I knew that Del and Rhonda were trying to help, but paying attention to their conversation was too difficult. I was mildly surprised at my own calm heart. If there were such a thing as numbing sadness, I was filled with it. They continued to argue about whether Stu were a dickhead and whether I were or should be, upset. I decided not to think about what Renee's sudden appearance meant.

Not thinking about it used up almost all my active brain function. I longed to transport myself home and deeply into the bottle of gin tucked away in an upper cupboard at the trailer, the better to continue not thinking.

Unfortunately, I was slated to help Neil chaperone the high school chem-free party, this year christened "The Night of the Disco Dead." Even more unfortunately, if the kids had to be "chem-free," so did the chaperones.

I had no choice but to stay sober.

So I longed, instead, for a diversion of my own, forgetting about the advantage of the devil we already knew.

While Del and Rhonda sorted out my feelings, a silver Lexus pulled up and parked in front of the cafe.

The driver's side door swung open and a handsome young man of about twenty-five with sleek brown hair, wearing a London Fog raincoat and a dissatisfied expression, stepped out. He stood squinting at the cafe, took one last puff on a cigarette, and tossed it to the ground.

The passenger door opened and a pair of white thigh-high go-go boots emerged. The boots were attached to a sturdy pair of long legs, that were, in turn, attached to a solidly built, not-entirely-young woman wearing a pair of hot pants and a matching silver-studded vest over a white ruffled shirt that barely contained a bosom of heroic proportion. Easily six feet tall, she added to her considerable height with another four inches of brassy blond upswept do that looked like a hair tumor spouting out of the top of her head.

The woman pointed excitedly at the cafe and said something to the young man, who only grimaced and squinted more.

"Guys," I said softly to Del and Rhonda. "I think we got company."

They paused to look out the window, jaws dropping.

"Jesus Christ," Del said, breathing sharply. "What in the hell is that?"

"I don't know, but I expect we'll find out real quick," I said, standing up.

4

....

Prince Albert in a Can

I suppose we should be grateful that trendoids from either coast have yet to *discover* South Dakota and turn it into the overpriced rural hell that portions of Montana, Wyoming, and Utah have become.

The success of the movie *Dances With Wolves* did put us under the national microscope for a while, and Kevin Costner is still trying to turn a small western corner of the state into a resort paradise. But even his money and boyish good looks have not been enough to overcome the locals' steadfast resistance to "being improved" by anyone.

On our side of the Missouri River, without an over-promoted Mount Rushmore to draw in the tourist dollars, there is even less to tempt the rich and trendy.

Which is pretty well how I like it, though I do wonder sometimes what real outsiders think when they find themselves in the middle of the Big Empty. Are they awed by the majesty of endless rolling plains? Do they appreciate glorious unobstructed sunrises and sunsets?

Are they impressed by inhabitants who thrive despite the wild extremes of a climate so variable that our thermometers need a 160-degree range just to register the annual high and low temps?

I doubt it.

I think they see dusty, dying main streets, empty highways, and a dearth of nationally recognized franchises. The stark beauty of northeastern South Dakota is not generally visible to the untrained eye.

We know that. And we automatically mistrust anyone who pretends otherwise.

"Why, isn't this just the cutest little place in the whole world?" the tall blond apparition gushed in a drawl so broad and bad that it had to be fake.

They stood just inside the doorway of the cafe.

"Isn't it, Brian? Isn't it just the most darlin' thing ever?"

Brian, at least I'm assuming that the young man in the trench coat was Brian, said nothing. Still wearing the squint he'd used to examine the outside of the cafe, he checked out the interior. He apparently found nothing to his liking inside either.

Rhonda, however, had found Brian to her liking. Forgetting she wasn't in Kansas anymore, she flipped her braids back over her shoulders and ushered the pair to a window booth and handed them menus.

"*Oooh*," the woman squealed, taking in the three of us for the first time. "Y'all are dressed up just like the Little Rascals. Brian, will you look at that, they're all dressed like the Little Rascals."

Brian hadn't been enthralled with his companion's first analysis. He ignored the repetition while studying the menu.

This did not faze the woman. "Why, there's Spanky." She pointed at me. "With shorts and hat and all. And Darla in her adorable little dress." She pointed at Rhonda, who was mostly looking at Brian and not paying attention to our odd, loud customer. "And"— she turned to Del, a look of confusion drifting quickly across her smiling face—"one of the other characters," she finished quickly, waving a hand.

Red-haired Del, whose resemblance to Alfalfa was minimal even on days when she wasn't wearing green face paint and a skin-tight black dress, was not amused. She closed her eyes, sighed, and shuffled over to the counter, parked herself on a stool, and pointedly swiveled it away from the booths.

Loud-and-Blond's eyes narrowed for the briefest of moments as she registered Del's snub, and then the expression was swept away in another wide smile. "Do y'all always dress like this?" she asked Rhonda.

"It's Halloween," Rhonda explained, arranging placemats, silverware, and water glasses on the table. "Each of the businesses on Main Street chose a movie to represent today."

"See, Brian, I told you, the Little Rascals," she said in triumph.

Brian grunted.

Rhonda raised an eyebrow at me, wondering if we should correct her. I had no intention of even getting into this conversation.

"Well, I understand costuming, it's a very important part of my business." The woman dug into a big black shoulder bag and came up with a handful of business cards and gave two to me and one to Rhonda. "Whoever designed yours did a good job. I'd like to give my compliments to the owner, if I may."

"Aphrodite's out just now, but we expect her back any minute," Rhonda said absently, reading her card with a small frown, flipping it over to see if there were anything printed on the back.

I looked at mine. In large flowing script it read: *Alanna Luna, Ecdysiast Extraordinaire*. Below the name, in smaller plain print, was an Oklahoma City address, and a phone number.

Ecdysiast. That explained the hot pants. And the bosom. And the theatrical overconfidence.

I had never met a real live stripper before. I certainly would have pictured someone not nearly so big, loud, or middle-aged for the job, though I suppose demand is low for the Kate Moss Table Dancers. At least in the Midwest. I had no doubt that Madam Alanna would be easily seen, in all her naked glory, from even the back rows of any smoky bar.

I wondered if Brian were her dancing partner, or manager, though from the pained expression on his face when he realized that I understood the word *ecdysiast*, I thought not.

Evidently, Rhonda's first-year sociology course hadn't touched on that particular cultural phenomenon. Still confused, she chirped, "Can I get anything for you folks?" mostly at Brian.

For the first time Brian looked up, and said with something that might have looked like a real smile if you hadn't seen one for a while, "Kinda dead in here, isn't it, Dorothy?"

With her back still toward the booths, Del snorted. Rhonda flashed a startled look sideways. I shook my head. No point in driving away our only customers by telling them just how dead things had been.

"People come in cycles," Rhonda said, taking out her pad, not looking at me. "Sometimes the place is jumping. Sometimes it's quiet as a grave." She winced at her own allusion.

"That's all right, honey," the woman said, patting Rhonda on the arm, "we like it quiet. Don't we, Brian? Get top-notch service that way." She flashed a brilliant smile at the empty cafe.

Brian ignored her, looking at his watch. "Should we wait?"

"I suppose," Alanna said, sighing. "Just coffee for now."

Since I had nothing else to do, and my services as stand-in cook were not yet required, I clomped behind the counter to get a coffee pot. Catching my eye, Del silently poked a finger down her throat. I tossed a card on the counter in front of her, which she read with eyebrows arched to the max. She stole a peek over one shoulder at the pair, in amazement.

The phone rang again. Del ignored it. I was filling cups.

Rhonda answered, listened briefly, then said loudly and angrily, "You should be ashamed of yourself. Can't you think of anything better to do with your time?" She slammed the receiver down, muttering to herself. "*Mikehunt, Mikehunt*, has anyone seen *Mikehunt*."

"What in the hell was that?" Del asked, surprised out of her pout.

Rhonda's eyes blazed. "Prank calls again. Only this time it was a grown-up." She was thoroughly disgusted. "I mean, I fell for the earlier ones, but no way was I going to go around asking if anyone had seen Mike Hunt. You'd think an adult would know better."

"Um, excuse me," Brian said, with a swift glance at his companion. "I think that call might have been for me."

"Huh?" Rhonda said.

"That call," he repeated. "If they asked for a Mike Hunt, then it was for me."

"But, but . . ." Rhonda faltered, looking to us for support. "I thought . . . Well I thought your name was Brian."

"It is," he said, smiling for the first time. "I'm Brian Michael Hunt. Most of my friends call me Mike, but Mom here insists on Brian."

I jacked up my assessment of Alanna's age another couple of years.

He held out a hand to Rhonda, which she shook, blushing furiously.

"I'm Rhonda, uh, um, Mike," she said. "Rhonda Saunders." She pointed at me, "And this is Tory Bauer, and Delphine Bauer is sitting over at the counter."

"Pleased to meet you," Brian Michael Hunt said. "Since we started out with Brian, why don't you just call me that?"

"Oh God," Rhonda said, suddenly too embarrassed to meet his eyes, "I hung up and didn't take a message. I yelled at that poor man for no good reason. I'm sorry. I am so sorry."

Brian smiled again. It was bright and friendly and just a little forced. "That's all right. It was probably my grandfather, explaining why he isn't here to meet us."

Rhonda, thoroughly chastened, was silent. The pause stretched to an uncomfortable length.

I took up the conversational thread. "You're meeting your *grandfather* here?"

Alanna jumped in, leaving Brian/Michael free to look at Rhonda, and Rhonda free to continue to look anywhere but at him. "Yes. In fact, I'm surprised Daddy isn't here already. Maybe he stopped in earlier. A smallish older man, balding, dressed nicely?"

Del, Rhonda, and I froze.

Oh shit.

Del and Rhonda waited for me to continue.

"Your father was going to meet you here at the cafe?" I asked, just to make sure I'd heard her right. "A smallish, older man, balding, nicely dressed?"

Alanna and Brian looked at each other, confused.

"Yes, have you seen him?"

I thought probably we had. How many smallish, older, balding, dead strangers were we apt to see in one day?

Del and Rhonda maintained their silence, the chickens.

I took a deep breath. "Well, we *might* have seen your father," I said, desperately trying to decide what to say next.

Just then Aphrodite came in the door, carrying a sheaf of legal-size documents and other papers. Norman Oberle, who I'd thought had continued on with his bread route long ago, was with her, a protective arm slung around her shoulders.

"Aphrodite," I said carefully, indicating Alanna with a free hand. I hadn't noticed, until then, that I was still carrying the coffee pot. "This woman is looking for her father . . ."

I paused, trying to figure out what to say next. But I didn't have to say anything because Aphrodite took one look at the ecdysiast, dropped her jaw and the handful of papers, stumbled backward, and was just barely caught by Norman.

I looked at Del, shocked.

Rhonda looked at Brian and shrugged.

Ms. Luna looked at Aphrodite and uttered a piercing, joyful cry.

"Mom!"

5

....

The Invisible Woman

I am of the opinion that waitresses, the good ones anyway, are born not made. Like artistic or musicial or athletic talent, the ability to carry three plates of eggs over easy, two cups, and a pot of regular without injuring yourself, or bystanders, is innate.

Unfortunately, as with car mechanics, plumbers, and sewer workers, our skills—though necessary to society at large—are simply not appreciated by the general public, or aspired to by the nation's young. Scam artists and incompetents color the national perspective. And the punishment for doing a difficult job well is invisibility.

Not that Del, Rhonda, and I, goggling between Aphrodite and Ms. Alanna Luna, considered ourselves outstanding in our field. We were simply professionals doing our job invisibly.

And like true Delphi natives, our job at that moment was to soak up every detail of the tableau unfolding in front of us. Del and Rhonda were still on duty, and had every reason to stand there openmouthed. Though my shift had officially ended an hour earlier, it would have taken a stick of dynamite to move me after Alanna's outburst.

Rooted to the spot, I stood with a pot of coffee forgotten in my hand.

Norman broke the silence first. "Honey?" he said to Aphrodite, concern in his voice, eyes glued on Alanna. Or perhaps on Alanna's chest. "Honey, are you okay?"

A small gargling sound came from Aphrodite.

In the ordinary course of events, a male directing a term of endearment toward our curmudgeonly employer would have provided hours of discussion possibilities. This just wasn't a slow news day.

As if to remind us, Alanna cried again, "Mom!" and then rushed forward, applying a headlock that, given the difference in their heights, could have involved the inhalation of copious amounts of silicone-filled ruffle on Aphrodite's part. Or at the very least, serious eye injury.

"What do *you* know about this?" Del asked me quietly, watching the tearful Alanna hug a very startled Aphrodite.

I sat the coffee pot on the table behind me. "Not a thing," I whispered back. "You?"

She shook her head, leaned over to Rhonda, and asked the same question.

"For a mother and daughter, they sure don't look alike," Rhonda said by way of an answer.

I had noticed that myself. And evidently so had Brian, who was watching the scene with undisguised amazement.

"Brian, honey, come over here and meet your grandmother," Alanna said, motioning as she loosened her stranglehold on Aphrodite's neck. She grinned widely, wiping tears from her cheeks in an exaggerated motion.

While her emotion seemed genuine, I couldn't shake the feeling that Alanna was, and had been, putting on a show, that this little scene had been staged, though for whose benefit I could not imagine.

"Mama, this is Brian," Alanna said, positioning Brian directly in front of Aphrodite with a forceful shove. "And Brian, this is the woman who raised me, the one who married my daddy when I was only two years old. She's the only mother I ever knew."

Well that at least explained how Junoesque Alanna came to be the progeny of short and round Aphrodite and her equally short, though heretofore unmentioned, husband.

Not knowing what else to do, gruff and usually monosyllabic Aphrodite mumbled a sentence-long greeting. She shot a deer-in-the-headlights glance at me, walked on the papers she'd dropped, sat in the nearest booth, and looked down at her hands.

"Rhonda, why don't you get pie for everyone," I said, figuring that any activity was better than standing around with our mouths open. "I'll get fresh coffee. Norman, you just slide in with Aphrodite, and Ms. Luna, you and your son can sit here and talk. Del . . ." I paused, unable to think of anything for Del to do.

"I'll put on some music," Del said, shuffling over to the counter against the far wall where the old portable tape player sat under the unused air conditioner.

She punched a button and Bach's "Toccata and Fugue" blasted from the speakers.

We had forgotten that it was Halloween. And that we were all wearing costumes. And that a man who had evidently been Aphrodite's husband, and therefore Alanna Luna's father, had died less than two hours ago in the cafe bathroom. I shot a desperate glance at Del, who flipped the stereo over to radio, from which now came the funereal tones of Paul Harvey spinning out another interminable monologue.

Sighing, Del spun the dial, found Patsy Cline belting out "Crazy," shrugged helplessly at me, and shut the radio off. "Who needs music anyway?" she gamely asked the ceiling. "Here," she said, grabbing the coffee pot from where I'd set it. "I'll do the coffee, why don't you . . ." She hesitated, looking around the cafe for inspiration, and then smiled. "You can pick up all those papers."

She pointed at the pages that Aphrodite had dropped. They were scattered from the bathroom door almost to the kitchen.

"I just can't believe he's not here yet," Alanna said loudly, looking at her watch, and then craning her neck to look out the window. "Daddy is always punctual. As you remember," she said to Aphrodite, grinning.

Norman cleared his throat. "Well," he said, "your, um, mama, uh, mother, uh"—he swallowed—"step-mother might be able to explain about your late daddy."

Del snorted, and then quickly covered the sound with a muffled cough. Rhonda clanked the pie plates a little more loudly than necessary, and I turned and knelt to gather the strewn papers. Though we had all three wanted to see this scene play itself out, Aphrodite's explanation about Alanna's "late" father was a personal communication. One apt to be accompanied by some large-breasted Okie lamentations.

Suddenly I wanted to be away from the cafe. Away from the sad news I was going to have no choice but to hear. Away from the grief that was sure to follow.

As I've mentioned before, it is a good idea to be careful what you wish for.

Crouched behind the till, trying not to listen to Aphrodite's gruff and hesitant voice, I belatedly realized that I was holding, and unconsciously reading, legally drawn divorce papers. Divorce papers concerning Aphrodite M. Ferguson, estranged wife of Alfred R. Ferguson.

Native snoopiness notwithstanding, I was embarrassed to be stuck in the middle of these entirely private proceedings. Forcing my eyes away from the page, I reached and grabbed a few more papers as Aphrodite said, ". . . and then Tory opened the bathroom door . . ."

Not wanting the hear the rest of the sentence, I crawled behind the counter for the last scattered sheets.

"As I live and breathe," Del said loudly and exaggeratedly.

I stopped and peered over the counter to find Del looking directly at me, and Rhonda staring out the window furiously.

"I do believe that Stuart McKee is walking over to the cafe from his Feed and Seed Store," Del said clearly.

I heard her words but did not attach any particular meaning to them.

"In fact," Del said even more forcefully, "he's just getting ready to come through the screen door. Right into the cafe." She widened her eyes. "*Now.*"

She tilted her head toward the kitchen and gestured.

I was not tracking quickly or well. It took another fraction of a second before I realized that on top of dead bodies, and reappearing wives, and divorce papers, and bad costumes and melodramatic scenes, Stu McKee was just about to step into the cafe.

That broke my paralysis.

The cafe door swung open as I scrambled, still on my knees, through the swinging half-door that divided the cafe from the kitchen. Crouching, and cursing my own cowardice, I hurried down the hallway, through the back door, and out into the chilly fall afternoon.

I was halfway home before I realized that I was still clutching an armload of legal documents.

6

....

Native Born

Popular myth has it that no matter how long you live in a small New England town, unless you were born there, you'll never be completely accepted by the natives. And by natives, I mean the European interlopers who established residence in the last five hundred years, not the indigenous folk who were unceremoniously booted from their own land.

Here on the plains, the native-booting interlopers haven't been around long enough to get snobby about who belongs and who doesn't. If you can last a decade, especially if you can refrain from reminding us how wonderful Nebraska, or Iowa, or Wisconsin was, you're automatically a member of the club.

Once you're in, the rest of us sometimes forget that it wasn't always so.

"I just figured she'd always been here," Neil Pascoe said, sitting cross-legged in front of the stereo in the big main room of the library he runs from the first floor of his house, deftly inserting a CD into the slot and punch-

ing a couple of buttons. The speakers pulsed with the
liquid beat of Andrea True Connection's "More, More,
More."

I winced. Contrary to popular belief, the seventies
produced some pretty good music, but I'd never learned
to appreciate the finer points of disco. Neil grinned and
turned the volume down.

"Well, *I* can't remember a time when she didn't run
the cafe," he said as he shuffled through the haphazard
assortment of CD cases, tape cassettes, and old LPs.

We were recording the background music for the evening's high school Halloween party, choosing selections
from the extensive collection Neil had amassed in the
years following his big lottery win.

"It's no wonder you don't remember," I said, leaning
against the overstuffed chair next to the stereo, thinking
back. "I started working for her while I was still in high
school." Neil was around ten years younger than me,
which would have put him about in kindergarten when
Aphrodite moved to Delphi.

I handed him a tape of the Village People, which he
accepted with a nod. I would have preferred to hide out
at the trailer and brood, or better yet drink heavily until
it was time to chaperone "The Night of the Disco
Dead," but I'd already agreed to help Neil record the
music for the evening's festivities. And besides, sobriety
was required of all the participants, student and adult.
That was the whole point of the evening.

So after sneaking out of the cafe and skulking home,
I'd stashed Aphrodite's papers in a dresser drawer,
ditched the Munchkin suit, and walked across the street
to Neil's library.

In the past hour and a half, interrupted only by oc-
casional library patrons, we'd recorded more awful music than I'd ever heard in a week during the Disco
Decade, and hashed over everything that had happened
in the cafe that morning.

Well, not quite everything.

Neither of us mentioned Stuart McKee. Or his wife.
Though certainly Neil had heard about Renee McKee's

unexpected reappearance in Delphi. Neil heard everything.

"I don't remember Aphrodite's arrival myself," I said. "I was still in school too, and not exactly paying attention to the grown-ups. One day she was just there, running the cafe, smoking over the grill, scaring the bejabbers out of young waitresses. Including me, until I realized she was all bark and no bite."

"And you don't remember any husband?" Neil asked, punching a series of buttons to record "YMCA."

Visions of pretty young construction boys filled my head. And dancing cowboys. Not to mention hairy-chested policemen with shiny chrome handcuffs.

"Nope," I said. "Or any large-busted daughters with a propensity to take off their clothes for money, either. I'm sure I'd have remembered that."

"So, the marriage broke up before she came to Delphi, then."

"As far as I know, no one knew there had been a marriage. Or if we did, we forgot," I said, reaching for the Bee Gees in the music pile. "Do 'Stayin' Alive' next."

He made a note on the legal pad balanced in his lap. "So she'd been separated from her husband and stepdaughter, living here alone in Delphi for more than twenty-five years, violating county health ordinances and terrorizing the waitresses—"

"And serving terrible food in generous portions to the public at large," I added.

"—perfectly content . . ." Neil ignored my interruption. "And then this week, after all this time, she finally decides to dump the guy?" Neil wrinkled his glasses up on his nose, and ran his fingers through his dark, prematurely graying hair. "Pretty suspicious timing, dontcha think?"

We considered that for a minute as the unintelligible lyrics of the Brothers Gibb filled the room. This time my mind's eye saw a young John Travolta strutting in a white suit.

"My guess is that the timing had everything to do with making eyes at Norman Oberle," I said, grinning. "I know her alleged husband ate breakfast in the cafe this morning, but it was a madhouse, and I don't think Aphrodite even saw him before"—I waved my hands around a little—"well, before we found him. And if *he* saw *her*, he didn't give any indication. At least that I could tell. I think it's probably a coincidence."

"Hmm," Neil said noncommittally. "And so it's not likely that Aphrodite murdered her former husband?" He raised an eyebrow.

"In the bathroom, with the lead pipe?" I laughed. "Not likely. The EMTs seemed to think he'd had a heart attack. No one treated this as anything but a routine, unfortunate occurrence. No questioning, no crime scene protocol, no flapping yellow ribbons."

"Well, I didn't think so either, but *you* have been known to go down that road."

Donna Summer lamented the last dance. Last chance for love.

"Did you at least read the legal stuff you accidentally walked out with?" He didn't look at me, or emphasize the word *accidentally* as he fiddled with stereo knobs, but I knew that he knew why I ended up in the street with a handful of official papers that weren't mine.

I blushed for the flimsy excuse I'd given for having the papers in the first place. It's not that Neil doesn't know about Stu and me. All of Delphi knows about Stu and me. I just didn't want to say it out loud. "Didn't seem right to read them," I said finally.

Neil peered over his glasses at me. "Turning over a new leaf?"

No one in Delphi ever apologized for snoopiness, especially Delphi's Designated Finder of Dead Bodies.

"Nah," I said, straightening the fringes of the area rug under the chair I was leaning against. "It's just that Aphrodite always kept to herself, and with all the rest going on this morning . . ." I paused, remembering more than I wanted to. "I mean, it just didn't seem proper to snoop through her papers too."

Neil grinned. "It's not. But that never stopped anyone before."

"Chalk it up to a latent sense of honor," I said, laughing. "Speaking of which, I should call Aphrodite and tell her that I have them."

We heard voices in the hallway. Neil turned the stereo down and stood, saying over his shoulder, "Good idea, get 'em back where they belong before temptation overwhelms you."

I turned the stereo down again and dialed the cafe as Neil greeted whoever had come into the library.

"Delphi Cafe, whaddaya want?" Del growled into the phone.

"Oooh, we're imitating New Yorkers now?" I asked.

Del blew a pretty good imitation of a Bronx cheer. "You thought it was busy this morning, you ought to be here after we find a dead body in the cafe."

"Been there, done that," I said.

"Well, you haven't been and done when Aphrodite's in this kind of mood, or"—Del lowered her voice and spoke quietly into the phone—"with this dipshit daughter of hers lording it around. You ought to see the men, drooling like they've never seen silicone tits before."

Del didn't like sharing the spotlight with anyone. If the guys in Delphi were going to drool over bosoms, she wanted them to be hers.

"What's she still doing in the cafe?" I asked. I'd pictured a tearful revelation, a mournful Alanna Luna, a speedy decamping of both her and her son.

"Beats the fuck outta me," Del said. "She's making noises about sticking around too."

"You're kidding," I said, amazed. "Staying? Here in Delphi?"

"That's what I said."

This was a new wrinkle, one that bore some consideration, and discussion with Neil. Which I planned to do as soon as I got off the phone and he got rid of whoever was chatting with him in the foyer.

"Hmm," I said, trying to think the implications over. "That's very interesting."

Del grunted.

Through the phone, I heard laughter in the background. Male laughter and a Southern female giggle.

Del growled.

"So did you have a reason to call, or was this just a social visit?" she asked.

"Actually, I need to talk to Aphrodite," I said, "and tell her that I walked out of there with all those papers this afternoon."

"Well, Herself is not speaking to mere mortals at the moment," Del said. "She hasn't left the kitchen for the last hour. In addition to the sudden interest everyone in town has in seeing the very bathroom where someone died, we also have to get food ready for that stupid school thing tonight."

"That's right," I said. I'd forgotten that Aphrodite was catering the disco party. "Well, maybe I'll just bring the papers over right now."

"That wouldn't be a very good idea," Del said, abruptly changing her tone to sticky sweet.

My heart sank.

"Stu's still there, huh?"

"Yup, all afternoon. Stuck like a barnacle on a boat. Like ugly on ape. Like—"

"I got the point already," I interrupted.

"Yup, all by his lonesome. All afternoon. Watching the door like a lost puppy dog," Del continued nastily.

Yeah, like a guy whose estranged wife moved back in and the only way he could see his girlfriend was to wait around her place of employment.

The last thing I wanted was to have some sort of public confrontation with Stu. I thought for a moment. "Well, Aphrodite will be in and out at the school tonight. Tell her I'll just bring the papers along and I'll give them to her there. Tell her I didn't mean to take them."

"She'll be so excited," Del said, as more laughter broke out behind her. She hung up without saying goodbye.

I looked at the phone for a moment, wondering if it wouldn't be better just to go to the cafe and get the scene with Stu, whatever it was going to be, over with.

My cowardice got the better of me even before I replaced the receiver.

Blowing out all my air, and forcing myself not to think about anything at all, I sat down and sorted through more music since Neil was still busy. I resisted the urge to stick a James Taylor song in the middle of the tape. I also resisted the urge to record ''Afternoon Delight,'' though neither the idea nor the expression was shocking by nineties standards.

I didn't have to hear the song to remember that most of my recent delights had been of the afternoon variety. Or that those were likely coming to an abrupt halt.

I sighed, and then settled on a slow song, figuring the kids would appreciate the excuse to feel each other up.

Lost in the rather frightening memory of swirling polyester and platform shoes and glitter balls as Neil Sedaka crooned ''Laughter in the Rain,'' I didn't realize Neil had come back into the room until he interrupted my reverie.

''Ah, Tory, ah . . .''

Maybe it was ESP. Maybe it was just that I knew it was going to be One of Those Days. Or maybe the soft and uncharacteristic hesitancy in Neil's voice that gave it away.

Whatever it was, I was almost prepared when I looked up from the stereo.

Or at least as prepared as I ever could be, to look up directly into the eyes of Renee McKee.

7

....

Rated PG

I stopped watching soap operas years ago, having become permanently disgusted with the genre in general, and *Days of Our Lives* in particular, after rooting and waiting forever for Don and Marlena to get together, only to sit openmouthed as their long-delayed relationship disintegrated almost immediately.

Then again, maybe it was the high concentration of impossibly coiffed, impeccably dressed, amazingly attractive denizens of towns that always seem to be named Springfield or Mill Valley that turned me off.

Or perhaps it was the overacting and overreacting that spoiled them for me. Too many long meaningful glances and arched eyebrows—pregnant pauses choreographed to overwrought music.

Or maybe I just plain outgrew 'em. I don't know.

But whatever the reason, I don't watch soaps anymore.

Unfortunately, that doesn't mean that I get to avoid them. Del watches her morning shows and tapes the afternoon ones religiously—and subjects me to detailed daily synopses. Rhonda keeps me abreast of the current ''real-life'' MTV versions. Even Aphrodite watches occasionally.

So though it's been a long, long time since I've made the daytime drama couch potato trip, I was still perfectly able to recognize a Soap Opera Moment when I found myself smack in the middle of one.

And how much more Soap Operatic can you get than being confronted by your married boyfriend's estranged wife? And their five-year-old son. In the town library. Sitting on the floor. With disco music boogie-oogie-oogie-ing in the background.

Talk about your pregnant moments.

I shot a controlled, carefully neutral look up at Neil, furious that he hadn't alerted me in time to beat a hasty retreat. Through a window if necessary.

He shrugged imperceptibly, misery writ large on his handsome, flustered face.

I would have forgiven him instantly, if I'd been capable of doing anything.

Which I wasn't.

''We've met before,'' Renee McKee said softly. Wearing a loose tunic sweater and leggings with scrunched heavy white socks topping expensive boots, she looked as fashionable and as out of place in Delphi's library as she had everywhere else in town during her short residence. ''Why don't you go look at books,'' she said to Walton, not taking her eyes off me. ''I'm sure the nice man has a children's section.''

The Nice Man knew when he was being dismissed. With an arched eyebrow, Neil silently asked if it were all right to go.

Though there was little in the world that I wouldn't rather do, including setting my feet on fire, than let Neil leave me to face Renee McKee alone, I'd learned from the soaps you can't postpone life's inevitable moments except for commercials.

There didn't seem to be any commercials handy, so I nodded at Neil, who beamed a look at me that I assume was meant to bolster my courage.

It didn't work.

"Do you mind if I sit down?" Renee asked.

I nodded, or shrugged, or somehow indicated that it was fine and dandy with me if she sat down. I'm good at nonverbal lying.

She gracefully folded herself into a cross-legged position across from me on the floor, which was surprising. I'd expected her to choose one of the overstuffed chairs and assume a position of height and power.

After all, she was the Wife. And I was the Other Woman. .

But she sat on the floor, smoothing her sweater over her knees calmly, as though we were good friends about to have an intimate conversation.

And I sat frozen, forgetting to breathe.

I could hear Neil in the other room, laughing and talking with Walton, who seemed to be having a wonderful time.

"I'll keep this short, and to the point," Renee said quietly. "But I need your honest answer."

She tilted her head to the side ever so slightly, pausing, then raised an eyebrow a hair, waiting for my reaction.

Incapable of speech, I nodded, not entirely sure of my own meaning, making myself as ready as I could for whatever was coming.

She nodded back. "Okay then." She inhaled deeply, perhaps more unsettled than she appeared. "What I need to know is . . ." She paused again. Another pregnant one. "Are you in love with Stuart?"

If I had, in my wildest imagination, put together a list of questions for Renee McKee to ask me in a situation like this, that one would have been at the bottom of the pile. Way behind every question that was easy to answer, and even behind the hard ones that required a bullet fired straight into the heart of the homewrecker.

I sat back sharply, looking away, and then back into her eyes.

And finally said, "I don't know."

She'd ambushed the truth out of me.

Renee looked away this time, chewing a lower lip. Then she faced me again, and nodded. "Well, that's what I needed to know. Thank you for your honesty."

She stood up quickly and clumsily, called for Walton, and was gone before I'd even processed the fact that she'd left.

Or the fact that I belatedly realized that I hadn't been honest.

I scrambled to my feet, and hurried after her, intent on catching up, though unsure of what I meant to say.

"Renee," I called, startling the several small costumed children who'd come into the library to trick or treat. And their smugly smiling mothers. "Wait."

But she was already out the door and off the porch and into the street.

Already dodging a group of junior high boys who merrily tossed lit firecrackers at each other, to Walton's intense delight.

Already exchanging tight-lipped niceties with Norman Oberle in front of our trailer. She stood, facing into the wind, plainly wishing to escape as the dust blew into her eyes and whipped her hair around.

As I stood on Neil Pascoe's porch, ready to call or wave, the words died in my throat. I dimly realized that I was again in the middle of a genuine Soap Opera Moment as the steady prairie wind pasted Renee McKee's loose tunic sweater to her already rounded belly.

8

....

Rodent Romance

I was too young during the Age of Disco to realize that what goes around, comes around. Literally, figuratively, and fashionwise.

Not that it was my fault. Who would guess that tight and shiny print shirts with long pointy collars were going to come back in? Or that platform shoes would find a resurgence. Or, God help me, hip huggers.

Besides, my own personal wardrobe of polyester and Qiana would not have provided a costume for the evening's retro-hip festivities. No amount of squeezing would have forced me into anything I'd owned back then.

Luckily, the size and preservative nature of the average South Dakota housewife (not to mention the indestructibility of double knit), ensured that there were plenty of pristine examples in my size to borrow. A little closet scrounging had yielded a pair of powder-blue elastic-waist bell-bottoms, a maroon vest that draped nearly to the floor, and a white blouse that could have come from a stage production of *The Pirates of Penz-ance.*

It was a look that resembled Maude more than Abba. My hair was another story entirely. The best I'd come up with, after a series of experiments, was a center part with the bangs sort of foofed back.

I was no Farrah Fawcett, lemmee tell ya.

I was no lighthearted high school party chaperone either, though I'd done everything in my power to become one.

While it had seemed like a couple of years, I'd stood on Neil's porch, voice dying in my throat, only long enough to process Renee's condition, and for my traitor brain to count backward. A pregnancy that showed in October had to have begun in July, or perhaps even earlier.

Which sort of rendered moot the announcement I was going to make to Renee.

And with that calculation, I'd purposely closed my brain down. No more thinking. No more counting. No more analyzing my own feelings. Or anyone else's.

I'd finished recording music with Neil, forcibly cheery, babbling constantly, not letting him get a word, or a question, in edgewise. I occasionally peeked out the window, relieved that Renee had disappeared.

Norman had stood by himself uncertainly in the street a while longer, and then crossed over to bang on the door of the trailer Del and I shared. When no one answered, he'd scratched his head and then trudged back toward town.

I stayed in the safe haven of Neil's library, avoiding contact with the rest of humanity, until Norman had finally gone. And Del had come and gone. And Presley had come and gone, sideburns glued in place, gold chains around his neck, wearing a white linen suit.

Neil, who saw all and heard all and understood all, allowed me to cower and chatter. And when I decided it was safe to leave, he gave me a swift hug at the door and let me go without a word.

So dressed in my Beatrice Arthur suit and faux-Farrah hair, Aphrodite's legal papers stuffed into a manila envelope and rolled into my non–disco era coat pocket, I walked to the gymnasium, studiously not contemplating the cyclical nature of the universe.

I didn't think about how I had married a philanderer and how his philandering had actually caused his death in a car accident. I didn't think about how awful it felt to be Wronged. And I didn't think about the fact that I'd knowingly taken up with *another* philanderer, and how this time I was the Other Woman. And I sure as hell didn't think about the fact that the philanderer might actually decide to have sex with his own wife and turn me back into the injured party.

Nosiree, I didn't think about any of that.

I hung up my coat in the coat room with the rest, took a deep breath, and joined a group of other grown-ups. We shouted small talk over the music, as the glitter ball twirled above a high school gym whose perimeter was dotted with folding tables covered by refreshments, carved pumpkins, and assorted games to amuse theoretically sober teens between their awkward imitations of the Hustle.

It was just good luck that my cousin Junior, the party's organizer, was too busy fuming over the food and the volunteers and the evening's prizes to pay much attention to my love life.

Or probable future lack thereof.

"What are you doing over *here*?" she demanded sharply enough that the rest of the chickenshit chaperones quickly dispersed, leaving me to stand and face Junior's wrath alone.

"Just waiting for you to tell me where to go and what to do," I said. I remembered to smile.

She peered at me grimly, with one hand pressed into her lower back. Junior wore an outfit that could have come directly from the seventies. Or it could have been brand new. With maternity clothes, it was hard to tell. She surveyed the room with a frown.

As far as I could tell, there was nothing for Junior to frown about. Neil sat behind the audio equipment at a table at the far end of the gym, playing one loud, hideous song after another, interspersing them with DJ-style chatter and prize drawings.

Others congregated around tables, playing games and exclaiming over the prizes, which were actually bribes amassed by local businesses—gift certificates for meals and movie rentals, savings bonds, portable stereos, VCRs, and even a small color television. The chamber of commerce definitely wanted to keep the windows of Delphi unsoaped and the outhouses untorched.

The rest of the costumed young wandered, or stood in small clumps, drinking punch and laughing. A fair number were gobbling Aphrodite's barbecue sandwiches as she glowered at them from behind another table crammed with standard South Dakota buffet fare: chips, pickles, baked beans, potato salad, and whatever home-made goodies could be cajoled from already overworked mothers.

So far, the civic ploy seemed to have worked. The gym was crowded and the kids appeared to be having a good and noisy, but generally well-behaved, time.

Maybe Junior's displeasure was preemptive, a preparation for whatever disaster was in store.

"Relax," I said to her. "Things are going swimmingly."

"That's what you think. The full lighting in here is too bright and the battery lights we have won't work in the pumpkins, so someone decided to use candles instead." She gestured emphatically at the dozen or so lighted and unlighted Jack-o'-Lanterns scattered around the gym. "The fire marshal would shut us down in a second if he knew."

"So blow the candles out," I said. "Pumpkins don't go with the disco theme anyway."

"I do," she said, exasperated. "But as soon as I blow them out, the kids relight them."

As she spoke, the flash of a lighted match sparkled in a dark corner on the other side of the gym, and another pumpkin face leered into life.

"See what I mean? Come on." Junior pulled me by the arm. "You can help blow them out. And confiscate any lighters you see. And take down names."

"So I'm on Nazi Match Patrol, huh?"

Pregnant Junior marched steadily through the dancers as she led me across the floor. "Would you rather be in charge of the hamsters instead?"

"Hamsters?" I thought I'd heard her wrong.

"Yes," she said, exasperated, stooping to lift the lids and blow out three glowing pumpkins. "Hamsters."

"Hamsters?" I repeated. Was that some new slang for unruly teenagers?

"Are you deaf?" Junior demanded. "Hamsters. Yes. Hamsters. Some idiot donated a couple of male hamsters and a cage with all the trimmings to be given away as a prize tonight."

"That sounds cool," I said, figuring I could be generous since this was a high school party, and there was no chance that Presley would be bringing rodents back to live with us at the trailer.

"Cool?" Junior repeated, plainly shocked. "It's disgusting. Don't you know what people do with hamsters?"

"Use them to make baby hamsters?"

"Oh, for crying out loud Tory, I said these were males. Don't you know anything?"

"Evidently not," I said, deciding not to tell Junior that I'd spotted another pumpkin lighter on the other side of the room.

Intent on her outrage, Junior didn't notice either the flare of the match, or the couple nearby stealing smooches as they danced. And she obviously didn't see Ms. Alanna Luna sashay into the gym and jiggle her way over to Aphrodite's table, though many of the young men, and a few of the older ones, did.

Keeping a bland but interested look on my face as Junior droned on, I tried unobtrusively to decode Alanna's wildly swinging arms and Aphrodite's stoic refusal to look directly at her, tuning in near the end of Junior's tirade.

"With PVC pipes!" She gestured emphatically. "And you know some impressionable child in Delphi will try it. And then we'll have the PTA and PETA both down on us."

"What?"

Exasperated, Junior repeated a rumor I'd heard years ago concerning a certain handsome movie actor and a use he allegedly made of small furry animals, aided by a length of plastic pipe and a willing friend.

"That was gerbils," I said laughing, remembering that I'd had a pretty serious crush on that particular actor right about in the middle of the disco reign. "And you know better than to believe that shit, don't you, Junior?"

"Watch your language," she said sharply. "This is a school function."

"You know better than to believe that *nonsense*, don't you, *Junior*?"

"It's been documented," she said, surveying the gym, eagle eye out for match lighters and rodent self-abusers. "On the Internet."

"Oh, and we all know that everything there is the absolute truth," I said solemnly.

She peered at me closely, but I crossed my heart and hoped to die if the conversation went on any longer.

Neil, perhaps picking up on the rodent wavelength, played "Muskrat Love"—the good version by America, not the Captain and Tennille. I squashed a smile.

"All right, you think it's so funny, you can take care of them."

I shrugged. Watching hamsters had to be more interesting than listening to Junior rehash old slander. "You're the boss," I said, and followed her back across the gym.

As I passed Aphrodite's table, I leaned over and told her that I had her papers in my coat, and would get them to her sometime during the evening. Alanna squealed in delight when she saw my costume, but I just waved and scurried off to follow Junior.

"Pretty jolly for a woman whose father died this morning," I said to myself. Out loud, apparently, because eagle-eared Junior turned suddenly.

''I was going to ask you about that,'' she said, peering over at Alanna, who seemed to be chattering continually.

''I don't know nuthin' 'bout nuthin','' I said, wondering how Junior had made the connection between Alanna and the dead man so quickly.

Silly me. In Delphi, gossip crackles through the air at the speed of light. And if Junior was wondering about Alanna, it would only be a matter of moments before she brought up Renee, whose pregnancy was probably already common knowledge.

''Oops, there goes another match,'' I lied.

''Where?'' Junior whipped her head around.

''Over there,'' I pointed vaguely at an innocent bunch of kids across the room.

''Damn,'' Junior muttered, forgetting that this was a school function. ''You just keep things in control here.'' Before leaving, she rattled off the drill for giving out prizes—a highly complex and organized system of her own devising.

I didn't listen because I caught a movement out of the corner of my eye, and was momentarily stunned to see Aphrodite swing an open-handed slap that connected solidly with Alanna's cheek.

Alanna seemed stunned too. As were the kids standing around the refreshment table who had witnessed the blow, watching with jaws hung in surprise and mouths frozen in big open O's.

I shot a glance at Junior, but she was too busy castigating a group of boys who frantically pantomimed innocence, to notice the altercation.

By the time I looked back, Alanna, with mascara streaks already running down her face and an angry red hand mark outlined on one cheek, had run crying from the gym.

Aphrodite is gruff and she is stern and she is not sweet. But I had never known her to be anything but fair. And not once in the nearly three decades that I have known her, has she ever struck another person.

It would be safe to say that I was shocked.

It would be safe to say that Aphrodite was shocked too. She stood immobile behind the table, face unreadable, spatula in hand.

"Hey, what the hell was that all about?" a young voice asked from nearby.

"Watch your language," I said absently, still staring at Aphrodite, rattled enough to play chaperone. "This is a school function."

"Yeah, and that was Aphrodite Ferguson actually hitting some woman," Presley Bauer said in a voice filled with either horror or respect. I couldn't tell which. "That was the coolest damn thing I've ever seen."

I sighed. At thirteen, Del's son Presley wasn't exactly up to speed on the workings of civilized adult society.

And at thirteen, he had no business being at a high school function.

"You better get out of here before Junior comes back," I said sternly. "She's on a tear tonight, and if she finds out that you sneaked in here, she's liable to report you to the principal. Get you in big trouble."

Presley, in full John Travolta drag, grinned widely. "She can't do a thing about it. I am here legitimately." He pronounced that last word slowly, with a satisfied grin on his face.

"Oh? And exactly how can you be here legitimately?" I asked, giving a cursory inspection and a nod to a signed prize certificate that had been thrust under my nose. The happy winner walked off with lunch for two at the Delphi Cafe, redeemable anytime within the next three months. "This here party is strictly for the high school students."

"For the high school students," he agreed, laughing, "and their dates."

He preened, drawing himself to his full height, which wasn't very tall yet, but was still taller than me.

"And which high school girl was silly enough to ask you to be her date?" I asked, knowing that once Junior got wind of cross-school dating, she'd put a stop to it immediately.

Presley leaned over the table, waggled his eyebrows, and gestured over his shoulder at senior Mardelle Jackson, and then stood back, enormously proud of himself.

I raised an eyebrow in Mardelle's direction.

She grinned and shrugged. "Ya gotta admit he's kinda cute." She slung an arm around Presley's shoulder.

He blushed.

I wondered if Mardelle, whose Daisy Duke costume consisted of tight cutoff jeans, high heels, and a tube top, was simply being kind in inviting Presley. Despite the difference in their ages, the two had been friends forever.

On the other hand, Presley had lately been mesmerized by the height, depth, and breadth of Mardelle's chest. And he wasn't grinning like a boy being granted a favor by a longtime friend.

He was grinning like a horny thirteen-year-old whose wildest dreams had all come true.

I sighed.

"So are you here to pick up a prize, or just to keep track of the adults?" I asked.

"Pick up a prize," he said, grinning even more widely than before. If that were possible. "I just won the hamsters."

"Jesus," I said to the ceiling.

"Hey, Mardelle, check this out," Presley hooted over his shoulder, pointing at the hamster cage.

The allegedly male hamsters, engaged in paying pretty close attention to each other at the moment, were unaware of the spectacle they had created for a wildly laughing crowd of high schoolers (interspersed, I now realized, with a few other junior high faces—also flushed and grinning wildly.)

I had never before realized how fascinating quadruped mammalian procreation might be to adolescent bipeds.

"What's going on?" Junior demanded, pushing her way through the crowd that had congregated in front of the prize table. When she saw what was causing the commotion, she stopped dead still, face pale, lips set, eyes focused and furious.

She turned to me accusingly. "I was told that they were male," she said furiously.

I shrugged, miming my own lack of responsibility for amorous rodents, same sex or otherwise.

Junior grabbed a cotton throw, one of the donated prizes, and tossed it over the hamster cage. And then angrily turned to disperse the crowd.

I stifled a laugh and backed into Mardelle, who had mysteriously appeared on my side of the table. She stood with the lid to a carved pumpkin in one hand and a flaming match in the other.

I looked at her, confused.

And then I noticed several others poised likewise, jack-o'-lantern lid and lit match in hand, scattered around the gym.

In the confusion following the impromptu live-sex rodent show, I think maybe Neil and I were the only ones who saw Mardelle give a small nod to the others. She turned to me and said quietly, "Duck." Then she and her cohorts lowered their matches.

And before I could process what was about to happen, and certainly before I could duck, in a nearly synchronized harmony of noise and orange pulp, each and every pumpkin in the room exploded.

9

....

Smashing Pumpkins

It would be pretty tough to research the subject scientifically, but I would venture to guess that the percentage of control freaks is relatively high here on the Great Plains. I can back up that assertion with close observation, and a longtime familiarity (not to mention a genetic link), with residents who are bound and determined to bend human nature and Mother Nature to their whim.

Maybe meteorology is to blame. In a state where the weather never stays the same, people are reduced to trying to impose continuity on each other. Schedules and plans are written in stone, and only the severest weather extremes are allowed to disrupt carefully wrought scheduling.

People themselves are automatically expected to conform. They are supposed to follow the rules and obey the laws and meet, but not exceed, expectations.

They are expected to behave.

Since the citizenry generally does what is expected, people like my cousin Junior Deibert are able to fool themselves into thinking that they wield some kind of control over their world and fellow creatures.

They bustle through life, managing and deciding and organizing the major and peripheral details of everyone's lives. For the most part they are allowed this kind of license because we're secretly relieved to have someone else sweat the small stuff. And because the controllers pretty well steamroll their way into positions of power.

But even control freaks miscalculate.

In order to circumvent, through the party, the usual round of petty vandalism that passed for juvenile self-expression, Junior had the food and the prizes and the music and the costumes and the chaperones and the hamsters subdued, if not completely tamed.

Unfortunately she forgot to take adolescence into consideration. And she forgot to take Halloween into consideration. And most of all, she forgot the combustible mix of hormones and cherry bombs and pumpkins.

And since she skipped adolescence entirely, growing straight from a prim and proper child into a tight-lipped adult, Junior never knew that it was fun to discombobulate the grown-ups.

Junior was, at the moment, thoroughly discombobulated.

She was also pretty well spattered with orange pulp.

In the very brief silence following the last of the small explosions, she stood like Sissy Spacek, wide-eyed and dripping, trying to catalog what had just happened.

Scattered around the gym, I heard the first tentative giggles. I don't suppose there was any malice, but as students and chaperones alike discovered that there were no injuries and no real damage that could not be remedied by a shower and a washing machine, relief turned to outright laughter.

Though she was still frozen, I knew that Junior would, any second, regain the use of her faculties, and unleash her considerable wrath on innocent and guilty alike. And she wouldn't need Carrie's psychic powers to make a hash of us all.

''Hurry,'' I said to Mardelle, who stood openmouthed, staring at Junior, ''grab a rag. Something. Anything, and look like you're cleaning this mess up.''

''I didn't know it was going to hit anyone,'' she said weakly. ''I just thought it was going to make some cool noise.''

''Too late to worry about that now,'' I said under my breath. ''Get busy, before Junior figures out who's responsible.''

I motioned to the relatively unscathed Presley. ''Did you know about this?''

''Uh-uh,'' he said, transfixed, staring around him. ''Honest.'' He looked at me and squinted. ''You need a washrag too.''

I realized that I was covered with goop. And since the majority of people in the gym had been congregated around the various tables and corners, where, incidentally, the pumpkins also seemed to be concentrated—so was everyone else, except for a few diehard dancers and Neil, who had been safe behind the stereo equipment.

''I'm not worrying about me right at the moment,'' I said. ''The best thing you can do for Mardelle and yourself is to look busy. And innocent.''

Looking innocent was one of Presley's gifts, his face shifts automatically into cherub mode. Looking busy was another thing entirely, but he did give it an honest effort as Junior began sputtering.

I shot a look up, expecting light bulbs and windows to start exploding. But the only explosion was another string of firecrackers that had been set off, apparently, right behind Junior.

Before the noise and smoke cleared, and as the tentative laughter rippled through the crowd, Junior herself exploded.

''That is enough!''

Loud and clear, her voice cut a cold and complete swath through the mumbled conversation and laughter. She beamed a fierce terrible glare that stopped everyone in his tracks. ''Not a single person leaves this room until this mess is cleaned up!'' Without benefit of microphone or podium, she transfixed every eye and ear in the place.

Years of church and community leadership and motherhood and natural bossiness had forged in Junior not only the desire to mold others to her will, but the ability.

No one, not even the guilty, who had foolishly stayed to see the result of their pyrotechnics, tried to leave.

"You!" She spun around and pointed at one hapless, and possibly innocent, young man, who wilted on the spot. "Go and find the mop closet and bring back all the mops and buckets you can. You!" she focused on another. "Don't just stand there, help him."

Too startled to protest or hesitate, the two young men sprung into action.

And so did everyone else. Mops were procured, buckets were filled, garbage cans were located, and rogue giggles were never completely muffled.

Junior quickly and efficiently organized the workers, who bustled, treating the pumpkin cleanup as a game. Someone turned the mercury lights on, and in the full light, we swabbed the room and ourselves as best we could. Neil provided a subdued soundtrack and we proceeded apace.

I was presented with two garbage cans filled with assorted pumpkin pieces, and had not a clue as to what to do with them.

I scouted the room for Junior, and finally found her, by herself, in a corner, behind a corn shock, facing the wall. She was taking swipes at the front of her shirt with a washcloth.

"What should I do with the full garbage cans?" I asked briskly.

Evidently I startled her, because she jumped and dropped her rag.

"Uh," she said, turning even further away from me, "um, I think you can just put them outside somewhere." She waved me off, still facing away.

That answer wasn't detailed or bossy enough for Junior, who never gave vague instructions.

"Isn't there a specific place we should put the cans? Like by the Dumpsters or something?" I persisted.

"Yes. Anywhere," she said, still not looking at me. She swiped at her face with the rag and sniffed slightly. "You decide."

I stood frowning, unsettled by a Junior willing to let someone else decide.

"Are you all right?" I asked quietly.

"Yes of course I'm all right," she said sharply, sniffing again.

"No you aren't," I said, realization dawning. "You're crying."

"Don't be ridiculous," she said, turning to me, glaring with red-rimmed eyes. "Why would I be crying? Just because I worked my heart out on this party? Just because I tried to help the community, and the kids both? Just because they're working on my pipes?"

That last one threw me. Junior crying was strange enough. Junior veering into non sequiturs was unheard of.

"Huh?"

"Pipes!" she said fiercely. "They came today and tore up my kitchen and they didn't get finished and not only do we not have a functional sink, we don't have running water anywhere else either."

"What are you talking about?" I wondered if that last string of firecrackers had overloaded her circuits.

"You don't know what it's like," she said to the wall. "They put me in charge of everything."

I would have interrupted to disagree, but she didn't give me a chance.

"And I have to keep track of all the details and organize everything and keep everyone informed. But do they extend me the same courtesy?" she asked shrilly, shaking her head, tears snaking their way down her face. "Nooooo. This kitchen thing has been in the works for months—and today, *today*, they decide, is the day to begin. But they forgot to tell Clay and me. If we'd known, we could at least have had the cupboards cleaned out."

"Junior, you're not making any sense." I shot a furtive glance over my shoulder to see if anyone had

noticed our conversation, probably hoping someone
would interrupt. But everyone was busy cleaning and
talking and laughing. There were even a few kids dancing again.

"I'm the preacher's wife," she said, like that explained everything.

I looked at her blankly.

"Even though we live on the farm, and not in the
parsonage, the church still provides the kind of mainte-
nance that it would if we lived in town," she said, trying
to dislodge a hunk of pumpkin from her hair. "The
council decided long ago that we needed new cupboards
and a sink and linoleum, and then let the rest of the
congregation know that donations of raw materials
would be appreciated.

"Evidently"—she rubbed a hand under her nose and
sniffed again—"the new flooring arrived today, and the
plumber was free and the cabinets were in. Only no one
told us that we were going to have to vacate the house
while they did the work."

"So things are in sort of a jumble, huh?"

Junior snorted. "We can't complain because everything is given by the congregation. And since it *is* donated, we get the ugliest patterns, and mismatched door
handles. The shit no one could sell gets palmed off on
us for a dandy tax deduction."

I was stunned. Not because the good Lutherans of
Delphi would foist their rummage sale rejects on their
own reverend for a tax advantage, but because Junior
was being indiscreet enough to use bad words to complain about it.

She continued working up steam for a full-blown rant.
"Since the labor is also donated, we have no say over
when it starts. Or when it's completed. We might be
without water for a whole week," she said bitterly.
"And since I'm not officially employed by the church,
I can't complain, or even ask to be consulted. Because
then I'm being ungrateful."

Having as little to do with organized religion as possible, I'd never realized the hazards of being married to

a minister. Or the pressure of receiving donated goods. Or having to be publicly perfect. On the other hand, Junior generally handled the odd combo of running the world and being at the mercy of Clay's congregation fairly well. At least well enough that I had never suspected a conflict.

She sniffed again and suddenly busied herself picking more pumpkin off her clothes, not looking at me.

Spattered, tearstained, enormously pregnant, and probably exhausted, Junior looked less like a dynamo than a young girl who suddenly found herself in over her head.

I was completely astonished to find myself fighting twinges of sympathy for her. If you had asked me an hour ago if I would enjoy seeing Junior get a comeuppance, I would have applauded enthusiastically. Now, dejected and dirty and sad, I mostly felt sorry for her.

Pity is a dangerous emotion. It makes you do stupid things.

Behind us the cleanup went on. Aphrodite, whose table had been mostly pumpkin-free, was serving barbecue sandwiches again. In the middle of the brouhaha, Norman had materialized. He had helped Aphrodite reorganize her table. They worked together comfortably, occasionally laughing and carrying on a lively conversation that evidently used words of more than one syllable.

The party seemed to be putting itself back together, taking the interruption in stride.

Mardelle and Presley, and the rest of the coconspirators, scurried around the gym, eradicating the evidence of their prank, shooting furtive glances in our direction as they worked.

Junior was immobile and miserable. And vulnerable and pathetic. And human.

It was a look she usually kept well hidden.

"It's not such a big deal, if you come to think of it," I said indicating the room, over which hung the pervasive odor of squash and gunpowder. "This will all seem better in the morning," I said, amazed that I was trying to cheer her up. "You'll probably even laugh."

Junior ignored that last comment. "This is going to turn into one of those *stories*. The kind they repeat year after year, and I am always going to be the Bad Guy. It'll get bigger and bigger and funnier and funnier. And I am going to look more and more ridiculous. And we'll never catch them," she said. "The ones who did this. They won't turn themselves in, and no one else will tattle."

I felt a small stab of guilt because I already knew who was guilty and had no intention of ratting on anyone.

"You know something like this was inevitable. No pumpkin in Delphi survives Halloween intact," I said lightly. "It's not as though they were aiming for you personally."

"Yeah, right," Junior snorted.

She had a point. Junior so annoyed everyone with her willingness to be the arbiter and controller of all that concerns Delphi, that the kids probably did blow up pumpkins just to annoy her. And to laugh at her.

I was surprised again by my completely involuntary urge to comfort Junior the Indomitable, who never seemed to need comfort. Especially from me.

"What you really need is a beer," I said, warding off her disgusted frown with a wave. "I know you can't have one," I said, making an instant, and probably stupid, decision. "But it's almost time to shut this thing down, and Neil and I had already planned to go to the bar for a drink afterward. Why don't you come along? You can have an O'Doul's or something."

She peered at me warily.

If it had been possible, I would have peered at me warily too. Neither of us are used to me being kind to Junior.

"Honest," I said, shrugging, knowing already that I would regret the invitation. "It'll do you good to get out a little. At least the bar has running water."

She squinted at me, and then nodded hesitantly, wondering, I suppose, where the punch line was.

Unfortunately, the punch line would come when I had to explain to Neil that not only were we going to Jackson's for a drink, but we were toting Junior along for company.

10

....

Good Deeds

Americans with a less uncluttered landscape might assume that our appreciation of life's small chuckles would be overwhelmed by the daily tedium of keeping one eye on the road for deer with a death wish and farmers who take their half out of the middle, and the other eye on the heavens, waiting for the Weather Gods to zap us with another tornado, lightning bolt, or blizzard.

Just driving twenty-five miles to the nearest bookstore or movie theater, not to mention a grocery store that carries more than one brand of shampoo, can wear down a person's ability to find humor in the absurd.

But that doesn't mean that descendants of slab-faced Northern Europeans can't appreciate the ridiculous. Consider the 'Ring Cycle,' and tell me that Richard Wagner didn't pass on more than his share of Teutonic goofiness.

New Yorkers and Californians, and even Minnesotans, blow off steam by dragging out the Armanis and

Vera Wangs and the 5.3-carat baubles, congregating to
see and be seen. We do the same thing, but we just go
about it in a slightly different way.

We know that our finery, suitable for high school
graduations and the nephew's wedding, would not im-
press swells from either coast (not to mention the Nor-
wegians on our eastern border), so we settle for
impressing the shit out of ourselves by wearing costumes.

Which is why I felt right at home wearing an outfit
that would have been stylish when the sale of Abba records had comprised the largest share of the Swedish
gross national product, into the only bar in Delphi, with
a bemused Neil and a morose Junior in tow.

It was Halloween, and believe me, no one was dressed
normally. At midnight the bar was still packed, though
the homemade costumes were a little worse for the wear.
And the costumees weren't in much better shape.

Neil, carrying all our coats, and Junior, letting a frown
be her umbrella, threaded their way to the back of the
room to look for an empty table and the nonsmoking
section—neither of which were in evidence. I stood at
the bar, waiting to order a pitcher of beer and a jug of
ice water from Pat Jackson, whose costume bore a strik-
ing resemblance to a very busy Pat Jackson.

"Tory!" a voice shouted over the laughter, and the
clinking glasses, and Brooks and Dunn blasting from the
jukebox.

I found myself being addressed by a Statue of Liberty
whose cardboard and glitter tiara sat decidedly askew.

"Nice hair, Rhonda," I shouted back.

"Cool, huh? I washed out the dye this afternoon, and
voilà," she said, shaking soft curls that now bore a strik-
ing resemblance to old copper. "It took me the rest of
the day to figure out a costume that would go with green
hair."

"Is it permanent?" I asked, wondering what Aphrodite would think of a verdigris waitress.

"That'd be cool. I sorta like it this color."

She was wrapped, toga-style, in a green sheet, and her face, arms, and shoulders were smeared with the same goo that Del had used earlier for her Wicked Witch incarnation. In one hand she held a big green flashlight. In the other she unsuccessfully juggled a textbook and a mug of beer.

"Psychology?" I asked, reading the book's title.

She laughed. "It was the only green book I had."

I jumped back before she spilled more on me.

"Here, let's rearrange a bit," Brian or Michael Hunt said to Rhonda, gently taking the flashlight, and transferring the book to her now-empty hand. The mug stabilized.

Rhonda beamed at me, and winked conspiratorially. She could fall in love faster than any drunken twenty-year-old national monument I knew.

Brian beamed at me too.

He was dressed in khaki slacks with a brown leather belt, a short-sleeve safari shirt, Doc Martens, and a sort of highway trooper hat. I didn't know if he were in costume, or just wearing a little something he'd picked up at Banana Republic on the way to Delphi.

He caught me checking the outfit and bowed.

"Park ranger?" I guessed.

"Tour guide." He laughed.

✦ This was the first time I'd seen him since my cowardly exit from the cafe as the demise of his grandfather was being announced. Though I'm no good at that sort of thing, a word or two of condolence seemed to be in order.

"Say, uh, Brian . . ." He'd introduced himself as Brian, and that's what Rhonda had called him, so I decided not to muddy the waters with "Michael." "I'm awfully sorry about your grandfather . . ."

The smile disappeared from his face even before I let the sentence trail off unfinished.

"Yeah, well." He flicked his eyes away from mine and continued. "It goes like that sometimes."

"I'm really sorry. If we'd known who he was, we could have—"

He interrupted. "Not to worry," he said with a small, tight, false smile. "You couldn't have known, and even if you had, nothing would have changed. He'd still be dead." He clamped his mouth in a straight line, not looking at me. "Will you excuse me for a minute?" Brian said suddenly, setting his empty mug down on the bar. "I'll be right back."

Without looking back, he headed around the far end of the bar, toward the phone and the bathrooms.

I raised an eyebrow at Rhonda, who shrugged.

"He's a guy. They don't do grief well," she said calmly, sipping her beer.

I had thought he looked more angry than grief-stricken, but I wasn't taking psychology. And I didn't know him as well as Rhonda did. Or as well as Rhonda was obviously intending to know him.

"Whatever," I agreed, paying for the pitcher of beer that had finally materialized on the bar. Rhonda refilled her mug from my pitcher with a grin, and then wandered off.

Carrying the tray, with the pitcher, three glasses, and a carafe of ice water, I carefully made my way, avoiding suddenly flung arms and lit cigarettes, back to the table Neil had snagged, which sat in the midst of several sets of theme costumes.

At the long table to his right was a group of Television Bumpkins. Maybe they were supposed to be the cast of *Hee Haw*, or *Petticoat Junction*. They could even have been representing *Green Acres*, I couldn't tell. At any rate, there was lots of gingham and eyelet lace, overalls, straw hats and "y'alls."

On the other side was the inevitable band of middle-aged Indians, whooping and drinking and passing out cigars, calling them Peace Stogies. Male and female, they wore gunny sacks and cheap braided wigs with construction paper headbands and pheasant feathers sticking up in back. There were lines of eye-shadow war paint drawn on their cheeks.

Political correctness has not yet reached the north central plains.

As I excused myself past most of the tribe, a shapely Indian maiden grabbed my arm.

"How'd you get stuck with sourpuss?" Del asked, indicating Junior.

"Long story," I said, sighing. "Don't you think it's time to shit-can the Indian getup? This is the nineties, you know."

"Why?" Del asked. "There aren't any real Indians here to object. Besides, we're paying tribute to them."

It would do no good to explain that saying "how" and calling yourself a squaw was insulting. Ours is a culture that automatically assumes that no offense will be taken if none were intended.

I changed the subject. "Busy night."

"Yeah, everyone's here," Del said disgustedly.

"What do you mean 'everyone'?" I asked, heart sinking.

In my impromptu quest to introduce Sunshine and Happiness into Junior's evening, I had forgotten that Stu might take it upon himself to visit the bar too. Or that his wife might come along for company.

"Well, Ron's over there." Del pointed. "Right next to sweet little wifey."

At another table, Ron and Gina Adler sat with a group of similarly dressed Romans and their ladies. The sight of no-chin, knobby-kneed, short and skinny Ron wrapped in a sheet, with a length of plastic ivy wound around his head, cheered me considerably.

Ron, who seemed to be fully aware of his ridiculous appearance, and Del's derision, shot a harried, blinking glance our way.

Del snorted. "And our illustrious newcomer is over there." She pointed toward the far end of the bar where Alanna Luna, dressed in full Highland gear that somehow managed to make tartan and knee socks look girlish and salacious at the same time, held court.

Alanna casually leaned back, one arm draped on the bar (the better to emphasize her truly enormous chest) as she laughed and flirted. A crowd of males in various states of inebriation hovered around her, mesmerized.

"Bitch," Del muttered.

A few feet away from Alanna, Brian dialed the pay phone and then glanced back at her. Though the look lasted only a second, I could have sworn that some kind of signal passed between mother and son.

"Interesting," I said.

"Interesting, my ass. The town is going to hell in a hand basket," Del said, disgusted.

"It's worse than that," I said, laughing at Del, which can be dangerous. "Are you allergic to hamsters?"

"No, why?" she asked suspiciously.

"Just wondering," I said over my shoulder as I sat the tray down on our table.

Junior observed it all—the room, the tray, the conversation with Del, and my bright phony smile—with an expression of unalloyed distaste.

I shot a desperate look at Neil, who grinned in return. Like Mr. Knightley championing Jane Fairfax in *Emma*, Neil has always maintained that Junior would be my ally if only I would let her.

His was the minority viewpoint.

"Well, this is fun, isn't it?" I asked heartily. It was a stupid question, but someone had to say something since Junior continued to frown, and Neil seemed to think grinning constituted his entire contribution to the conversation.

"There's smoke in here," Junior said.

"Well, it's a bar," I said. I wanted to say: *No duh.*

"Too much smoke," she said.

There was no arguing with a statement so obviously correct. Smoke hung over the dimly lit room like a fog. And since I couldn't even disagree with Junior, I busied myself pouring beer for Neil and me, and water for Junior.

"Lots of people here," I said noncommittally, sitting in the chair with my coat draped across the back, which, thank God, was on Neil's other side—away from Junior. We were far enough from the bar not to have to shout over the jukebox, which now blasted the Eagles, in slow-dance mode.

Several couples were slow dancing.

Junior only nodded and sipped her water.

"This is all your fault," I whispered to Neil.

"Mine?" he whispered back, denying responsibility.

"Yours," I declared. "And *you* are going to pay."

"Hey," he said softly, so Junior couldn't hear, "you did a nice thing. I'm proud of you."

"Yeah, we'll see how you feel in another hour," I said sourly.

We sat for a while in comfortable silence, watching the costumes and the dancers, squinting through the smoke, refilling beer mugs, shooting surreptitious glances at Junior to see if she had cracked a smile yet.

Junior did seem to be loosening up. Occasionally she leaned over and said something to Neil that I couldn't hear, which was fine by me. I was content to sit and drink. Being in a smoky bar with Junior was better than sitting home alone with my own thoughts.

Which was a scary enough thought all by itself.

Junior said something to Neil that got his attention. He sat up straight and looked over her head and mumbled something back.

"What's up?" I asked, trying to see around, or through, him.

"Nothing," he said quietly.

Junior got up and came around Neil and sat in the empty chair on my other side. I was now sandwiched between them.

Neither one would look at me, and I was just about to demand a goddamn explanation when the jukebox went suddenly silent and the lights, if possible, dimmed even more.

"What's going on now?" I asked, thoroughly confused.

"Who knows?" Neil nodded at the bar, grinning.

I shot a glance at Junior, who avoided my look entirely by pouring herself some more water. I could tell that they were pleased by the coming diversion, whatever it was.

Before I could say anything, a couple of never-used track lights, installed in a frenzy of 1970s modernization, clicked on, spotlighting the bar, and one of the most amazing things I've ever seen. Or heard.

11

The Little Bang

Just so there's no doubt, let's get this straight—I am a liberal.

I support gun regulation and unlimited funding for education. I go for the separation of church and state in a big way. I see no reason to censor the content of books, television, music, movies, or the Internet when each and every citizen has the opportunity to close the covers, change the channel, leave the building, or power down.

It goes without saying that I am pro-choice.

It's okay with me if the government takes more money from the rich to give to the poor. Hell, they can even take more of my money, though I don't qualify as the former, and the difference between me and the latter isn't worth arguing about.

I love the spotted owl.

I would no more be caught reading George Will than agreeing with Rush Limbaugh or listening to Paul Harvey.

When the word *liberal* became a pejorative, I wore a pin to work that read, "The Only Good Conservative Is a Dead Conservative."

I will defend to the death your right to be a doofus in public.

And I especially have no problem with grown-ups doing whatever they wish with their own bodies and/or other consenting grown-ups.

So why was I appalled by the spectacle before me?

There were, after all, no children present to witness what I assumed was about to happen as Alanna Luna stood on top of the old oak bar, in full Highland regalia, arms wrapped around a bagpipe.

That's right, a bagpipe.

I shot a look over at Del, who shook her head in disgust. Across the room, Rhonda seemed equally mystified, though not nearly so repulsed.

Sitting beside me, Neil chuckled.

"This is going to be great," he said.

"What's going on?" Junior asked, confused.

With the exception of Brian, who was nowhere in sight, Neil, Del, Rhonda, and I were the only ones in the bar with even an inkling of Alanna's profession.

And with the apparent exception of Neil, not a one of us was interested in a demonstration of her skills.

The bar fell silent. Drinks sat undrunk. Cigarettes went unlit, or burned in ashtrays, ignored. Conversations died mid-sentence. Even Pat and Pat Jackson, husband and wife owners of the bar, stood stock-still, in open-mouthed, staring surprise.

"I came to your fair town, a weary traveler," Alanna proclaimed to the stunned crowd in a loud, clear, and, nearly as I could tell, authentic Scottish brogue. "Searching for my family and looking for a home."

Del duckwalked over to our table and knelt on the floor beside me and whispered, "Can you believe this shit? If she says *begorra*, I'm gonna throw something."

Alanna continued. "I found instead great sadness and loss. And so I dedicate this performance to my darling

da.'' She ended by bowing her head in what appeared
to be a moment of prayer.

While most in the building had no idea what, or who,
Alanna was talking about, all heads bowed in unison.

Del was not in a reverent mood. ''Her *da*? She actually said *da*?''

Alanna looked up at the ceiling and said, ''Pop, this
one's for you,'' inhaled deeply, and commenced playing
a passable version of ''Amazing Grace'' on the bagpipes, which startled even Del into silence.

It takes a lot to surprise us here in Delphi, but a larg-
ish, middle-aged blond dressed schoolgirl-demure in a
white blouse and kilt, standing on top of a bar, reenacting Mr. Spock's funeral scene from whatever *Star Trek*
movie, did the trick.

Though, as the saying went—we hadn't seen nothin'
yet.

I had no sooner concluded that Alanna really was per-
forming nothing but an odd, albeit heartfelt, tribute to
her recently deceased father, when she tossed her bagpipes to a very startled Ron Adler, who, wide-eyed,
caught the instrument gingerly, and held it like an infant
with far too many arms and legs.

With nothing in her hands, the wheezing bagpipe
strains of ''Amazing Grace'' still filled the room as
Alanna had begun to move, slowly and sinuously, ro-
tating her shoulders, arching her back, rolling her head
with her eyes closed. In perfect rhythm with the hymn,
her movements might have been mistaken as moderately
sensuous stretching exercises in preparation for a religious aerobic workout.

''Where's the music coming from?'' Junior asked, not
taking her eyes off Alanna.

''There's a portable rig and speakers set up at the end
of the bar,'' Neil said, leaning over me to talk to Junior.
''See.'' He pointed. ''She's got a tape going now. That
is a *great* sound system.''

Neil was right. If I hadn't known otherwise, I would
have sworn that an actual piper were tootling away.

I was vaguely heartened to know that Neil was impressed with Alanna's stereo, since Alanna herself was so impressive.

And judging by the reaction of the crowd, everyone in the bar *was* impressed.

Well, the men were, anyway.

Though the melody didn't change, the tempo picked up and took on a bump-and-grind back beat as Alanna slowly and deliberately began to remove bits and pieces of her outer clothing.

The audience didn't know who she was, or why she was taking her clothes off, but they certainly appreciated the performance. Stunned silence turned first into tentative applause, and then into enthusiastic whooping, as tartan garters and red knee socks and a fringed sash flew through the air, into the laps of costumed men whose wives wore universally sour expressions.

It wasn't just the wives whose faces registered disgust. Girlfriends and significant others and casual friends all displayed an extreme displeasure. Del's narrowed eyes telegraphed outright malice.

Rhonda seemed to be the only female in attendance who wasn't disturbed by the increasingly undressed Alanna, probably because her romantic hopes were currently focused on the one male in Delphi who would not be mesmerized by the performer. She watched Alanna unbutton her blouse with a rapt and studious expression that was not so much neutral as downright amazed.

I realized I was frowning when Neil grinned at me.

"This doesn't bother you, does it?" he leaned over and asked.

"Of course not," I said quickly, consciously smoothing the furrow between my eyebrows. "Why would it upset me?" I squashed my annoyance at Neil's obvious enjoyment.

Why did the notion of a large-breasted, attractive woman taking her clothes off to the wild enthusiasm of the assembled males upset me?

I had not a clue, but I was seriously displeased.

"Good," Neil said, taking my lie at face value. "Because there is a lot of skill on display here."

Del, who was eavesdropping, snorted. "Surgical skill, you mean. You can't tell me those tits are for real."

"I mean dancing skill," Neil said. "I'm talking talent. Can you take your socks off while standing up and dancing at the same time?"

Del, whose skills were not a proper subject for discussion in a public place, was not wowed by anyone else's ability to take clothes off artfully.

The noise level rose. Recorded bagpipes still played, but the song had somehow segued from "Amazing Grace" into a sort of Highland fling. Alanna's gyrating tempo picked up. Her blouse was long gone, draped around the neck of a sheepishly grinning young man, though an up close and personal glimpse of her heaving bosoms had been delayed by a red plaid Wonderbra that lifted and separated the superstructure in a truly heroic fashion.

"Anybody got a dart?" Del asked. "I bet they'd pop like balloons."

"This . . . this . . . spectacle . . ." sputtered Junior, as the kilt dropped to reveal a pair of red silk tap pants. "This has to be stopped."

"Yeah," Del said, in uncharacteristic agreement with Junior. "Go and pull the plug on her stereo."

"Plug, hell," Junior said sharply. "This is illegal. I'm calling the police."

She was up and out of her chair and heading for the phone before we realized what was happening.

"Oh Jesus," I said to Neil. "I'd better stop her."

Neil nodded. Even Del nodded.

Regardless of how we felt individually about being regaled with an impromptu performance of Alanna Luna's undeniable skills, none of us wanted the sheriff called.

You need official permission for this sort of entertainment, and the Jacksons, who had not asked for a spectacular ending to their Halloween festivities, would

bear the brunt of official displeasure. Perhaps even by
losing their liquor license.

In addition to which, the community embarrassment
would be large and uncomfortable—I could see the
headlines now: DELPHI BAR CAUGHT IN BIG BUST. State-
wide amusement at our expense would be sharp-edged
and long-lived.

If this went public, we'd never live it down.

I raced after Junior, realizing, as I neared her, that the
pay phone on the wall was already ringing. Probably
some wife checking up on an errant husband.

The hooting and clapping rose to new levels as
Alanna, down to a tartan G-string and red-and-black glitter pasties, took the low road, undulating to the final
strains of "Loch Lomond."

Junior answered the phone, with one hand covering
her free ear completely.

"What?" she shouted into the phone. "Who?"

A hand grabbed my arm and spun me around.

"Tory, I need to talk to you. Now," said Stu McKee,
who had materialized out of nowhere.

Though I had done my best to forget it all, Stu's sudden appearance brought back everything that had happened today—from the terrible surprise of seeing him
with his wife, to the revelation of Renee's pregnancy, to
the aching sadness I had been fighting ever since.

My heart beat painfully in my chest as I regarded the
man whose body I had memorized but whose mind and
heart I knew not at all.

I looked down at his hand clamped around my arm,
and then back into his eyes, but said nothing.

Beside us, up on the bar, in defiance of every law
pertaining to the exposure of certain intimate female
body parts in establishments that served liquor, Alanna
deliberately removed one of the pasties and tossed it into
the wildly cheering crowd.

Oblivious to what was going on around him, Stu loosened his hand, but did not let go of my arm.

"Not now, Stu," I said sadly. *Not ever*, I thought.
"Please."

I had no idea what to say to him anyway. Avoidance and delay were my favorite courses of action, and I saw no reason to change tactics now.

"Listen, I've been trying to get hold of you all day to explain . . ." he said.

"Explain what?" I said, suddenly angry. "Explain that your wife has moved back in with you? Explain that she's pregnant with *your* child?"

He had to have read my lips because he could not possibly have heard me over the crowd noise. "It's not . . ." He shook his head.

Stu was suddenly spun roughly around himself. By Neil, who had evidently followed me to the phone.

"Can't you see that she doesn't want to talk to you?" Neil asked, voice steady and soft. So soft that we shouldn't have been able to hear him, and yet we heard every word over the din as the second pasty went airborne.

Neil and Stu stared at each other angrily for a moment. Neil dropped his hand, but not his eyes.

Stu looked back at me, somber green eyes locked on mine. Eyes that had crinkled with laughter. Eyes that had looked down on me from above, filled with tender passion. Eyes that had haunted my dreams and destroyed my equanimity long before anything happened between us.

Eyes so sad that I could no longer bear their gaze.

I looked away.

"Go away," Junior said forcefully to Stu, phone in hand. She stood close to me. "She doesn't want to talk to you."

Stu stepped back, perhaps waiting for me to protest.

I wanted to. I wanted to turn the clock back, to gather him in my arms. To continue as we had been. To forget that the relationship had always been wrong, no matter how right it felt.

And I almost did.

Instead I stood, saying nothing.

The moment lengthened. Stu swallowed, nodded, and stepped back, and with a last, searching glance, turned away.

"Here," Junior said, handing me the phone.

Breathing heavily, and barely able to comprehend what had just happened, I looked dumbly from Neil to Junior to the receiver I held in my hand.

We seemed to be in a silent cocoon, I knew that the commotion in the bar had not stopped. Alanna was still gyrating on the stage to the noisy enjoyment of nearly all who watched.

Rhonda appeared at my side and placed an arm around my shoulders. Del hovered behind her. Neil and Junior tightened around me in a protective circle.

"It's for you," Junior said.

"The phone," Neil explained gently.

I looked at it, confused, and then held the receiver to my ear.

"Hello?" I said.

"You need to get over here," Aphrodite said gruffly. "Right now."

"Huh?"

"I'm at the cafe," she said, as if that explained everything.

Or anything.

"Are you all right?" she asked me, as Alanna took her final bow to a shower of tossed coins and dollar bills.

"No," I said. "Are you?"

"No," she answered.

12

....

The Big Bang

If I had known that wearing a Munchkin costume was going to be the highlight of this particular Halloween, I'd have done my best to enjoy it more. Looking ridiculous is usually enough, all by itself, to ruin my day, but this one had been a downhill tumble right out of the bucket. A real pisser whose brief lulls had only served to dim my emotional radar and leave even more vulnerable to the next attack.

A day that started out with a stupid outfit, and progressed through a dead body, another stupid outfit, an undressed interloper with big boobs, and what, on the surface anyway, looked to be a rather large romantic upheaval, was not a day destined to be remembered fondly.

Thank God it was almost over. Officially, at least, it was November 1, though the kids who continued to launch lit firecrackers and uncarved pumpkins out of car windows hadn't seemed to notice the passing of October.

Mother Nature knew it, though. It was a clear and starry night, which meant temps would sink well below freezing. The wind, as always, blew sharply, tearing at uncovered fingers and ears. I pulled my coat close around me and shivered on the two-block walk from the bar to the cafe to meet with Aphrodite.

Which promised even more unpleasantness. In our long association, Aphrodite had never summoned me off-hours, at least not for anything more pressing than to assist with an early start to the Salisbury steak and scalloped potatoes.

Scrupulous as she was about cooking and serving bad cafe food, even Aphrodite did not normally begin preparations in the middle of the night. Something was up.

And judging by the tone of her voice, and the unusual events of the day, it was serious.

I entered the cafe through the front door, assuming it would be unlocked since Aphrodite was expecting me.

A light from the far recesses of the kitchen spilled over into the cafe, dimly shining on the indifferently polished stainless-steel divider, and reflecting dully from the napkin holders on the counter. The rest of the long narrow room was dark.

I've spent a good portion of my adult life in this room. I know it by heart. I could negotiate its obstacles with my eyes closed. But in the half-light spilling from the kitchen, it looked foreign. And a little eerie. Without the hiss of the fryers, the clank of porcelain and silverware, the opening and closing of the door, ringing of the phone, and the constant laughter and chatter, the silence of the cold cafe was unnerving.

"Aphrodite?" I called. "Where are you?"

"Back here," she said, from a booth in the far corner of the cafe. The red glow of her cigarette traced an arc in the darkness, and then glowed brightly as she inhaled.

"Should I turn the lights on?" I asked, squinting in her direction, unable to make out more than her solid form, sitting alone next to the window.

"Nah, they'll just want to eat if you do."

The bar would be closing down very soon; lights in the cafe would shine like a beacon, drawing drunken revelers with the promise of bacon, eggs, and toast.

It would be easier to leave the lights off, and avoid the hassle.

"What's up?" I asked, slipping into the booth opposite her.

Aphrodite didn't answer at first, though she continued to inhale and exhale, looking out the window. Sitting across from her, I could make out her expression, which was somber.

Finally she looked at me. "Been some day."

Aphrodite is perfectly capable of multisyllabic conversation, but she prefers not to waste energy with unnecessary speech, relying on understatement to make her point.

"No shit," I said.

I could be a monosyllabic understater myself, when the situation called for it.

But not for long. Especially on a day like this.

"He really was your husband, then?" I asked.

"The jerk," she agreed.

"I don't suppose he just accidentally showed up on your doorstep, though."

Aphrodite snorted, stubbed out her cigarette, and lit another one. She inhaled deeply. A car drove past, its headlights momentarily lighting her face, making shadows in her red beehive hairdo, illuminating the cigarette with the usual lipstick marks, flashing brightly on the ring on her left hand.

"Not him," she said, disgusted. "Or Cheryl and Mike either."

"Cheryl and Mike?"

"Well, Cheryl was her name back when Gus and I got married," Aphrodite said. "She was just a little shit then. I didn't know she'd changed it. Mike is her kid."

Ah, Alanna and Brian.

"Well, Cheryl Ferguson probably isn't the best name for an exotic dancer," I said, shrugging. Though a naked woman by any name would still garner plenty of attention. Especially in Delphi.

"Not Ferguson. Hunt. Cheryl Hunt."

"Huh?"

"Cheryl Hunt is her name. Mike's dad was Bill Hunt." She stopped for a moment, frowning. "Or maybe it was Bob. Doesn't matter. He's gone now."

"Dead?" I asked.

"Nah, just divorced. Like everyone."

"Well, not everyone," I said softly.

I, personally, was a widow. Neil and Del had never married. Stu seemed destined not to divorce. "You're still married. Or at least you were until today."

"I'd rather be divorced. It'd be easier," Aphrodite said ruefully. "Especially . . ." her words trailed off as another car drove past slowly.

In the dark we could see the red fuse as a string of lit firecrackers was tossed from the open car window. They popped and bounced harmlessly against the sidewalk, each explosion making a small light in the darkness.

"Speaking of which," I said, patting my coat pockets for the manila envelope, "I have all your papers here. I wasn't snooping, honest. But I couldn't help seeing divorce papers as I picked them up."

"It was in the works," she said. "Gus knew. I think that's why he came."

My pockets were empty.

"That's funny," I said, mostly to myself, searching again, feeling the lining of the coat, standing up to see if I was sitting on the envelope. "I'm certain I put them in this pocket."

I checked the pocket again, just to make sure.

It was still empty. Maybe I'd left the envelope at home.

"Damn," I said. "I thought I had all that stuff right here."

"Doesn't matter," Aphrodite said, shrugging. "Gus is dead, no point divorcing him now."

"I'm sorry," I said, embarrassed. Leaving the cafe with the papers had been bad enough. I would feel doubly stupid, and probably criminally liable, if I had lost them.

More to change the subject than anything, I asked, "Is it going to cause any problems here since, uh, Gus, was discovered in the bathroom? I mean with the police and all?"

"Nah," Aphrodite said. "He had a bad heart. Had it for years."

"So you kept in touch?"

"More than I liked. He wrote or called. Once a year or so. He wanted to try again."

"You mean, you and him?" I asked, surprised. "Together? Now?"

Aphrodite had been separated from her husband for going on thirty years, and he'd been pining away the whole time? I was nearly swept away by the romance of the notion.

"I never wanted to," she said, squashing that notion. "When I split, it was for good. But getting divorced was a lot of trouble. And it cost too much. We just left things the way they were."

"Until lately," I said, specifically remembering divorce papers among the legal shit.

"Yeah, well," Aphrodite smiled sheepishly. She slid out of the booth and paced a little. "Ya see, Norm and me . . ."

Aphrodite was a jewel-free woman, but I suddenly remembered the reflected sparkle of the ring in the headlights.

"You're getting married?" I asked. "You and Norman Oberle?"

Aphrodite nodded, grinning widely.

Now I *was* swept away with romance. Norman Oberle and Aphrodite Ferguson were getting married. Lost in the moment, I jumped up and gave her a big hug, which made her squirm.

"When did he ask? Where will you have the ceremony? Have you set a date?"

I was delighted. We hadn't had a cafe wedding for ages—in addition to being genuinely happy for Aphrodite, a little voice in my brain said that planning her wedding would keep me plenty busy, which would help me to forget the rest of the day's unpleasant revelations.

"Don't have a date yet," she said, stepping out of hug range. "We were waiting for the divorce to be final first."

"Well, you don't have to do that any more," I said, thinking out loud. "Though, I suppose you should wait a decent interval. You can have the reception right here in the cafe . . ."

I would have gone on and on deciding her colors and ordering balloons and streamers, I suppose, but even in the dark, I could see that her expression had changed.

"Well, that's why I called you over here. To talk to you about the cafe," she said quietly.

"What about the cafe? Why should your getting married change anything here?"

"It's not me getting hitched," she said sadly. "It's Gus dying that matters."

"Good Lord, why?" I asked, confused.

She started to reply, but an explosion so loud that it rattled the windows interrupted her.

We'd been hearing them on and off all day, but this one was the loudest yet.

"Out back," Aphrodite said, frowning mightily. "Damn kids."

I followed as she marched through the kitchen and out the side door into the back parking lot, which was empty except for Aphrodite's van.

The old metal Dumpster that sat against the back wall of the cafe belched wisps of blue smoke, and the smell of gunpowder hung on the air.

"Cherry bomb?" I asked.

"M–80," she said.

M–80s were real firecrackers, not cutesy fireworks for juvenile pranksters. They made a powerful explosion, and a really big noise, and because of that, were highly sought after even though they were illegal.

And with good reason. If held in hand, an M-80 could easily blow off several fingers. In a worst-case scenario, an M-80 foolishly lit and carelessly tossed, could kill.

It could also start a fire.

I ran back into the cafe for the fire extinguisher, just in case, but the smoke coming from inside the Dumpster had already dissipated.

In the meantime, Aphrodite patrolled the perimeter of the parking lot. Assuming, I imagine, that no juvenile would waste the big stuff on an unobserved explosion.

"All gone home by now," she called from beside her van, and then bent over to pick something up. "Hey, come and see this."

She waved me over, holding an object up in the moonlight.

It was a large flashlight. In the moonlight we could see that it was green.

I took it from her, frowning.

"Tory! Is that you? Are you all right?" Neil shouted, rounding the corner of the cafe at a dead run. "I was on my way home and I heard the explosion." Concern, and maybe even real fear, was in his eyes.

"We're fine," I said, trying to reassure him. "We were inside when the Dumpster blew. An M-80, we think."

"No damage," Aphrodite said. "Just damn kids."

"Thank God," Neil panted. "I was afraid something had happened to you. And Aphrodite, of course."

Aphrodite grinned and nudged me.

I ignored her.

More voices echoed from around the cafe. Evidently the Dumpster explosion had been loud enough to have been heard in the bar, which caused every ambulatory patron to stumble on over for a look-see.

Including Alanna Luna, fully dressed again.

Aphrodite's smile disappeared when she saw her step-daughter. "No time to talk now," she said to me quietly, opening the door of her van and climbing inside. "We'll finish this in the morning."

"I'll get rid of the crowd," I said, sighing. "That'll give me time to make sure the Dumpster really isn't on fire."

"Thanks," she said, leaning an elbow on the open window frame. "I'll go now."

"Fine," I agreed, nodding. Whatever she had to tell me about the cafe could wait until morning.

Neil was explaining to the disappointed crowd that there wasn't anything left to see, when Aphrodite turned the key to start the van.

I was already several feet away, and had turned around to wave at Aphrodite, whose engagement ring glittered in the moonlight, when her van burst into a ball of flame in an explosion so massive that I was blown backward, off my feet, and into the air.

After which the world went silent.

13

....

The Last Ghost of Halloween

November 1, Early a.m.

Part of the appeal of murder mysteries is that they let us pretend that death can be held at a comfortable remove. We'd all like to live in a universe where nasty surprises come only to those who deserve them, or to those we don't know very well, and therefore won't mourn. At least not for long.

We like dramatic denouements as long as they're followed by neat and tidy explanations. We don't like loose ends. Or ambiguity. Or variations from the formula.

We buy into the notion that the Good Guys always win and that the Really Good Guys will still be around for the next book.

The problem with real life is that it doesn't follow the happy ending rules. It's messy and unpredictable, and unlike some of my favorite fictional escapes, sometimes the Good Guys die.

A part of me knew, even lying on the hard-packed dirt parking lot behind the cafe, in the baking heat from the burning van, that Aphrodite, definitely one of the Good Guys, could not have survived the explosion.

Though for just a moment, I thought she stood over me in the silence, cigarette in mouth. Silhouetted against the flames, she pointed at the cafe, and then turned and nodded somberly at Nicky, who was next to her.

Nick, looking as good as ever, blew a kiss in my direction and winked, then he and Aphrodite stepped back into the milling crowd.

"Tory!" someone shouted. The voice was muted, as though from a long distance.

"Tory!" The voice came again, closer this time.

There were people standing around me. Sounds, far away at first, were beginning to filter in. I could now hear pounding feet and distant sirens, as well as the crackle of the flames.

"Aphrodite," I shouted after her, struggling to sit up, searching the crowd wildly.

Someone told me to lie still and try to stay calm.

"No, I have to find Aphrodite," I said, shrugging off the hands that were trying to hold me down.

"You need to stay put until the ambulance gets here," Stu, kneeling over me, said softly. "Please, Tory. You might be hurt."

Though my head ached terribly, and every part of my body felt bruised, and Stu's voice was barely louder than the ringing in my ears, I struggled to my feet.

"I'm not hurt," I said adamantly. "I need to find her. She was just here."

"How is she?" someone asked.

"Disoriented," Stu said. "She wants to go find Aphrodite."

"Jesus," Neil said. "Tory, hon, Aphrodite's gone. There wasn't anything anyone could have done to save her. It all happened too fast."

"You don't understand," I said sharply to both men, furious at their interference. And their patronizing tone. "Aphrodite *was* here, standing over me, just now. With . . ."

My voice trailed off as I stared at the flame-engulfed van. Aphrodite had waved at me while turning the ignition key. The explosion had been terrible and instantaneous. Its force must have knocked me out long enough to have a small, wistful hallucination in which both Aphrodite and my dead husband dropped by, on Halloween of all nights, to say hello.

Or maybe good-bye.

"You okay?" Del shouted in my ear.

I ignored her, watching the flames. The rural fire trucks had arrived. Uniformed volunteer firemen sprayed water on the charred vehicle, shouting instructions and encouragement at one another. The newly arrived EMTs waited silently for the firemen to finish so their job could begin.

"Is she okay?" Del demanded of Stu and Neil.

Stu said nothing.

Neil shrugged. "I think so. A little shock maybe."

I stepped closer to the van, needing to see the shape hunched in what was left of the driver's seat.

"No, Tory, don't," Del said, grabbing my arm.

I glared at her steadily until she dropped her hand.

The sheriff and a couple of deputies had arrived, and so had the television cameras. They filmed the fire, and the crowd, many of whom still wore their gaudy costumes.

The street in front of the cafe had filled with cars and townspeople who had heard either the explosion or the sirens that followed, and had come out to see what was going on. They shivered and talked quietly, horrified and wildly entertained at the same time.

A half-mile away on the highway, a steady line of headlights from the north streamed toward Delphi, looky-loos drawn by flames that would be visible for miles in the flat countryside.

With Del, Stu, and Neil behind me, I picked my way over hoses coiled on the ground, and around firemen. The fire was almost out though the van's metal framework was still hot, and water hissed and steamed from it. The charred interior was black, too dark, really, to

see details clearly. The acrid smell of smoke mixed with
the odor of burned fabric, and something else that I
didn't want to identify.

I stood for several minutes, still and silent in the middle of the motion and noise, and then turned.

"Could this have been an accident?" I asked the trio.
"Some sort of mechanical malfunction?"

"Sure, it could have been," Del said, hopefully.

"Maybe," Stu said. "We'll have to wait for the reports to know for sure."

Neil just stood, sad and unsmiling.

A pain washed over me, so strong that for a second I
thought I might be having a heart attack. I stood with
my eyes closed tightly as it faded, breathing in shallow
gasps.

With my back to the van, I surveyed the crowd, scanning faces for something, though I didn't know what.

Presley, who should have been home and in bed long
ago, stood stiff and pale, Mardelle Jackson's arm draped
protectively around his shoulder. Rhonda, in disheveled
Lady Liberty garb, still holding her textbook, wept dis-
consolately as Brian, with flashlight in hand, stood by.
His face, in the growing darkness, was unreadable. Not
far away, Alanna Luna, dressed and buttoned, wiped
away tears that looked as cold and hard as metal in the
moonlight.

Norman Oberle, half-dressed, without shoes, and out
of breath, pushed his way to the front of the crowd. As
he came to a standstill next to the van, his large and
homely face crumpled.

"Attention," a deputy said, voice carrying over the
murmuring of the crowd and Norman's soft sobbing.
"We'd like those who witnessed the incident to step
over and give statements. The rest of you folks go on
home now. Show's over."

A couple of TV cameras hovered nearby as the crowd
slowly dispersed. Those of us who had no choice stood
in the cold, clear darkness, waiting our turn to speak.

14

Fish-Eye View

When I was a child I often went fishing with my Uncle Albert Engebretson. The outings were more of a social than a sporting nature, since the few fish we caught were usually too small to keep. Uncle Albert would inspect the catch, congratulate me, and then release it back into the river. Mostly we came home empty-handed, but content.

One morning as we sat on the grassy banks of the James River, my pole dipped and bent alarmingly. I had hooked a big one, a carp much too large for me to handle, so Uncle Albert reeled him in. I remember the feeling of excitement as I leaned over to inspect the prize. My excitement turned to horror as I saw a trickle of blood from the carp's mouth, which was opening and closing in soundless gasps. Its terrified, glassy eye stared steadily into the sunlight.

"This one's a keeper," Uncle Albert had said, grinning. "Good job, Tory."

"What's wrong with it?" I had asked, uneasy.

"Nothing. He's just trying to breathe. We'll fix that in a second."

Before I had a chance to say anything else, Uncle Albert had picked up a pair of pliers and bashed the fish on the head. I squealed as he hit the fish again, and burst into tears.

My gentle and entirely baffled uncle had then pulled a hankie from a back pocket and knelt down to daub my face. "But honey, it's only a fish. They can't feel anything, and besides it happened too fast to know what was going on."

After that, I made flimsy excuses when Uncle Albert asked me to go fishing with him, and eventually he stopped asking.

It wasn't the fact that I had begun to view the enterprise from the fish's point of view that bothered me. It was that my uncle, a man who would never purposely hurt a living creature, had convinced himself that it was *only* a fish, and it didn't feel anything.

I have been fishing in the intervening years, and I have even enjoyed it. But no matter how many times I heard others say it, or tried to convince myself, I never did believe that death came too fast for the lowly creatures to feel.

Or the higher ones either.

"It was instantaneous," Neil said. He'd taken one look at my face and known my thoughts. "I'm certain that the whole thing was over too quickly for her brain to register anything, except maybe surprise."

I remembered that poor carp gasping and staring, and didn't answer as I draped my coat over the back of a kitchen chair. Below us, the library was dark and quiet. The rest of the house, and all of Delphi, was dark and quiet.

At the cafe, most of the costumed bar patrons, stunned and sleepy neighbors, and just plain gawkers had been sent home immediately. The rest were dismissed after giving detailed statements to the county deputies.

Unfortunately I had been on the scene long before the explosion. Since the officials wanted to know all about

the conversation inside the cafe, as well as my version
of what happened outside, I was not given permission
to leave the parking lot until almost four A.M., long after
the others had left. They had been especially interested
in the timing of the first explosion—the small one in the
Dumpster.

By the time they were done questioning me, the town
was quiet again. It somehow seemed appropriate that I
was the only civilian on hand when the ambulance drove
off, lights unflashing, siren silent, speed well under the
limit.

I had watched the taillights disappear before turning
to walk home. The night was crisp and clear, the stars
shone brightly. My breath plumed before me as I walked
the three blocks home, shivering with my hands stuffed
into pockets. Exhausted, I'd wearily climbed the porch
steps of the trailer.

Neil's porch light flashed three times. Certain that I
would be unable to sleep and grateful that he was still
up, I headed across the street.

"I was watching for you," he said, taking my coat
from the back of the chair and hanging it on a hook.
"You must be freezing. There's hot chocolate on the
stove. The real stuff—made with milk and everything."

Unwilling, or maybe even unable, to talk, I just nodded and wandered into his dark living room, curled up
on the couch, and stared into the darkness.

From the stereo, James Taylor sang softly about death
and hope. Neil set two steaming cups on the coffee table
and then covered me with an afghan. He sat down next
to me, put a pillow on his lap, and patted it.

I scootched over and laid my head on the pillow. Neil
settled a warm arm around my shoulders. Without
speaking in the darkness, we listened through to the end
of "Hourglass." Neil beamed the remote at the stereo
and started the CD over.

Somewhere in the middle of "Gaia," I said, finally,
"It couldn't have been fast enough."

Neil's arm tightened. "I think it could have. That was
a big explosion. The blast concussion probably killed

Aphrodite immediately,'' he said quietly. "And even if
it didn't, it would certainly have knocked her out. She
had to have been unconscious before the fire even
started."

As always, he knew what I was thinking.

"You can't be certain of that," I said, seeing the
flames again.

He gently smoothed a stray hair off my forehead.
"Tory, you were outside the van and you blacked out.
Think how much stronger the force would have been
inside."

I wanted to believe him. I wanted to block my mind's
terrible version of Aphrodite's last moments, an un-
speakable vision of fear and pain and searing heat.

I had no real notion of how much time had elapsed
between the blast and when I'd opened my eyes to see
Aphrodite's ghost looking down on me.

"How long was I out?"

"Two minutes minimum," Neil said. "She'd have
been out for at least the same amount of time. Long
enough for the fire to kill without her ever knowing what
was happening."

Neil was doing his best to reassure me. Unfortunately,
I didn't know if he were just being kind.

"I'm not saying this because I want to believe it,"
said the mind reader. "Did *you* have time enough to be
afraid between the blast and when it threw you eight
feet across the parking lot?"

There had not been time to think or feel anything. I
had heard the noise and was dimly aware of flying
through the air. I had not been in pain. I had not been
frightened. I only remember being briefly surprised before everything went black.

Neil took my lack of answer as an assent, which it
was, sorta.

"So what happens now?" I asked.

"I imagine they'll conduct an investigation. Catch
whoever set the explosive."

"Maybe it was an accident," I said, hanging on to a
small and futile hope.

"I don't think so," Neil said sadly. "Sitting vehicles don't spontaneously explode."

James sang on, soothing us through what was left of a long and terrible night. We talked quietly about inconsequential things. Neither of us said out loud what had been immediately obvious—the common knowledge that no one drove Aphrodite's van except Aphrodite. That the explosion had been a trap set specifically for her.

We didn't say it, but we knew that Aphrodite Ferguson, my boss and friend, had been murdered.

Sometime during James's fourth go-around, as the blackness outside gradually lightened, I dozed off with my head still nestled in Neil's lap. Neil must have dropped off too, because it was full light and the stereo was silent when the phone rang.

Grabbing his glasses from the coffee table, rubbing his eyes and yawning, Neil shuffled to the kitchen to answer the phone.

"Yeah, she's here. Just a minute," he said and then covered the phone. "It's for you. Del."

I sat up on the couch, confused.

"How did you know where I was?" I asked Del.

"Process of elimination," she said. "You weren't snuggled in your own bed and the McKees said you weren't menage-a-trois-ing with them, so I figured you were dallying with the millionaire librarian."

"Oh, Del," I said, disgusted. "You didn't actually call him, did you?"

"Of course not, dipshit. Considering the strange reappearance of the wife, and the rest of last night's fun and games—where else would you be but with Neil? I didn't interrupt the two of you, did I?" she asked hopefully.

"Don't be ridiculous," I said, running my fingers through my wildly disarrayed hair, unable to look directly at Neil, squashing the picture that popped into my head. "Did you call just to wake me up?"

"No, there are more important things going on besides your lack of lovelife, you know."

"Like what?"

"Like we better get over to the cafe right now," Del said impatiently.

"The cafe? What for? You're not thinking of opening, are you?"

That was one of the things Neil and I had discussed in the waning hours of the night—the fact that the cafe would probably be closed until Aphrodite's affairs could be settled.

"It's already open," Del said. "Rhonda just called to inform me that the joint is hopping and *Alanna*"—Del spat the name—"is cooking up a storm."

"*What?*"

"Just what I said. Alanna took it upon herself to open the cafe this morning. It might be a good idea if we get our asses over there and find out just exactly what is going on."

I was still confused. "What business is it of hers? She doesn't have anything to do with the cafe."

"Au contraire, my dear," Del said snottily. "According to Rhonda, Ms. Luna has announced to one and all that she is now the owner of the Delphi Cafe."

Del paused and let that sink in for a moment and then continued. "Don't you think we ought to check the situation out?"

15

....

Execute This

I'm not much for standardized rules of behavior. Something about the whole idea of institutionalized expectations for the conduct of others drives me nuts. Evidently, my inner child is a closet rebel.

Declare that fat women shouldn't wear horizontal stripes, and I'll look like an awning before you finish the sentence. Make a certain book off-limits, and guess which one will be on my bedstand before nightfall. Try to tell me that I can't set fire to the American flag, and see how fast I get out the matches.

But like all anarchists, I have my own unwritten rules. My taboos. My sacred cows.

Give away the ending to a mystery and I will be tersely unforgiving. Drop candy wrappers on the sidewalk, and I will politely remind you that there are garbage cans on nearly every corner. Be mean to small animals, and I will intervene—with a baseball bat if necessary.

Announce that you are the new owner of an established business, especially less than twenty-four hours after the death of the previous owner, and I will be horrified.

Patronize that business if you have been a steady customer of the aforementioned recently deceased owner, and I will bypass shock and denial, and the other steps of grief, and land smack-dab in the middle of fury.

Pausing just long enough to thank Neil, change from my wrinkled polyester finery, and brush my teeth, I stormed to the cafe with Del.

My vague hope that Rhonda had exaggerated was crushed immediately. Dusty pickup trucks and cars lined the street in front of the cafe. Out on the sidewalk, we could hear the normal sounds of a busy cafe in operation—clinking dishes, ringing register. Laughter.

That the locals in search of coffee and gossip weren't willing to forgo their morning constitutional for even one day out of respect for Aphrodite solidified my own barely acknowledged sense of loss into a white-hot anger.

I hesitated at the door, glancing at Del. She nodded grimly. Inhaling deeply, brushing hair off my forehead, I opened the door.

As grand entrances go, I don't suppose ours was all that impressive—a couple of disheveled, plainly upset women standing in a doorway, staring balefully at a room full of friends and neighbors.

But it got their attention, all right.

Forks froze midway to the mouth. Cigarettes burned unnoticed in ashtrays. Conversation died immediately. The cafe sat in unnatural silence as people carefully avoided looking directly at us.

Everyone except Stu McKee, who sat in a booth opposite Ron Adler. Ron had taken one look over his shoulder, blinked several times in quick succession, turned, and hunched down as if to hide. Stu, green eyes calm and focused, looked directly at me.

Too angry to be flustered by Stu's presence, I concentrated instead on transmitting my own sense of betrayal to the crowd. I willed them to feel shame for gathering, for eating and laughing. I condemned them all for sitting there as though Aphrodite were still in the kitchen, smoking over the grill. For acting like our world had not suddenly changed. For being alive when she was not.

Rhonda, whose faintly green-tinged blond hair had been pulled into a sloppy ponytail, had been pouring refills. She rushed down the aisle to us.

"I'm so glad you guys are here," she whispered. "It's been awful."

"And what are *you* doing?" I asked, pointedly glaring at the decaf pot clenched in Rhonda's hand. "Sucking up to the new boss?"

Rhonda, whose red and puffy eyes widened in surprise at the unexpected attack, looked down and blushed. "No, it's not like that. I just wanted to . . ." She hesitated, shaking her head. ". . . to keep an eye on things here. Brian, um, sorta asked me to fill in for a while. I called you guys as soon as I could. I know it looks awful, me being here and all. I just thought one of us should stick around. You know, to figure out what was going on . . ." Her voice trailed off.

She looked so young and sad that I immediately felt guilty for snapping at her.

The cafe was still unnaturally quiet. People were eating and drinking and smoking again, but mostly they were trying to eavesdrop on our conversation as we stood gathered by the door.

Del leaned over to Rhonda and said, even more quietly, "So what, exactly, *is* going on?"

"I don't know," said Rhonda, plainly miserable. "I mean, *she* says the cafe is hers now that her dad and Aphrodite are . . ." Rhonda swallowed, her big blue eyes filled again, threatening to spill over.

"But how did she get the keys?" I asked. "You didn't give them to her, did you?"

"Oh God no," Rhonda said. "She said that Aphrodite gave her a set. And she says that Aphrodite made it clear that she was to run things if anything happened to her. Aphrodite, I mean." This time the tears did spill.

"What?" Del asked, loudly enough that several heads turned.

"Alanna made it sound like Aphrodite had some kind of premonition that she was going to die," Rhonda said, sniffling.

"Bullshit," I said flatly. "I was with Aphrodite last night. Just before . . ." I stopped and closed my eyes, left that sentence unfinished, and started over. "She wasn't having any premonitions then. Women who know that they are about to die do not announce their engagements. I'll bet Alanna found an extra set of keys at Aphrodite's house and made up the rest to get people to accept her."

"Engagement?" Del and Rhonda said together.

"Aphrodite and Norman Oberle . . ." I started to explain.

"Welcome, welcome, welcome," a loud and broadly Southern voice interrupted from behind us.

We turned to find Alanna Luna, hair piled high into a blond nest, wearing skintight jeans, an even tighter University of Oklahoma sweatshirt, and a broad smile. With a spatula in one hand, she performed a small bow. "I am so pleased y'all stopped in."

There was no trace of last night's Scottish brogue in her voice, and no hint of sadness in her eyes. For a woman who had suddenly and separately lost both her father and the only mother she had ever known, she was amazingly jolly.

"I think we need to talk, Ms. Luna," I said quietly.

"Alanna, call me Alanna," she said brightly and loudly, grabbing a clean cup from an empty table and holding it out to Rhonda, who filled it automatically.

"All right, *Alanna*," Del said nastily, "We'd like to talk to you. About the cafe."

"Well," she said, drawing the word into two syllables, "there isn't actually much to talk about. I know this might look unseemly"—she gestured at the packed booths and tables—"but the unfortunate and terrible deaths of"—here she stopped and wiped a phony tear from a completely dry eye—"of my wonderful parents have left this town without a central gathering place. The best way I can honor both of them, and preserve tradition, is to keep this establishment open.

"And the best thing you can do," she said, staring at Del and me directly, "is to help me run the cafe just like before. You can have your old jobs back, just like normal."

Alanna not only intended to run Aphrodite's cafe, but she expected *us* to work for *her*. I was speechless.

Luckily, Del was not.

"And the best thing you can do is go fuck yourself," Del hissed.

Conversation in the cafe had again died completely. Every ear was tuned to our conversation at the door.

Alanna's smile stayed in place, but her eyes narrowed and her voice lowered. With almost no trace of Southern joviality, she said quietly to Del, "Listen, honey. This place is mine now. You wanna work with me, fine. You don't wanna work with me, that's also fine."

"Mom," Brian said softly. He'd been in the kitchen, listening like everyone else. "Maybe you should talk to the ladies in private."

"I don't think there's much to talk about," I said to Brian, recovering my voice. I was surprised to hear how calm and reasonable I sounded, that my anger and loathing didn't leach out with every word. "Your mother says that she owns the cafe now. With all due respect, I think we'll wait for an opinion from Aphrodite's lawyer on that point before we proceed further."

"Go ahead, talk to a lawyer. He will only confirm what I've already told you," Alanna said evenly, with no trace of an accent. "My dear father is dead and I have inherited his interest in this cafe. It's mine and I intend to run it. If you do not wish to work for me, then there is nothing more to discuss."

"We'll see," I said to Alanna. Without considering the long-term consequences, I turned to Del and said, "There's not much point in sticking around, is there?"

"Nope," she said to me. She then continued, loudly and clearly. "As far as I can see, there's no reason for anyone to stick around.'' She glared at the eavesdroppers, sparing no one, withering poor Ron Adler with her acidic stare.

The last person she looked at was Rhonda, who stood uncertainly, coffee pot still in her hand.

''Are you coming?'' Del demanded.

Rhonda glanced uncertainly at Alanna, who stared triumphantly back at us, evidently assuming that Rhonda's attraction to Brian would overrule her loyalty to us.

It almost did. Rhonda shot a beseeching look at Brian, who shrugged imperceptibly, and then at us.

With a sigh, she sat the pot down on the counter, mumbled an apology to Alanna, and then turned to us. ''Let's go, then,'' she said quietly.

With one last glare, an unspoken challenge for those inside to join us, we followed Del into the cool November morning.

''This is too much,'' Rhonda said, beginning to cry again as we stepped out on the sidewalk. ''First that dead guy yesterday. And then Aphrodite last night. And now we don't have jobs anymore. I mean, I can live at my folks' farm while I go to school. But what are you guys going to do? There aren't any other restaurants for you to work in, and you're too old to find new jobs.''

She dissolved into miserable tears. I gingerly patted her on the back and let her sob on my shoulder. I shot a glance over her head at Del, wondering what, exactly, were our elderly employment prospects.

Del just shrugged.

''So what do we do now?'' I asked out loud, still comforting Rhonda.

''Beats the shit outta me. You're the smart one of the bunch. You knew Aphrodite best—do you think she left the cafe to Steel Magnolia in there?''

I didn't feel like the smart one of any bunch. And considering that until yesterday, I hadn't known about either a husband or a stepdaughter, I didn't feel as though I had known Aphrodite either.

''She didn't say that Aphrodite left the cafe to her, she said her dad did,'' Rhonda sniffed.

"I thought Aphrodite owned the cafe free and clear," Del said, pulling her coat tight around her and shivering.

Aphrodite had certainly not discussed her financial situation with me. I had automatically assumed that she had the title to the cafe.

I had also assumed that she would live forever.

I have been known to be wrong.

The cafe door opened and Stu McKee stepped out, zipping up his jacket.

He didn't smile when he saw us. "Good, you're still here. We need to talk."

"Oh for chrissakes," Del said disgustedly. "Can't you leave Tory alone for a while? She's had a rough night."

I silently applauded Del. Things were complicated enough. I had no desire to enact any personal dramas on the sidewalk in front of the cafe in the cold sunlight.

"This is *not* about Tory," Stu said, voice hard with anger. "This is about Aphrodite. I assume you *do* want to talk about Aphrodite, don't you?"

Del had the grace to look abashed. I blushed too, for my own mistaken assumptions. Rhonda dug in her coat pocket for a Kleenex and blew her nose loudly.

"Yes," I said quietly. "We do want to talk about Aphrodite. Do you know anything about what happened to her?"

"No," he said softly, looking directly at me. "But I couldn't help overhearing the conversation you were having inside."

"The whole town could have overheard the conversation inside," Del said impatiently. "Get on with it."

The cafe door opened behind us again. This time Ron Adler came out. "Who needs a cafe anyway?" he asked, blinking. "Solidarity and all that."

Del actually smiled at him. He blinked even more furiously.

To me, Stu said, "You mentioned something about contacting a lawyer. Do you know who to call?"

"Unfortunately, no," I said. "But after we found the, you know, body, yesterday, she disappeared for a while

with Norman Oberle. She came back a little while later
with an armload of legal documents. She must have had
a lawyer.''

"That's right," Del said. "You had the papers. Did
you see who drew them up?"

"All I saw for sure was the divorce stuff. I didn't
notice any signatures anywhere. I was going to give
them back to Aphrodite last night—but they disappeared
before I could do it."

"What do you mean, they disappeared?" Del asked.

"I put them in a manila envelope, and then stuck the
envelope in my coat pocket," I said. "And they were
gone when I checked for them later."

"You mean someone stole them?" Rhonda asked,
shocked. "Someone just took them out of your pocket?"

"I don't know what happened to them," I said. "I
could have dropped them on the road. They might have
fallen out at home, for all I know. I hope that's what
happened, because that would give us the name of Aphrodite's lawyer. And the lawyer can tell us exactly
what's going on with the cafe."

"Yeah, and whether we can ride that bitch out of
town on a rail," Del said, glaring at the cafe.

"How are we going to find out who her lawyer was?"
Rhonda asked. "We can't just call every attorney in the
county and ask if Aphrodite Ferguson were a client."

"They might not be able to tell us anything even if
she were," I said. "Client confidentiality and all that.
Maybe we should ask Norman."

"Actually, that might not be necessary," Stu said.

We all looked at him.

He looked at the ground and continued. "Well I've
been seeing a lawyer myself. And last time I was in,
Aphrodite came in right after me. I think she had an
appointment."

I filed a zillion questions about why Stu might have
been visiting a lawyer for some other lifetime, and went
ahead with the only important one.

"Who were you seeing?"

"Darla Hoffart."

Darla was a local gal, young and newly graduated from the University of South Dakota's Law School. Loan-poor and without offers from what passes for powerful law firms in our part of the country, Darla lived in Aberdeen, but had set up a roving practice in several small towns. She spent a couple of days a week in each community, building a meager business in wills and estate management and litigation between squabbling neighbors.

And, possibly, divorce cases.

"Shit, she was here yesterday. She won't be back until next week," I said.

Darla's days in Delphi were Tuesday and Saturday. No weekends off for budding attorneys.

"She gives clients her home phone number," Stu said softly.

Darla was young, smart, and fairly cute. Carefully not wondering if Stu had her home phone for other than business reasons, I said, "Can you give me the number?"

"Sure." He smiled. "It's at the store. Come on. You can call her from there."

Marveling at the circumstance that forced me to depend on Stu, I followed him across the street to the Feed and Seed Store. Everyone else followed me.

He unlocked the door and motioned us inside. Flipping the fluorescent lights on, he rummaged behind the old wooden counter.

"Here it is." He handed me a business card printed with Darla's home and assorted office numbers. He picked up the old black rotary phone and faced it in my direction.

"Now?" I asked Del.

Del shrugged in assent.

"Why not?" Rhonda said. "Might as well find out for sure."

"Go ahead," Ron said, blinking.

Stu just nodded.

I lifted the receiver and dialed her home number, which rang three times before a canned message began playing.

I covered the mouthpiece. "Damn, got her machine. I'll leave a message," I said to everyone during the recorded spiel.

The phone beeped.

"Hello, Darla. This is Tory Bauer. You know, from Delphi . . ."

Everyone has answering machines these days, and I still feel like an idiot talking into them.

I continued speaking into the phone as the rest listened intently. "I am, uh, was, a good friend of Aphrodite Ferguson, who, uh, died last night. I know that you can't tell me much due to client confidentiality and all that, but I was hoping—"

"I'm here. I'm here," a voice interrupted, out of breath. "Oh God, Tory. I am so glad you called. I have been trying to get hold of you for the last hour."

She's there, I mouthed at everyone.

"Hi Darla," I said, realizing what she'd just said. "Why have you been looking for me? Did the news reports give out my name?"

"Huh?" Darla asked. "No, there hasn't been anything about you on the TV or radio. But I did hear the terrible news about Aphrodite this morning and I've been trying to call you ever since."

"But why?"

Unless she was psychic, Darla would have no way of knowing that we'd need to talk to Aphrodite's lawyer.

"Because we need to talk over Aphrodite's affairs, that's why," Darla said.

"Well, *we* certainly want to talk over Aphrodite's affairs, especially the regarding the cafe," I said, confused. "But why would you want to talk to me?"

"I figured you'd want to get things rolling as quickly as possible," Darla said matter-of-factly.

"What things?"

"Well, I assumed you'd want to get organized, considering that Aphrodite named you the executor of her estate."

"What?"

"Do we have a bad connection?" Darla asked. "I said I figured you'd want to meet today because, as executor, you have a lot of work to do."

"No, I heard that part," I said. "This just comes as a sort of a shock, that's all."

"You mean, you didn't know?" Darla asked, plainly surprised. "Aphrodite didn't tell you, didn't even ask you if you wanted the job?"

"She never said a word," I said, waving off the curious questions being whispered at me from all sides.

"Well then she probably never told you the rest then either," Darla said.

"What rest?" I asked with a sinking heart.

"You better sit down for this," Darla said.

"I am," I said, lying. There weren't any chairs nearby.

"Not only are you executor of Aphrodite's estate. You, Tory Bauer, have personally inherited her interest in the Delphi Cafe."

16

....

The Law Is a Ass

I can laugh at a good (or bad) lawyer joke the same as everyone else. But having had little official contact with the species, I don't share the rest of the country's premeditated contempt. Sure, big-name lawyers who defend celebrity creeps and then go on to multimillion-dollar book deals irritate me too. And I can work up a healthy head of steam over suing fast-food establishments whose hot coffee is actually hot.

But that kind of egregious use of litigational skill isn't common here, where the people are too busy, and too poor, to indulge in courtroom dreams of large settlements.

And the lawyers are too dependent on the goodwill of the entire community to invite the enmity of large chunks of the population by encouraging frivolous lawsuits.

Besides, nearly every one of them has an eye toward a future run for public office, and it doesn't take a genius to realize that memories are long in this part of the country.

Of course, memory is a knife that can cut both ways in Delphi. We are sometimes slow to grant our children status as fully functional adults. Especially in a profession that is still considered a bastion of middle-aged male propriety.

Given the conservatives' reluctance to entrust their affairs to anyone at all, establishing yourself here as a young lawyer is hard enough. Doing it when you're female is even harder.

Especially in your hometown, where everyone remembers your stint as a high school cheerleader. And your summers spent waiting tables in Aphrodite Ferguson's Delphi Cafe.

I could only hope that Darla Hoffart were a better lawyer than she had been a waitress.

With papers strewn about her on the living room floor, she looked impossibly young to have satisfactorily completed the aggregate courses that the University of South Dakota requires before awarding a Juris Doctorate.

It had not seemed incumbent on me, standing in Stu McKee's Feed and Seed Store surrounded by grieving, curious, and furiously blinking questioners, to announce that I was now perhaps one-half owner of the cafe. At least not without any corroborating evidence.

Rhonda, still sniffling, had left to break the news of her unemployment gently to her hardworking parents. Del and Ron disappeared, possibly together, while I said an awkward good-bye to Stu. By unspoken agreement, we decided to postpone ironing out the rest (and perhaps the last) of our relationship difficulties.

I'd had no time to contemplate the intricacies of relationships, or inheritances, or anything else since Darla had appeared on the trailer doorstep in record time, proving that lawyers sworn to uphold the law still might treat speed limits as guidelines only. She'd suggested meeting at home, rather than her small office in town.

Wearing a baggy red USD sweatshirt, with the additional logo, ''First, let's kill all the lawyers,'' printed on the front, blue jeans, and tennis shoes, she'd refused a Coke and immediately folded herself comfortably on the floor and began arranging papers from a large cardboard box into assorted piles. Her light brown hair was twisted up in back and held in place by one of those many-toothed clipper things, though tendrils had escaped around her face, and ends that were probably supposed to be tucked in spiked straight up on top.

I'd offered her the kitchen table as a work area, but she chose the floor, saying that it was larger, and more comfortable to boot.

Not being much of a floor sitter, I perched on the edge of the green vinyl couch and watched as Darla adjusted her tortoise shell glasses and selected something from the top of one of the piles.

"You can start with this," she said, handing me a document.

The top of the page said: *Last Will and Testament*.

"Are you sure I should be reading this?" I asked. "What about client confidentiality?"

Without looking up, Darla said, "For all intents and purposes, you *are* my client now. Being named executor of Aphrodite's estate means that until said estate is settled, you are the legal representative. So not only do you have the legal right to be privy to all of her affairs, you have the *obligation* to make yourself familiar with all this stuff. You will be held accountable." She flashed a small smile at me. "There will be a test later."

"Oh goody," I said faintly, skimming the document.

I haven't read many wills, but this one seemed like standard fare, being of sound mind and body, blah, blah, blah. It wasn't very long or detailed, but sure enough, Mrs. Tory (Atwood) Bauer had been named executor by one Aphrodite Ferguson, with the full privileges and duties as conferred by the signature below.

"How come I didn't know about this?" I asked.

Darla shrugged. "Permission from the executor designee is nice, but not required. I just assumed that the two of you had talked it all out ahead of time."

"Aphrodite never said a word. This came as a total surprise."

"That's odd," Darla said around the end of a pencil clenched firmly in her teeth. "She always spoke very highly of you. Made it sound like you were real close. The daughter she never had, and all that."

"Close to Aphrodite mostly meant that she didn't growl, not that she shared secrets."

"I take it you didn't know about the marriage, then?"

"Or its impending dissolution," I said, shrugging. "I worked with her for more than twenty years. I suppose I knew her better than almost anyone. And I didn't know anything."

Aphrodite had been my boss and my friend. I trusted her and I loved her. The fact that she may have felt the same way about me came as a total shock.

"Have you got to the good stuff yet?" Darla asked, standing up and stretching. "You know, I think I will take you up on that Coke."

"Help yourself," I said absentmindedly, skimming through the rest of the will. "Here it is," I said out loud. " 'A 50 percent interest in the Delphi Cafe shall be transferred directly to Mrs. Tory (Atwood) Bauer.' "

I sat back on the couch, amazed.

From the kitchen, Darla, ice cube tray in hand, said, "Looks like you're now the proud owner of one-half of one cafe. After we perform the rest of the legal mumbo-jumbo, that is. Congratulations."

"But I don't want to be half-owner of the cafe," I said weakly. "Especially not this way. I have no idea how to run a business."

"The law assumes that you will get the hang of running an inherited business."

"If the law assumes that," I said, "then the law is a ass."

"That's on my other sweatshirt," Darla said, grinning, and then sat down again and continued seriously. "Listen, Tory, I have no idea why Aphrodite chose to trust me with her affairs, but she did. And she did it when almost no one else in Delphi would. So I intend to honor the memory of that wonderful crusty old broad by carrying out her wishes. She wanted you to have the cafe. You now have the cafe. Got a problem with that? Take it up with Aphrodite.''

Unfortunately, my last chance to do that had been while lying on the ground in the parking lot as I regained consciousness.

I rubbed my eyes. The emotional buffeting, the physical trauma, and lack of sleep were all combining to slow my process of assimilation.

''Why 50 percent?'' I asked, confused.

''Because Aphrodite only owned 50 percent of the cafe,'' Darla said simply. ''Her estranged husband owned the other 50 percent. And until last week, he stood to inherit everything in the event of her untimely death.''

''So between Aphrodite and her father, Alanna figured she would get 100 percent of the cafe,'' I said.

''Right, kemo sabe,'' Darla said, rummaging for another document, which she handed over. ''The will you are holding is new, and it supersedes any previous ones. Prior wills stated that, in the event of Aphrodite's death, all actual property went to Mr. Ferguson. They also stipulated in the event of his prior death, that everything was to go to one Cheryl Ferguson Hunt.''

Darla looked up at me.

''In other words, Alanna Luna,'' I said. ''And she had no way of knowing that there was a new will. She thought she got it all.''

''And prematurely announced that fact to the general public. I have yet to meet this paragon,'' Darla said. ''Am I going to enjoy her acquaintance?''

''I kinda doubt it,'' I said, thinking furiously, and coming to a most unwelcome conclusion. ''This means that we own the cafe together, doesn't it? Me and Alanna, I mean.''

''Yup.'' Darla grinned. ''Gonna be an adventure, huh?''

''No shit,'' I said, grimly.

I was not looking forward to explaining the good news/bad news to Del and Rhonda—that they could have their jobs back, but that they would be working for me. That we'd still be there, but Alanna would be there also, permanently. That I had inherited the cafe from Aphrodite, and they had inherited nothing.

Actually, that last was a bad news/bad news scenario.

The only other person specifically mentioned in the will was Neil Pascoe, who was slated to get all of Aphrodite's books for his library.

"What about her house?" I asked. There had been no mention of the disposition of property other than the cafe and the books. "I suppose Alanna still gets that."

"Well probably, but only because the house actually belonged to her father."

"You mean Aphrodite never owned her own house?"

"Nope."

"So Alanna's here. In Delphi. Forever." I sighed.

"That looks to be the case," Darla agreed.

"Pretty good timing, don't you think? Aphrodite's long-estranged husband, stepdaughter, and grandson all show up in Delphi on the same day, just in time to witness the death of the woman from whom they are about to inherit?"

Darla leaned back against a chair, and looked over the top of her glasses. "That thought had occurred to me."

"Do we even want to say this stuff out loud?" I asked her.

The "M" word hung, unspoken, between us.

"Well, there are things that as a lawyer, I don't want to say out loud. But I can say that it was most fortuitous for Ms. Luna that Aphrodite died before the divorce from her father was final."

"How so?"

"The dual ownership of the cafe was the result of a separation agreement signed by both Mr. Ferguson and Aphrodite. The agreement stipulated that Mr. Ferguson provide a house for Aphrodite, and that any profit from the business be split evenly. It also provided that neither could sell his or her interest without permission of the other."

"And the agreement would be null and void if the marriage ended?"

"Not exactly. The agreement would still be in place, but it's an old agreement, and completely unfair, tying two incompatible people into a permanent business arrangement. It was poorly written, with no provision for splitting the business in the event of a divorce. Aphrodite had already tried to dissolve the partnership by offering to buy out Mr. Ferguson's interest, but he had refused to sell. She came to me, seeking a divorce from Mr. Ferguson, but also to see if the agreement could be broken. I thought, given the omissions, that it was possible. Check it out for yourself." She handed me another document.

"So a divorce would have thrown a wrench into Alanna's inheritance?"

"Well, it would have slowed things down, that's for sure. Perhaps the courts would have upheld the old agreement. Perhaps not. But with a divorce finalized, and litigation in progress, it would have cost a lot of money for Ms. Luna to establish a claim on what she had assumed would be hers free and clear."

"They couldn't sell their individual interests, but they could dispose of them in their wills, huh? That doesn't make much sense," I said, looking over the dense legalese.

"I said it was an unfair agreement," Darla agreed.

"But all of this is moot now, right?" I asked. "Aphrodite died before the divorce was finalized or a sale of Mr. F's interest could be arranged. He still owned his 50 percent when he died. And when he died, Alanna inherited his portion."

"We assume that to be the case, though I haven't seen Mr. Ferguson's will." Darla shrugged.

"Lucky Alanna," I said quietly.

"It would appear so."

17

....

Free Will

Remind me never to be anyone else's executor.

Nicky, my late and still occasionally lamented husband, had had the sense to die deeply in debt. And therefore, except for slowly paying off creditors (some of whose existence I'd had no clue) and coming to the sad realization that there had been nowhere near enough insurance to satisfy the above, the settling of his estate had mostly consisted of promising to make good as soon as possible.

Things were considerably different in an estate complicated by estranged spouses and reluctant business partnerships.

Not to mention the sudden deaths of the parties of the first and second part.

An hour and several Cokes later, I ended up on the living room floor with Darla, though sitting cross-legged was beyond me. We had already gone over the basics: Did Aphrodite have insurance? (none applicable except for on the van); were there large outstanding business debts at the cafe? (not that we could tell from the financial statements and tax returns in her file); did she have any personal debts that would have to be satisfied from the estate? (nothing out of the ordinary—a Visa card and a revolving account at Lane Bryant, light bills and stuff like that); were there any other next of kin? (not as far as we knew).

Of course, we had already discussed the biggie: Was there any money?

The answer to that was: evidently not. As far as Darla knew, Aphrodite's bank accounts were all local. There were sufficient funds in the business account to cover the daily functioning of the cafe, and Aphrodite's own personal checking account seemed ample enough to keep her in bingo cards and cigarettes, which were her two primary interests.

"I know she used to keep a wad of cash in a zipper pouch in her van," I said. "Under the front seat. I assume that went up in smoke."

"Unreported cash?" Darla asked, making a note on a mauve legal pad.

"Probably," I said. "Aphrodite didn't discuss her accounting methods with us. But we always assumed that at least some of the cash from the restaurant went into her own personal emergency stash."

"Do you know how much was there?"

"It's only a guess, but we always figured that she had at least several thousand dollars salted away. Enough for a good shopping trip but not enough to run away to the Caribbean."

"I'll contact the police about the possible cash. If there are bits and pieces left, we can get replacement bills from the government. Though you'll have to pay taxes on the money, you know."

"Me? Why me?"

"You're executor, doofus. You're responsible for paying *all* the bills and taxes, and distributing the physical goods of the estate. You also have to see to it that ads are placed in the local paper informing those named in the will, and the general public, that they have a specific amount of time to get their bills in to you for payment by the estate. We also have to petition the court to accept the will, so you can get this here ball rolling.''

''Is that my job too?'' I asked, wearily. This executor stuff wasn't all it was cracked up to be.

Darla smiled. ''No, that's up to me. The day-to-day concerns of the cafe are your bailiwick, though.''

''I figured that would have to be a joint thing with Alanna,'' I said.

''After probate, and the estate is settled, then you two will have to hammer out some sort of working agreement. But until then, as executor, you're da boss.''

''If the police don't care that it's open, there doesn't seem to be any point in closing the cafe now,'' I said. This morning I would have kept the place closed forever. But, as little as I wanted to admit it, Alanna was right about the cafe being a monument to Aphrodite. ''Could anyone legally object to running the cafe while you perform your legal maneuvers?''

''Only the other owner. And the other owner has already publicly stated her intention to keep the establishment open. But, officially, it's up to you.''

''Gosh, I love the perks of real power,'' I said tiredly.

''You know, you can refuse the position. The court can name a surrogate.''

I thought about that for a second, mightily tempted, and then shook my head. ''Aphrodite wanted me to do this. It's the least I can do for her.''

''Good girl,'' Darla said, chewing on the bow of her glasses. ''Let's see, I think we have it almost all covered for today.''

I stood up, slowly and noisily, joints popping and cracking, and stretched. ''It was nice of you to come down on a Sunday. Making weekend house calls isn't exactly a general part of most lawyers' routines.''

''Hey.'' She grinned up at me. ''What else do I have to do? It's not like I have a shitload of clients. Or a social life. Besides,'' she said softly, ''Aphrodite was my friend too. And anyway, you'll get a bill for my services. Right along with all the others.''

"Just part and parcel of the duties of the jolly executor, right?"

"Right."

Down the hall, Presley's door opened. Wearing a rumpled white T-shirt and a pair of flannel boxers, he shuffled into the living room, squinting and rubbing his eyes.

"Well, look who decided to make an appearance," Darla said, laughing.

She stood up easily and gracefully, and slung a companionable arm around Presley's shoulders.

Embarrassed to have been caught with a serious case of bed-head, Pres smiled uncertainly at Darla, and then said to me, "You didn't say we had company."

"Well, I didn't figure you wanted me to wake you up just to tell you," I said, beginning to stack the assorted papers. "Do these stay here?" I asked Darla.

"Not my files. But you can keep a copy of the will and some of the other stuff," she said, ruffling Pres's hair, which made him squirm.

On his way into the kitchen, Pres glared at me. I shrugged—not my fault that he overslept to find a cute lady lawyer lying in wait. He tiptoed through the papers.

"What's all this stuff?" he asked.

"Aphrodite's legal things," I said, which reminded me of something. "Are these all copies of the papers Aphrodite got from you yesterday?"

Maybe it wouldn't matter that I couldn't find the originals, if I already had duplicates.

"Huh?" Darla said, not looking up. "I didn't see Aphrodite yesterday. Her appointment was on Tuesday. Yesterday was pretty dead. I went home early." She paused for a minute, realizing what she'd just said, and winced.

In the kitchen, Presley noisily fixed himself a bowl of Fruit Loops. When Darla wasn't looking, he furiously finger-combed his hair. Satisfied with his reflection in the refrigerator, he carried his bowl into the living room, tiptoeing back through the papers to seat himself on the couch. "Why are all of Aphrodite's papers here?" he asked with a mouth full of cereal. "I mean, on our living room floor?"

"Tory and I are working out what has to be done next," Darla said. "That cereal looks good. Mind if I have a bowl?"

"Sure." He grinned, bed-head forgotten. "Can we turn on some music in here? Or the TV?"

"No TV," I said sternly. "We still have work to do. But I suppose we can have the radio on. Oldies channel only."

"Jeez," Presley grumbled.

"Yeah, jeez, Tory," Darla said from the kitchen. "We'd rather have no music at all than that dinosaur stuff."

Outnumbered, I laughed. "Oh all right, but absolutely no Sheryl Crow." Actually, I didn't mind Sheryl Crow, I just wanted to let them know I wasn't an uninformed dinosaur.

We turned the radio on, and you-know-who was worrying about the sun coming up on the Santa Monica Boulevard. I sighed.

"I figured you and Mom would be at work," Presley said.

"Well, there've been some changes at work," I said.

"Oh," Pres said, abashed. "You mean with what happened last night. The explosions and all."

"Were you there too?" Darla asked, inhaling her cereal. The kid definitely needed to be fed.

"Sorta," Pres said, concentrating on his bowl. "We were driving around last night. We were on the other side of town when we saw the smoke and the flames. And then we saw the van." He stopped and swallowed. "And we saw that Tory'd been hurt or something. And we saw that lady, the new one with the big . . ." He hesitated for a second, remembering whom he was talking to. "Anyway, that new lady and that guy who is her kid standing there, and all the rest of the people. But we didn't see the explosions."

"Who's this *we* you keep talking about?" Darla asked, getting back up. She took her and Presley's bowls and set them in the sink. "You aren't old enough to drive yet, are you?"

"Presley had a date last night," I said. "With Mardelle Jackson."

"Woo woo," said Darla, waggling her eyebrows. "If I'da known you were interested in older chicks, I'd have asked you out myself."

Pres blushed.

Talking about Mardelle had reminded me of some of last night's other festivities.

"Speaking of dates, where are the hamsters?" I demanded of Pres.

"You mean Mulder and Scully?" he asked, grinning. "They're in my room."

Automatically, I sniffed. Expecting, I suppose, some aural evidence of rodent inhabitants.

All I got was a faint whiff of cigarette smoke. Not unusual in a house with a chain smoker.

The phone rang. I answered it as Darla followed Pres to his room to inspect the hamsters. Judging from their laughter, the furry pair were reenacting last night's amorous escapades.

"Hello," I said.

"Hi there, did you get any sleep at all?" Neil asked.

"Not yet," I said. "Doesn't look like I'll get to for a while, either." I wearily eyed the stack of papers still on the living room floor. "I still have lots to do."

"Well, if you get a break, come on over. I have something to show you."

"Actually, that wouldn't be a bad idea," I said. "I have plenty to show you too."

18

....

Men in the Moonstone

There isn't an American alive who hasn't dreamed of hitting it big. Entire industries have grown and prospered by cashing in on that fantasy. From the folks who take a half-hour of Sunday morning TV to explain how they'll exchange your $1,500 for their insider tips on buying real estate with no money down, to carefully coifed ladies driving horrendous pink Cadillacs, whose purpose in life is to talk you into selling makeup—the pitch is always the same: You can get rich—right now, lemmee tell ya how.

And like all fantasies, the dream is a good deal more romantic than the reality.

The only person I ever knew who actually got rich without working his ass off for the money was Neil Pascoe. He hit it lucky years ago in the Iowa lottery long before state governments began routinely using gambling as a revenue enhancer.

His millions, accumulating in installments stretched over a twenty-year period, haven't made Neil either happy or unhappy as far as I can tell. The money provided him with the means to do what he wanted to do (and would surely have done, regardless). Other than that, it hasn't seemed to affect his life at all—he keeps a low profile, and for the most part, people hereabouts forget just how much money he has moldering in the bank.

The resentment factor is pretty low, considering that the average income in the county is something like 20K.

According to the tax returns and other assorted documents I had carried over to the library, my income was just about to take a giant leap forward—to almost the county average.

We're not talking the big time here—and we're not talking free money either. I was going to have to work at least as hard as I had always worked. But I had a sinking feeling that the resentment factor was going to run pretty high when news of the new joint ownership of the cafe became common knowledge.

"The plot thickens," Neil said. He was leaning back in the swivel chair behind the massive oak desk in the first floor of his library, skimming through the files I'd brought over. "Which are the ones you picked up in the cafe yesterday, and which were in Darla's files?"

"All of these are from Darla's files." I explained about the missing envelope, and that I had searched at home again for it, with no luck. "Darla says that she didn't see Aphrodite yesterday, so those papers came from somewhere else. Probably her house. I know that there were divorce documents in the bunch, because I saw them. But I don't know what the rest of the stuff was. Most of the sheets were legal size, like these." I indicated the papers on Neil's desk. "But there were some smaller pages and at least a couple that were handwritten."

"It'd be nice to get hold of those papers, you know," Neil said, looking over his glasses. "Since you're the executor, you could read them now without feeling guilty about snooping."

"I'll keep looking. The envelope didn't fall out of my pocket at home, and it wasn't lying in the street. Maybe I lost it at school or the bar."

"And maybe you didn't lose it at all," Neil said seriously.

"What do you mean?"

"Maybe the envelope was taken," he said simply. "By someone who also had an interest in Aphrodite's affairs."

Neil had a point. Unfortunately there wasn't any way to prove how the papers disappeared until we actually found them, and we couldn't find them without knowing how they disappeared.

In the meantime, we had more than enough to keep our minds occupied, without worrying about papers that might or might not have been stolen.

"What's Del going to think about all this?" Neil asked. Meaning the will and the inheritance.

I sat back in the chair next to the desk and sighed. "She'll be happy for about fifteen seconds just because this messes up Alanna's big plans to run things. And then it'll occur to her that *she* didn't inherit anything. And then the shit's gonna hit the fan."

"You think she'll resent the change in the power structure?"

I just looked at him.

"Stupid question, huh?" he asked, grinning.

"No one's going to like the fact that you and I are the only ones specifically mentioned in the will."

Neil pushed his glasses up on his nose. "Of course they're going to hate you. It has now been proven that Aphrodite loved you best. But do you think anyone will actually care that she left me her old books? If they have an interest in the books, they can check them out from the library."

The CD in the stereo changed from Vivaldi's *Four Seasons* to *Marvin Gaye's Greatest Hits*, both of which were an improvement on the music I'd had to listen to at the trailer until Darla left.

"*What* you got is irrelevant," I said. "They're going to hate it that you got a little. They'll like it less that I got more. But most of all they're going to be pissed that they didn't get anything at all."

He sat up straight, and pushed a bowl of almond M&Ms over to me. "I suppose you're right. Oh well, they'll get over it. Eventually."

I grabbed a handful of candy. "Most of them will, I imagine." I was being optimistic—I had my doubts about Del getting over anything. "At least until Alanna and I run the cafe into bankruptcy court because neither one of us knows how to operate a food service enterprise."

Neil grinned. "That's where you're wrong," he said, fishing in a desk drawer for a small stack of papers. "Our Alanna seems to have had experience running all kinds of service enterprises."

The papers were photocopies of assorted newspaper articles and a couple of official-looking documents.

I raised an eyebrow at Neil.

"I did a little investigating this morning," he said, holding up a business card. "Remember this?"

It was Alanna Luna's card. The one that had an address and phone number printed on the reverse side. I'd left it with him.

"It seems that Delphi's newest independent businesswoman hails from Rockville, a little town in the panhandle of Oklahoma. Population 895, which is fair-size for Cimarron County."

He handed me a sheet with a reprinted newspaper article that reported the opening of the Moonstone Cafe. The small nightclub would feature food and drink, as well as some locally renowned exotic dancers, including, not incidentally, the new owner of the establishment, Cheryl Hunt, known internationally as Alanna Luna.

"So Rockville, Oklahoma, is big enough to support both a supper club/strip joint as well as a weekly paper?"

"Not really." Neil laughed. "The *Rockville Reporter* is sort of an area newspaper—it covers events in the entire county. I think it squeaks by mostly on advertising and community goodwill. The Moonstone Cafe didn't fare quite as well.''

He handed me another page. This one had a photo of several shouting women and a couple of ministers, picketing outside a dilapidated building. The caption read: ''Angry citizens protest nude dancers at local nightclub.''

''Looks like the good wives of Rockville didn't like their men being entertained by large-busted strippers any more than the ladies of Delphi,'' I said, grinning even though I had also not been amused by Alanna's performance.

''There's more,'' Neil said, giving me a couple more sheets.

''Oho,'' I said, laughing as I read of several arrests of prominent local citizens. Some local men had been arrested for participating in a high-stakes poker game— the kind that is illegal everywhere except Las Vegas. But others, including the mayor and the president of the First Rockville Bank, had been arrested for consorting with, as the paper delicately put it, ''ladies of perhaps uncertain repute who may have asked for money in exchange for their delightful conversation.''

''Oh God, she's a hooker too,'' I said.

''Well, she wasn't arrested *in flagrante delicto*,'' Neil said, smiling. ''But we can probably infer that she at least arranged for the services.''

''A facilitator, right?''

''Something like that. That was the beginning of the end for the nightclub.''

Another article reported a police investigation into the operation of the Moonstone Cafe. Allegations had ranged from prostitution, to tax evasion, to illegal gambling, to serving alcohol to minors. Unfortunately the investigation had been hampered by the precipitous disappearance of the establishment's proprietress, along with all the account books and what was assumed to be a very large amount of cash.

"I didn't think they looked like genuine Lexus drivers," I said. "How did you get this stuff, anyway?"

"The *Rockville Reporter* comes out weekly, on Tuesdays. Which means the owner, who also happens to be the manager, editor, chief typesetter, and star reporter, as well as archivist and fax machine operator, works all day Sunday to get each issue ready for the printers on Monday. And he answers his own phone."

"And apparently he doesn't mind being interrupted on his busiest day with frivolous requests to search the back issues," I added.

Neil munched on some more M&Ms. On the stereo Marvin wondered what was going on.

I wondered that myself.

"Actually he was delighted to fax this stuff to me," Neil said. "There had been a great deal of speculation as to the disappearance of one Cheryl Ferguson Hunt. These were just the articles he remembered off the top of his head. He's sure there're more. He promised to search the whole archive for anything related to any member of that family and ship me anything he finds in the next few days, in exchange for an exclusive on developments here."

"What sort of developments is he expecting?" I asked, confused.

"This might explain," Neil said seriously, sliding the last fax over to me.

I caught a whiff of something. I sniffed the air, and then the paper, unable to locate the source of the smell.

"You letting people smoke in here now?" I asked, finally identifying the odor.

"Never," Neil asserted. "Why?"

I sniffed the paper again, but the smell seemed to have evaporated. I shrugged and looked at the article.

It was a cover story from about ten years ago. The photo featured a small, smiling, balding man whom I immediately recognized as Aphrodite's late husband. He stood with his arm proudly around the shoulders of a gangly boy of about fifteen.

The headline read; WW2 MUNITIONS EXPERT PASSES KNOWLEDGE TO GRANDSON.

I looked up at Neil. He gestured for me to read on.

The story reported that Alfred "Gus" Ferguson, owner of a small explosives supply, was training his grandson, Michael Hunt, son of Rockville residents Cheryl and Robert Hunt, to take over the business one day. "The boy's a natural," the article quoted the proud grandfather as saying. "He picks up the details like he was born to it."

"It's cool," young Michael had replied. "I like blowing stuff up."

My jaw hinged open, and I looked up at Neil.

He started to say something, but the library door slammed open, and Presley, winded and wheezing, burst into the room shouting, "You guys, you guys. You gotta come quick!"

Startled, we jumped up. "What? What's going on?"

Presley, still gasping for air, said, "There's a fight in the street in front of the cafe. A big one. Mom and that new lady are punching each other out!"

19

....

Nose Guard

No one likes to admit it, but there is, inside each and every one of us, a rubber-necking jerk who cannot pass by a car wreck without checking for blood on the windshield.

Oh, we'll swear that we're only on the scene to offer help, and we'll complain about other looky-loos getting in the way of the folks who really belong there (like us). And we'll deny forever, to ourselves and to everyone else, the secret thrill we feel when we come up on wreckage around the bend of the road.

However much we protest to the contrary, we want to see. And we want to see it all.

The same pretty much applies to fights, though even the most civic-minded of us have a hard time convincing anyone of the altruistic motives behind emptying into the street to watch a couple of desperadoes duke it out.

Not that I would have condescended to stand in the street to see just any pair of fighters. If it had been an ordinary altercation, Neil and I would have repaired to the tower in his attic and watched the whole thing with binoculars.

But this was Del and Alanna.

Del had taken an immediate dislike to Alanna, though that was probably more an antipathy to silicone than a genuine personality clash. And it was obvious after the confrontation in the cafe this morning that Alanna had no very cordial feelings toward Del.

But it had not occurred to me that their animosity might boil over into the physical.

And it had certainly not occurred to me that I might be required to get in the middle of their battle.

Nicky'd had faults aplenty, but he was not an abusive man. With the exception of an incident with Butchie Pendergast in the third grade, I had never in my life been punched. And I had never been angry enough to take a swing at anyone.

Believe me, I had no desire to change that particular status quo.

Though we could hear the shouting and see the crowd several blocks away, we weren't able to make out the participants clearly until we pushed our way, panting, through to the middle.

In the center of a roughly fifteen-foot circle, dusty, sweaty, and panting in ragged white puffs, stood a medium-size redhead and a large blond, shouting hoarse obscenities at each other. Del, dirty and bedraggled, had a ribbon of blood running from her nose, and a darkly swelling lip. The hair that had been carefully piled on top of Alanna's head was skewed to the side like the Leaning Tower of Ivana. The knees of her jeans and the shoulder of her sweatshirt were torn, the exposed skin was raw and bleeding.

Each circled. Each swung furiously at the other without connecting.

Neither paid the slightest attention to the cheering crowd, which had no interest whatsoever in stopping the sideshow.

Well, most of them, anyway.

"Jesus, Tory," Ron Adler shouted, so agitated that he didn't blink at all. "You gotta get in there and stop them. They're gonna kill each other."

"Me?" I shouted back. "Why me?"

"Because you're the only person Del will listen to," Ron explained, wincing as Del ducked an easy swing, and then landed an open-handed slap on Alanna's shoulder.

"Del never listens to anyone," I said, not wanting to watch the spectacle, but uncomfortably fascinated just the same. "How long has this been going on?"

"Beats me," he said, shrugging. "Del and me was at the garage . . ." He paused and blinked rapidly and actually blushed.

I sighed. Ron and Del's mutual aggression pact must have been set aside long enough for a quickie in the stalls.

". . . she left about ten minutes ago, and then pretty quick we all heard shouting." He waved his hands and shrugged. "They were already at it by the time we got here."

"I saw Del talking in the street with Presley," Stu said, disgust plain in his voice. I hadn't noticed him earlier, but was vaguely pleased to know that he wasn't enjoying the fight.

I looked around for Presley, but he was nowhere to be found.

Neil was seriously disgusted. He frowned at the highly amused crowd. He frowned at the pair in the middle. He frowned at Stu.

"Well, someone's gotta get in there," Neil said to Stu, "and stop these two idiots."

Stu sighed. "I suppose you're right."

Neil and Stu circled around them warily. Del shrieked and made a lunge for Alanna. Neil caught her mid-air, his arm looped around her middle, her arms and legs gyrating madly, as she screamed like a banshee.

At the same time, Stu grabbed Alanna from behind, pinning her arms to her sides. She twisted her head around and tried to bite him.

The crowd applauded, hooted, and whistled.

With his hands full of Del, glasses knocked sideways on his face, Neil glared at the crowd.

Amazingly enough, the onlookers seemed to remember that they were not unruly pack animals. Confronted thusly by the most civilized man in Delphi, they suddenly remembered that they had something else to do right at the moment. One by one, they shuffled a little and began melting back into the bar and the cafe. They retreated to the garage and the grocery store.

Neil and Stu, however, still had their hands full of squirming, furious, shouting women.

Feeling not the slightest guilt for having stayed out of the way until all the stray punches had been rounded up, I knew it was my turn to go onstage.

"What the hell is going on?" I demanded of Del.

"You calm now?" Neil asked her quietly.

She glared at him but nodded.

"Promise?"

Del nodded again, and Neil loosened his grip.

Straightening her shoulders and shaking her hair, Del swiped her hand under her nose, inspected her blood-streaked hand, and shot another venomous glare at Alanna. "She," Del spat, pointing, "she . . ." Del sputtered and paused, and then continued, ". . . said some bad things."

"Oh for chrissakes, Del," I said, disgusted. "Don't you know there's no such thing as fightin' words?"

"Yeah, well you didn't hear what she said."

"So she impugned the honor of your mother. So what?"

"It wasn't *my* mother she impugned," Del said with a small, superior grin.

By then Stu had let Alanna go, but he stood nearby, ready to grab her again if it proved necessary. To no avail, Alanna had tried to restore a little verticality to her topknot. She dusted off what was left of her jeans and UO sweatshirt while glaring at me.

"What do you mean?" I asked Del.

The street had nearly emptied again. Only Ron Adler remained, blinking nervously. At a safe distance, in front of her parents' bar, Presley stood with Mardelle Jackson, watching.

Keeping Alanna in her sight line, Del continued. "She said, and I quote, 'What more can you expect from the daughter of a money-grubbing bitch?' "

Del's imitation of a broad Okie drawl was pitch-perfect, which caused Alanna to howl and lunge again. Stu and Neil each grabbed one of her arms.

She stopped struggling, so they let go again.

I was certainly confused. "Whose mother is a money-grubbing bitch?"

"Yours," Del said triumphantly.

"*Mine?*" I asked incredulously. I looked at Neil, who shrugged. I looked at Stu, who shrugged. I even looked at Alanna, but she only glared back. "My mother worked for every penny she ever earned."

"Not according to Gypsy Rose Lee over there," Del said, continuing to quote Alanna in a snotty drawl. " 'She had to have learned money grubbing at her mama's knee for her to be so damn good at it. And since she sucked my poor mama dry over the years, I can only assume she learned from the best."

"*What?*" I was too flabbergasted for more than one syllable.

"Deny it, go ahead and deny it," Alanna shouted at me. "You mighta been able to fool the rest of these hicks, but I know a pro when I see one."

"I don't know what the hell you're talking about," I said, facing Alanna squarely.

"Like hell you don't. You been sucking money from my mama all these years. She paid your bills, she helped you out, she gave you loans, and what do you do to repay her?"

"What?" I repeated. I had been reduced to a one-word vocabulary.

"Sweetpea here says that you stole money from Aphrodite," Del translated helpfully.

I could only stare at Alanna incredulously.

"She also says that you fooled Aphrodite into putting you into her will."

This time I stared at Del. "How did you hear about the will?"

"So you don't deny it! You can't deny it!" Alanna shouted.

"Just shut up a minute," I said over my shoulder. "Who told you?"

"Presley, of course," Del said. "He heard you and Darla at the trailer."

We all turned to look down the street at Mardelle and Pres, who did his best to duck into his own shoulders.

"And you trotted over to announce the news to the cafe?" I asked Del.

Del smiled again. "I wanted to wipe that shit-eating smile off her face. It worked too. You shoulda seen her when I said that she didn't own the cafe free and clear."

From behind me, Alanna said, "Thief."

"And so you swung at her defending my honor," I said to Del.

"Well, not at first. At first I laughed at her. And then I called her a couple of names. And then she said that your mother must have been a pretty piss-poor whore to have given birth to you."

"And *then* you hit her?" I asked, beginning to feel the urge myself.

"No. I laughed some more, and went out the door and said, 'Her mom might be a whore, but she's your boss now—so what does that make you?' And then she tackled me in the street."

Trying to fathom Del's logic was an exercise in futility, so I let it go. "Well at least you didn't do any damage inside."

"Worrying about the inventory already, dearie?" Del asked nastily. She might theoretically enjoy the fact of my inheritance, but there would still be hell to pay.

I ignored her, rubbing my eyes, thinking furiously.

"Look, Alanna," I said finally. "I don't suppose that either one of us likes this arrangement much, but there's not much we can do about it. We're going to have to learn to work together. We need to do it for ourselves, and for Aphrodite.''

A speech like that should have been accompanied by a marching band and waving flags. By itself it didn't have any effect at all.

At least not on Del or Alanna.

"Gimme a break," Del snorted.

"You took what was rightfully mine," Alanna said. "You cheated my mama."

I'd had enough. I whirled around and shouted, "Listen you—I had no idea that Aphrodite was going to leave her part of the cafe to me. I didn't ask her to do it. I didn't want her to do it. It was entirely her decision! She was my boss and she was my friend. And I had to watch her die. Don't *you* give me any shit about anything." I was beyond angry now. I was furious. And unfortunately, my mouth was running way ahead of my brain. "Besides, *I* wasn't the one who magically appeared just in time to collect my inheritance." I ignored Neil's widened eyes, his signal that perhaps I might want to rethink any further statements, and continued. "And *I* wasn't the one who disappeared from Oklahoma with a bunch of missing money and a son who likes to blow things up!"

"Tory," called a voice faintly from behind me.

I turned to see Clay Deibert walking across the street from the church, smiling and waving. His smile turned into a large O of astonishment.

"Tory look out!" Neil shouted and lunged at the same time. And missed.

Momentarily nonplussed by my anger and distracted by Clay's sudden appearance, Stu and Neil both had relaxed their guard.

Taking advantage of their inattention, Alanna tackled me. Before I even registered what had happened, for the second time in two days I blacked out.

20

....

Contact Sports

I was gone the day they handed out the desire to trade broken knuckles for the privilege of smacking someone in the snotbox. Not only do I lack the gene that encourages participation in fisticuffs, I don't even want to watch anyone inflict damage on anyone else, one blow at a time. In that, I am evidently in the minority.

You don't have to be a scholar or a historian, or even a fan of Joyce Carol Oates, to realize that people have always enjoyed a good knock-down, drag-out fight. If they can't be in the middle, experiencing the rush that comes from beating the shit out of another human being, the spectators at least share the vicarious thrill of cheering for, and identifying with, the victor.

And it's not just the winners who feel that surge of power, a cleansing energy, in the post-combat glow. Even the losers seem to possess a beatific smile, beamed through missing teeth, their eyes shining through lids nearly puffed shut.

Seeing neither poetry nor beauty in hand-to-hand combat, and based entirely on several reluctant observations and no real-life experience at all, I had come to the conclusion that fighting was both stupid and painful.

I was now in the unfortunate position of knowing that I was absolutely right.

Not that I had been an actual participant in the altercation. My contribution had been to utter a short cry of surprise and a small "oof" as I hit the ground.

I came to almost immediately. The crowd seemed to have rematerialized around me as I lay in the street. Slightly wary of recurring hallucinations, I peeked through one squinted eye just to make sure that Aphrodite and Nick weren't standing over me again. Neither was to be seen, though for a second the smell of cigarette smoke convinced me that Aphrodite might be nearby, until I focused enough to realize that (1) I was being silly, and (2) Del was smoking.

Though it had at first seemed like hundreds of people, only Neil, Stu, Presley, Ron, Mardelle, and Clay Deibert hovered by anxiously.

"We really have to stop meeting like this, you know," I said wearily.

Neil laughed. "Are you all right?" He held out a hand to help me up.

"I think so," I said, standing slowly. I was a little dizzy and my head hurt like a son of a bitch. I dusted myself off, taking mental inventory of bruises and sore spots. There were plenty but none seemed serious. I was more worried about the humiliation of having been literally blindsided right in the middle of Delphi's main drag. I could hear the laughter already, as this story made the rounds.

"Where's Alanna?" I asked. She had not been among the worried hoverers.

"She stormed back into the cafe, shooed everyone out, and stuck the *Closed* sign in the window," Del said, lighting another cigarette. "Hasn't been seen or heard from since."

I shot a glance at the empty cafe, but could only see our reflection in the dusty window, and nothing inside. It looked deserted.

"Are you sure she's still in there?" I asked.

"Yup. Her and the kid both," Del said.

"Brian's here? I didn't see him before."

"He drove up just after Neil threatened to call the cops," Presley said. "That was a cool fight, Tory."

"*Cool* is not exactly the word I had for it," I said, gingerly probing the area around my left eye. There was no blood, but the whole side of my face was tender and swollen.

"I am so sorry." Clay spoke up for the first time. "I seem to have provided the distraction Ms. Luna needed to, um"—he smiled uncertainly—"inflict the final blow. I was with a parishioner, and didn't even know anything was going on until I came out into the street. I was just pleased to see you out here, Tory, since I was looking for you specifically. Can you come over to the church for a moment?"

The wooziness had almost disappeared, and the aches were receding slightly. I would love to have gone home for a comfy snuggle with an ice pack. But whether we liked it or not, there were a couple of things that Alanna and I had to work out concerning our business relationship. Putting off the rest of that conversation would only make the next meeting even more uncomfortable.

I thought that probably the fisticuffs were over for the day, and that it would be marginally safe to enter the cafe.

My cafe.

Well, half my cafe, anyway.

I squinted at the blank windows and came to a decision. "I'd better go inside and talk first, Clay. But it shouldn't take long. I'll stop over at the church when I finish here. Okay?"

He nodded.

"I have to go too, Tory," Stu said softly. "Got the store to run and all."

I looked him in the eye and saw only a weary sadness, as though he'd lately been in a fight or two himself. "Thanks," I said.

The word hung in the air between us.

No one else spoke until Neil broke the silence. "I want to thank you too," he said to Stu, holding out his hand. "You stepped in to help when no one else would."

Stu shook Neil's hand. Behind them, Ron blinked furiously as he whispered to Del. Probably explaining why *he* hadn't stepped in.

"You gonna be all right in there?" Neil asked me quietly. "Alanna's not stupid—she understood exactly what you were driving at when you brought up Brian and explosives in the same sentence."

"Mama Bear's got nothing on Mama Luna, I guess," I said, wincing at the memory of both my own angry stupidity and Alanna's reaction to it. "Well, if nothing else, I'd better apologize." I smoothed the hair back off my forehead. "I mean, I don't *really* think Brian killed Aphrodite. I mean actually, anyway."

"Are you sure?" Neil asked, cleaning his glasses on his shirt and squinting suspiciously at the cafe.

"Pretty sure," I said, though of course I wasn't. "But it doesn't matter, I have to go in there and talk to her. Might as well be now."

"Well, you just keep your wits about you," he said. "Pay attention, and be careful."

"*Neil*," I said, surprised. "Do you think he killed her?"

"I'm not ruling out anything," he said darkly. "But I figure you're safe enough—we all know you're going in, and if you don't make it over to Clay's office in about a half-hour, he'll know something is up."

"And if the cafe bursts into flames, he can call the fire department," I said ruefully.

It hadn't occurred to me to be afraid to face Alanna and Brian alone. I was just tired and embarrassed. And leery of trying to hammer out a working relationship with a woman whose preferred method of dispute management involved physical contact.

Now I was distinctly nervous.

"You want me to go in with you?" Del asked with a nasty smile. She was evidently feeling that after-fight rush. "We can take her on again if we have to."

"Nah," I said. "I'll try to work it out without any more bloodshed."

"Okay," she said, saluting. "You're da boss."

I thought I detected a little anger in her reply, though she smiled brightly, took Ron's arm, and ambled back down the street with him.

"I'm really sorry, Tory," Pres said, plainly miserable. "I didn't mean to start anything. Especially not . . ." He paused, indicating my face. "I thought Mom would be happy that you were going to own the cafe. And I thought that everything would go back to normal now."

He was too tall for me to sling an arm around his shoulders, so I slipped one around his waist and gave him a swift hug, which he allowed even though we were in the middle of the street and someone might have seen it. "That's okay, kiddo. We'd all like things to get back to normal, but I think we're going to have to find a new normal now."

"I want the old one back," he said, giving me a brief hug.

"Me too," I said, facing the cafe and exhaling.

21

....

Changes in the Status Quo

Aphrodite Ferguson had been a part of my daily life for going on thirty years. Tersely gruff, she'd stood in the cafe kitchen, smearing red lipstick on her cigarettes, flipping burgers, and intimidating the summer help for all of my adult life. Short and stocky, with her tightly teased, and studiously maintained, red beehive hairdo, she had been the foundation around which the Delphi Cafe had been built.

She was not exactly a mother-figure (I had a serviceable mother functioning in that position already), and not exactly my close friend, but Aphrodite and I had over the years perfected a working relationship that crossed the boundary from boss and employee, to . . . well, I don't know what. We knew each other's moods and we knew each other's skills and we knew how to work around the deficits in each other's characters.

It was a well-oiled, comfortable system. Like a good marriage of long duration, it had reached the point of self-maintenance.

And like the cliché, I had not appreciated it until it was gone.

I had been too angry this morning to realize the profound change that had already taken place. In the nearly empty cafe, the dishwasher was silent, the grill was cold, and the kitchen was smokeless. There was no laughter, no clinking of silverware, no monosyllabic conversation in the kitchen. The only sound came from the radio, which played music softly. The solid fact of Aphrodite's permanent absence hit me like a fist.

Or like a tackle from an ex-stripper.

Alanna, her hair returned to a semblance of its earlier height and glory, was sitting in a window booth, her elbow on the table and her chin propped on her palm. She didn't turn her head as I came in, but she was watching me just the same. Brian stood behind the counter, polishing napkin holders and straightening salt and pepper shakers. He acknowledged me with a noncommittal nod.

I stood by the till for a moment, trying to assimilate the changes in my life. And to work up the courage to start the conversation, since neither Alanna nor Brian had volunteered.

"I can't even imagine this place without Aphrodite. I'm going to miss her terribly," I said out loud, surprising myself. I had intended to talk business, to hammer out some way that Alanna and I could work together. I certainly had not meant to reveal anything quite so personal.

Without moving, Alanna shifted her eyes to me. I was surprised to see a tear coursing its way down her cheek. "Well, at least you had her all these years," she said quietly. "That's more than we had. Me and Brian."

Brian finished tidying up behind the counter. With a dishtowel slung over one shoulder, he efficiently poured two Diet Cokes, brought them around, and set them on Alanna's table. "I figure you two got a lot to talk about," he said to me. "And I have things to do"—he flashed a small smile—"people to see, miles to go and all that. So I'll leave you alone."

He leaned over and planted a kiss on his mother's forehead. "You going to be all right?" he asked softly.

She nodded but did not speak.

The tableau was intriguing. Was Brian a handsome young man being solicitous of his bereaved mother? Or was he a pyromaniac who had blown up his grandmother so that they could inherit the business?

Their performance didn't ring false, but it didn't feel real either. Brian seemed to be neither the conscientious young man nor the coldhearted murderer. I wondered what he really was. What they both were.

My aching head and swollen face were adequate reminders that Alanna was capable of doing more than weeping for her lost stepmother.

Brian nodded at me on his way out the door. He got into the Lexus and drove off toward the highway.

I hesitated for a moment, gathering my strength, and then sat down in the gray booth opposite Alanna.

We sat quietly for a long time, looking out the window, watching the sporadic traffic, each waiting for the other to speak. Finally I gave up and said, "Listen, I'm sorry. We're all in shock still, and no one is acting normally."

Alanna leaned back in the booth, with her eyes closed. She was crying soundlessly, tears spilling down her face.

I pulled a couple of napkins from the holder and slid them over to her side of the table. She accepted them with a nod, and then blew her nose.

My first thought was that the tears and the misery looked very real. My second thought was that she hadn't seemed all that grief-stricken by the death of her own father, so why this show for a woman she hadn't seen for many years? My third thought was to junk the analysis and just go with the flow because Alanna began to speak very rapidly and it took most of my concentration to follow her.

"I'm sorry." She blew her nose loudly and continued in a breathless drawl, "I don't know what came over me. That display was shameless, absolutely shameless. Are you hurt? I would just die if I hurt you. Did I hurt

Delphine? Oh my God, she will probably sue me. Will she sue me do you think? Oh my Lord, if she sues me for assault, and I go to jail, who will take care of Brian?''

Brian was probably of an age to take care of himself, but I figured that Rhonda would volunteer for the job.

''You probably don't have to worry about lawsuits,'' I reassured her. It was true, though only because the thought would not likely occur to Del.

She went on as though I had never spoken. ''This has just been such a shock. A complete and utter shock. We had such high hopes for this town. We wanted to move here and become part of y'all. The joy of seeing Mama again and then the terrible news about Daddy . . .'' Here she paused to daub her eyes with a soggy napkin.

The tears looked real, but her Scottish accent last night had sounded real too.

''And then losing them both so close together, and so unexpectedly. So horribly. Without even a chance to say good-bye. We were having such a wonderful visit too. Just getting to know each other again. Mama was so happy to see us, and so glad we were moving here.''

As I remembered, Aphrodite hadn't been all that excited to see them. Nor did she seem to be having a wonderful visit when she slapped Alanna across the face at the disco party last night.

Barely pausing to inhale, Alanna continued, bringing up her father and Brian and Aphrodite and her sadness and the terrible timing and how when God closes one door, He always opens another. All in a perfect drawl, all accompanied by frequent tears and heartfelt sniffles.

''And then this morning, when y'all came in the cafe I was so happy to see y'all, and then I was so horrified to find that you were angry with me, that I just snapped and said some things I shouldn't and I am so very sorry.''

That gave me the opening I needed to get the conversation back on track. Remembering that Clay was waiting for me at the church, and not wanting to sit through another repetition of apologies and excuses, I said, "There were a lot of things that shouldn't have been said this morning and this afternoon. Maybe it's just best if we forget about that for now and talk about what all this means."

"What all of what means?" she asked, tearfully looking down. Mindlessly, she shredded one of the unused napkins.

"The fact that we are both now joint owners of the Delphi Cafe," I said. "Or at least we will be when the court stuff gets finished. The fact that we are going to have to work together from now on, whether we like it or not."

"Oh," she said, tearing more small pieces from the napkin. She rolled them into tiny balls and arranged them in symmetrical piles. "That stuff."

I sipped my pop and let that sink in for a minute. Outside the usual Sunday traffic was increased, augmented I suppose by the looky-loos who hadn't yet inspected the parking lot, or who wanted to see where Del and the new lady had been fighting. There was lots of excited pointing as people drove past.

"It's for real then?" Alanna asked, her eyes narrowing slightly. "I mean, you getting Mama's share of the cafe? I thought Delphine might be saying that just to upset me." Her hands worked at the napkins furiously as she spoke.

We run across people who do that all the time in the cafe. They mechanically chew toothpicks, they bend straws, they tear napkins into little pieces—and we have to clean up the mess. I swear they don't even know that they're doing it.

But since Alanna wasn't allowing it to interfere with the conversation, I wasn't going to either.

"I don't have a copy of the will with me right now, but yes, she left me her *half*." I emphasized that word. "Fifty percent," I said, just to make sure.

"And are there any other surprises in her will?" There was less sweetness in her voice with every sentence. The piles of napkin balls grew.

"There wasn't anything else in the will at all, except that she wanted Neil Pascoe to have her books for the library. Aphrodite didn't mention the disposition of the furniture or her personal belongings. I'll have to ask her lawyer what happens to that stuff. As far as I know, the house itself is all yours, through your father."

Alanna nodded, a small smile playing on her lips.

"I don't suppose she had all that many books," I said. "But I'm sure that Neil can drop by tomorrow or the next day and get them out of your way."

"Oh that won't be necessary," Alanna said hastily, dividing the tiny balls into even more piles. "We're staying there already, Brian and me. And we can just pack those old books up in a box and bring them here to the cafe any old time."

She finished with a smile, one I didn't trust for a second.

"That still leaves the cafe, and how we're going to run it," I said.

Alanna's lips tightened. "Well, I certainly won't be one to argue with Mama's decision about what to do with her *part*," she emphasized that word, "of the cafe. She could have left it to anyone she wanted. But"—her eyes narrowed down even more—"I would have thought that you had already got   more than enough from Mama."

I imagine my eyes narrowed just a tad too. "Now, that's the second time you've said that. Just what exactly do you mean?

In all the years I worked for Aphrodite, she never gave me anything that she didn't give to anyone else. We all got minimal raises, tiny Christmas bonuses, and absolutely no workplace benefits. At least not the kind that showed up on tax returns.

"Oh yeah?" Alanna said sharply. "Did she pay everyone else's hospital bills too?"

I had to assume that wasn't a napkin-piling non sequitur.

"As far as I know, she never paid *anyone's* hospital bills," I retorted.

"Well, that's mighty funny because just last night Mama said that she couldn't advance me a loan because she had depleted her accounts. Depleted them to pay off your old hospital bills."

"What?" She'd caught me completely off-guard.

"Are you deaf, dear?" Alanna asked sweetly.

"No I'm not deaf. But . . . but . . ." I sputtered. "Aphrodite hasn't paid off my hospital bills. They were from an injury last summer. They didn't have anything to do with the cafe. I was paying them off myself."

Well, I had been trying to pay them off myself. In installments that would take me the better part of a decade to finish.

"She said that it was her fault that y'all didn't have insurance, and that she felt obligated to pay your bills for you," Alanna said in a clipped voice. There was no trace of dewy-eyed grief in her face. "Either she was lying to me, or you're lying to me. And I don't think Mama was lying."

"I have no idea why Aphrodite would say such a thing," I said slowly. Had it been a while since I'd received a bill from the hospital in Aberdeen? I truly couldn't remember. "But it doesn't have anything to do with running the cafe together. Which is what we're going to have to learn to do."

"For the time being," Alanna said darkly. She seemed to have run out of cheery patter. Absentmindedly she pulled another napkin from the holder.

"Yes, for the time being," I agreed. "I'm not an expert cook, but I can run the grill. How about you?"

"My skills lie in working with the public," she said, throwing back her shoulders to show off her considerable assets. "I can draw the customers in."

"Yes," I said. I was certain that she could. "But can you work with Del? Without resorting to violence?"

"I will not have that woman in my cafe," Alanna said. "I cannot be held responsible for my actions if she is nearby. Besides she quit this morning."

"And I rehired her this afternoon. Her *and* Rhonda," I said, hoping that they'd both consent to work again. I couldn't imagine having to spend the rest of my working days alone with Alanna.

"What gives *you* the power to rehire anyone?" she asked nastily, rearranging the piles. "We own this dump fifty-fifty, don't we?"

"Since your father was a silent partner, sharing only in the profits, right at the moment, your powers are limited," I said. Darla and I had painstakingly gone over this at the trailer. "According to their agreement, Aphrodite had the responsibility of day-to-day operations here, and those passed to me as executor of her will. After probate, we can work out an arrangement that will be satisfactory to us both," I said with a very small smile. "But for the time being, I am in charge of hiring and firing. And rehiring."

Alanna licked her lips. There was no Southern babbling now. No protestations of grief. No tears. Not even any paper shredding.

I took her silence, and her still hands, as assent.

"Shall we just pretend that today never happened?" I asked. "I'm used to opening and working the morning shift. If you want to come in early, fine. If you want to wait and take the afternoon shift, that's all right too. I'll contact Del and Rhonda."

Giving orders to Alanna was kind of fun. Unfortunately, giving orders to Del would probably be impossible. I just hoped I could talk her into coming back to work.

I had a sinking feeling that Aphrodite's absence was going to be the least of the changes at the cafe.

22

Subversion in the Ranks

For a person with no leanings toward any brand of organized religion, I derive an enormous amount of pleasure just stepping into St. John's Lutheran Church. Its high ceilings are lined with beams that were handwrought in a time when handwork wasn't out of the ordinary. The pews, burnished by generations of well-dressed rear ends, sit perfectly aligned in ecclesiastical symmetry. Soft light filters in from tall windows to make dancing shadows on the dark wood.

It radiates the austere security of a building that has survived everything that man and Mother Nature in South Dakota have thrown at it for a century. The silence invites contemplation. The beauty creates a temptation to linger.

It's calm and comfortable and peaceful.

Not so the annex. Built in the decade famous for disco music and platform shoes, the single-story, concrete-block, flat-roofed rectangle is tacked to the side of a building that might otherwise have been eligible for the historical register.

I didn't have to walk through the church proper to get to Clay's office in the annex, but I always made a point of doing so. Anything to delay stepping into Kumbayah Land.

The annex itself housed several Sunday school classrooms, the community meeting room complete with a full kitchen (which was also rented out for wedding receptions, baby showers, and rummage sales, church membership not required), a couple of storage rooms, and Clay's office at the end of the hall, which faced the street.

The hallway was hung with gold and avocado wall hangings depicting key biblical scenes and passages, all painstakingly cut out of felt and glued to burlap backing piece by piece. Judging by the color scheme, I assumed that no one had volunteered to make new ones for at least twenty years.

The big wall clock read close to five P.M. Clay was sitting behind a large modern desk, tapping intently on a keyboard and frowning at the monitor. The radio on the bookshelf behind him was tuned in to the rock oldie station; ''Gloria'' blared from the scratchy speakers. The office was decorated in Inspirational Modern, all chrome and glass with asymmetrical crosses and motivational posters dotting the walls.

Tall, blond, and handsome, Clay Deibert took his job and his calling seriously, with none of the on-display piety of television evangelists. He lived the life, but he didn't talk about it much. That was one of the things I liked best about him.

It almost made up for the fact that he was married to my cousin Junior.

He hadn't heard me come down the hall. ''Yoo hoo,'' I said from the doorway. ''Sorry I'm late. Things are a little hairy at the cafe right now.''

''Tory, come in and sit down. I didn't hear you. I've been working on this article for two straight days and can't seem to find the hook I need to finish it.'' He swiveled around and turned the radio down, and then looked up with a smile that was swiftly replaced with a frown. "Have you put any ice on that?" He pointed at my face.

"Not yet, I haven't had time. But I promise I'll go straight home from here and lie on the couch for the rest of the evening with a cold pack."

"I could get you one of those sports packs for now. We always have a few stashed in the freezer," he said, standing up.

"Nah," I said. "Thanks, but this won't take long. Will it?"

He grinned. "Nope. But at least let me get you some aspirin. I'll bet you haven't had time for that either."

"That'd be nice," I said gratefully.

While he rooted out a couple of Excedrins and a glass of water, I sat back in the chair with my eyes closed. Exhaustion was setting in, accompanied by a bone-deep achiness that went beyond being knocked around. So much had happened in such a short period of time, with such profound results, that I had not had time to track the changes properly. I had the feeling that I had already missed something important.

"I won't keep you any longer than necessary," Clay said, coming back into the room. He handed me the aspirin and a paper cup. "But I wanted to ask you about funeral arrangements for Aphrodite."

"Ask me?" I said, swallowing. "Why?"

"Well, Norman Oberle was in a little earlier, we talked for a while about it in the church. When I got back to the office, I saw everyone in the street talking, so I decided to come over and ask you on the spot what you want to do." He grinned ruefully. "I didn't realize until it was too late that I'd just missed the Gunfight at O.K. Corral. Well, nearly missed it anyway. I'm really sorry, by the way."

"That's all right," I said, rubbing my face. "I think we'll be able to work together without pads and helmets."

That's me, premature optimism all the way.

"I'm glad to hear it," Clay said, nodding. "It'll be good for the community to see that the cafe will go on as per usual after Aphrodite's funeral. What day did you have in mind for the services?''

I had not even thought about going to her funeral, much less planning it.

"Is that up to me too?''

"You're her executor, aren't you?'' Clay asked. "I'm certain Junior told me that.''

Trust Junior to have the whole scoop and nothing but the scoop.

I sighed. Darla and I hadn't gone over funeral details, so this new obligation was a surprise. "Yeah, I guess I am. What do we need to work out?''

Clay chewed a pencil eraser. "Well, if she didn't tell you her wishes, or leave them in writing somewhere, first you'll have to try to figure out what she would have wanted for a service.''

"As far as I know, she didn't leave any burial instructions,'' I said. "And she wasn't very religious.''

"Don't tell anyone I said this''—Clay smiled—"but sometimes the least religious people have the best funerals. There seems to be less hand wringing and more celebration of the life lived well. Aphrodite wasn't a member here, but she sat in on services once in a while. And Norman *is* a member, so we didn't think she'd mind having a memorial here. I'd like to do the honors, if I could.''

"Of course,'' I said, surprised. I hadn't known that Aphrodite ever set foot on any church property, except to go to the CCD hall to play bingo. "I'm sure she'd want you. You know, it's so strange to be planning her funeral. I can't even get used to the idea that she's gone.''

"I'm not sure that she is,'' Clay said.

I raised an eyebrow.

"I mean completely gone. I can't help feeling that a part of her is still here, making sure that we tie up all the loose ends. You know what I mean?''

I did know what Clay meant. Whether it were a symptom of denial or not, I felt that she was still here too, just out of sight, keeping track of everything. For a moment I felt as though she were standing in the hall, listening to Clay and me. I even thought I caught a whiff of cigarette smoke.

"That's pretty subversive thinking for a Lutheran minister," I said, shaking off my own case of the vapors.

He shrugged. "There are more mysteries on heaven and earth, and all that. None of us here have all the answers."

"I don't even have all the questions," I said, laughing. Though I had thought of a few. "I suppose I have to do the coffin shopping?"

"Eventually. But this won't be a full funeral with a burial," Clay said matter-of-factly. "The police won't release the remains until the investigation is finished. And perhaps not until after they've solved her murder."

I read enough murder mysteries to know that, I should have remembered. "You're the first one I've heard say the word *murder* out loud."

"I've been hearing it all over," Clay said softly.

"From Junior?" I asked.

"Well . . ." He hesitated, not wanting to indict his wife, I suppose. ". . . and from other people around town already. But mostly on the radio. The news reports have been announcing more unusual deaths in Delphi, and the very odd coincidence of both Aphrodite and her estranged husband dying less than twenty-four hours apart."

"I haven't been near a radio or TV all day," I said. "Have they named any suspects yet?"

"The radio and the police, or the people in town?" Clay asked with a smile.

"Both, I guess," I said, returning the smile.

"The police aren't naming names of course, but they say that they already have suspects in mind."

"Well, they always say that," I said, "just to make the guilty parties feel exposed. And, well, guilty." Though there was every possibility that the police had also connected with Neil's fax-happy newspaperman in Rockville, and knew what we knew about Brain Hunt's proclivity toward explosives. And his mother's recent possible absconding with cash and account books.

"And in town?"

"Well, mostly everyone is suspicious of the timing involved."

"I can understand that, what with Alanna showing up just in time to inherit," I said.

"Well, Alanna isn't the only one inheriting, you know," Clay said quietly.

I let that sink in, tightening my jaw.

"For what it's worth," he continued, "I don't think anyone actually suspects you. The comments have been few and far between, and all in jest."

I had known that resentment would run high over the cafe inheritance, but had not expected any real nastiness. Trust Junior to repeat it all.

"It reflects badly on us, but everyone is reeling from the shock. And there are people who speak without thinking. This will all blow over when the police find out who did this terrible thing."

"Yeah, if that ever happens," I said sourly.

Clay craned his neck and looked out the window over at the cafe. "Well, at least they're on the job." He pointed across the street.

A patrol car had just pulled up in front of the cafe. A uniformed officer emerged and tapped on the cafe door. Though I could only see her dimly, Alanna unlocked the door and let the officer inside.

Maybe they were narrowing their list of suspects down to those who had something to gain from Aphrodite's death.

Or maybe they were routinely questioning anyone who might shed light on Aphrodite's life.

In either case, I figured they'd come and talk to me.

23

·····························

On the Grill

MONDAY, NOVEMBER 2

As a tool for inducing visions, exhaustion is hard to beat.
I expect that it was some weary caveman who first discovered the correlation between not enough hours in between the furs and the tendency to see things that aren't
really there.

Throughout human history, native cultures have ex-
ploited this phenomenon, thinking it a link between this
world and the next, devising elaborate rituals to interpret
the resultant hallucinations as messages of great import
from the beyond.

Of course those visions were sometimes helped along
by fasting and the burning of native grasses or the in-
gestion of specific fungi. This system is still widely in
use on many college campuses (well, not so much the
food deprivation part), and those habits may go a long
way toward explaining the music popular on college radio stations.

Having slept not at all on Saturday, I had fully intended to sack out as early as possible Sunday night. But after Clay and I finally worked out an itinerary and a timetable for Aphrodite's memorial service on Tuesday morning, I'd spent fifteen minutes on the phone getting Rhonda to agree to come back to the cafe, followed by a full two hours of asking, cajoling, and finally begging Del to come back to work. By then, the police had made their way to the trailer, and we spent another hour going over everything we'd gone over already, in exactly the same words and with exactly the same results. After that it was absolutely necessary to give Neil an update on the afternoon's activities.

By the time I got to bed, I was too tired to sleep. I blocked the overwhelming memory of Aphrodite's burning van with a torturous remembrance of the good times Stu and I had had together. That, of course, led to the reappearance of Renee, and the realization that whatever else happened, the affair could not go on as it had before. Which was too painful to dwell on, so I switched channels to Alanna and the cafe, which flipped the station right back to Aphrodite's death.

I finally dropped off about twenty minutes before the alarm rang.

I was rumpled, bleary-eyed, and not tracking well, and two days of sleep deprivation had induced a nightmare vision of me in charge behind the grill, trying to cook breakfast for a capacity crowd.

Unfortunately, the only hallucination was the notion that I was in charge of anything at all.

"Tory, Willard Hausvik says his bacon isn't crisp enough and he'd like you to fry it a little longer," Rhonda said apologetically, sliding a plate across the stainless-steel counter that divided the kitchen from the cafe.

I had just burned the toast, spattered grease all over my shirt, and blistered my finger on a burner. I had six breakfast orders going at once, every one of them different. Every one of them with specific instructions. These eggs with hard yolks, those sunny-side-up. This bacon crisp, that sausage unsalted. I hadn't even begun the biscuits and gravy, or the short stack.

No wonder Aphrodite didn't talk much. There wasn't time for conversation with all these damn customers wanting their food cooked just so.

I took the plate and growled at Rhonda, who grinned. "You're a peach," she said, "imitating Aphrodite just to make me feel better."

"Who's imitating?" I mumbled to myself as Del pinned another order to the wheel hanging above the counter and gave it a spin.

She had dressed with special care. Despite the unusually early shift, her hair tumbled to her shoulders in a riot of perfectly arranged red curls, her preshrunk Garth Brooks T-shirt was tucked just a shade too firmly into tight jeans, which were in turn tucked into cowboy boots. A careful makeup application had covered the remains of yesterday's fight; her injured lip looked more super-model pouty than swollen.

There was no trace of Saturday's Wicked Witch. At least not on the outside.

"Step it up, Boss Lady," she said. "We got restless natives with rumbling tummies."

I slapped Willard's limp bacon back on the grill and furiously flipped the hard-yolk eggs before looking up at Del with a possibly murderous glint in my eye.

"Whoa," she said, in mock alarm. "Take 'er easy. You've done this before, you just have to hit your stride, that's all."

I had often spelled Aphrodite on the grill, or helped out with the cooking when things were unusually rushed. But she had always been in command, calm and competent. By myself I floundered, unable to remember where the spatulas were, or the proper order in which to cook two over-easy with a side of hash browns, links, and whole wheat toast.

I could serve that stuff in my sleep. Cooking it was another matter entirely.

Wrestling with the pitcher of pancake batter, I said, "If they get too restless, just tell them to take a moment of silence in honor of Aphrodite. And if that doesn't shame them into being patient, say I'll come out there and personally stick a spatula right up someone's ass.''

I could swear I heard a familiar snort of laughter from behind me. I whirled around, but of course nothing was there except a small haze of smoke caused by another piece of smoldering toast.

"You okay?" Del asked.

"Yeah," I said, shaking my head. "Just hearing things."

Rhonda pinned another order to the carousel. She exchanged puzzled glances with Del, who shrugged and picked up the plates I'd just pushed across to her.

"I don't think Ron wanted his eggs scrambled," Del said, looking down at the plates.

"Yes he does," I said, daring her to contradict me.

"Hokay," she said, blowing out all of her air. "Whatever."

I knew that Ron would accept what was served without argument or complaint. I had made a mess of his over-easy eggs twice, and didn't want him to have to wait for another attempt. I figured scrambled eggs *now* were better than the possibility of no eggs, ever.

"You want me to come back there and help for a while?" Rhonda asked hesitantly.

"Thanks, but I'll get the hang of it," I said, remembering to smile at her. "Just tell everyone that things will be a little slow until I get used to doing this."

My respect for Aphrodite grew by the minute. She had never seemed to be flustered by busloads of customers. The food served in the Delphi Cafe wasn't exactly good, but it was served pretty much as ordered, and it usually got to the table still warm. And very little of it was sent back to the kitchen.

"Uh, Tory," Rhonda said quietly as I wrestled a sheet of hot biscuits out of the oven. "There's a lady out here who wants to know if we have any fresh strawberries for her oatmeal. Which has lumps." Rhonda added unnecessarily, "She's from out of town."

"It's November, Rhonda," I said carefully. "There *are* no fresh strawberries in the Upper Midwest. But gimmee her bowl, and I'll mash the lumps out."

Sweat dripped into my eyes as I stirred the thickening sausage gravy, trying to remember how much pepper to use. Not enough and the dish would be blah, too much and it would be inedible. Cursing Aphrodite's tendency to work without a recipe, I decided to err on the side of bland.

"Tory . . ." Rhonda said.

"What now?" I asked, exasperated.

"A delivery guy just brought these for you," she said, handing over a huge bouquet of flowers that was rich with the smell of roses.

Though the kitchen faced the cafe and the view through the large opening into the dining room was not obstructed, I had not seen or heard anything that had happened beyond the grill all morning. I suddenly understood why Aphrodite was usually oblivious to activity in the cafe. One simply could not pay attention to both places at once. Even when a delivery man brought large bunches of flowers—a decidedly unusual occurrence.

So unusual that conversation had stalled in the cafe as heads craned to watch Rhonda hand the flowers to me.

"Must have cost a fortune." Del sniffed.

"They're pretty," Rhonda said. "Maybe you have a secret admirer."

"Not likely," I said, searching the bundle for a card. The flowers were beautiful. And obviously expensive. "Oh, here it is," I said, locating a small white envelope tucked deeply into the ferns.

Ignoring the rapidly thickening gravy and eggs sizzling into leather, I pulled out the envelope, which bore the hand-printed inscription: *To the Owner of the Delphi Cafe.*

The folded card inside was generically typical, illustrated with a sprig of lilac and loopy script saying "Congratulations."

I smiled, thinking that Neil had sent flowers to com-memorate the first day of the rest of my life, such as it was.

Balancing the flowers over an arm, I opened the card. When I saw what had been written inside, I dropped the flowers and the card and jumped back in confusion.

In disgust.

In fear.

Inside the card, printed in a bold black ink, was the word *BOOM!*

24

....

Straight Flush

Okay, so I already said I wasn't tracking very well. I was tired, and crabby, and overwhelmed, and occasionally hearing nonexistent laughter. My first morning as chief cook had been a painful process of trial-and-error—the customers' trials and my numerous errors—with Del and Rhonda running interference between the two opposing camps. I was beginning to hate the idea of my cooking just about as much as those who warily eyed hotcakes that could double as Frisbees and toast that could be used to draw on the sidewalks.

It was not an auspicious beginning for a new and fulfilling business venture.

The last thing I needed was a nasty prank of the note-in-the-bouquet variety.

That is, if I were lucky enough for it to have been a prank.

Rhonda, who was rapidly becoming accustomed to seeing me do irrational things, took my tossing the flowers on the floor in stride. She bent over and picked them up and fluffed the ferns a bit. "I'll just put these in water for you," she said, catching Del's eye meaningfully on her way out of the kitchen. "We'll put them on the counter out here for everyone to enjoy."

I turned to the grill and tried to attend to the assorted burning breakfasts, rapidly discarding about a half-dozen overdone eggs and some bacon that would have been crisp enough even for Willard Hausvik. The note and envelope lay where they had landed on the floor.

Still in the kitchen with me, Del leaned back against a stool and lit a cigarette. "Are you losing it?" she finally asked.

"I hope so," I said, not looking at her. "Tell me if the note says what I think it says."

Cigarette in mouth, she picked up and read the envelope, raising an eyebrow, and then opened the note.

"Oh," she said, quietly. "What do you suppose this means?"

"I'm open to any interpretation you can come up with," I said, cracking more eggs and adding pats of butter to the sizzling hash browns.

"You think it's a joke?" she asked.

"That'd be nice," I said, flipping the eggs and rearranging the bacon. "But I don't suppose it's a good idea to operate on that assumption. Considering." I pulled another order ticket from the carousel and read it.

"I suppose not," she said, inspecting the back of the card. "It doesn't say which florist it came from."

"Well there aren't very many around here," I said, popping bread into the toaster. It should be pretty easy to find out who had an order to deliver flowers to Delphi this morning." I lifted the eggs from the grill and slid them, intact, onto two plates. "Rhonda," I called through the opening. "Come in here a minute, would you?"

"Orders for me?" she asked brightly. "That was fast."

"Just a second," I said, arranging bacon alongside the eggs and hash browns and sliding two plates toward Del.

Del put the note and envelope down on the stool and took the plates. "Do you realize what just happened?" she asked, grinning.

"Outside of getting a possible death threat," I said, buttering the toast, "I have not a clue."

"Look at these plates," Del demanded.

Annoyed, wondering what I had done wrong now, I inspected them. "Everything looks fine to me," I said shortly.

"Exactly," Del said smugly, pushing through the swinging half-door that divided the kitchen from the rest of the cafe. Over her shoulder she said, "Don't think so much. Be the food."

I frowned after her, thinking that I was not the only one who was losing it.

Rhonda cleared her throat.

"Oh yeah," I said, remembering that I had called her over. I poured several dollar pancakes in a line on the grill. "What can you tell me about the guy who delivered the flowers?"

She looked at the ceiling, chewing her lip. "Well, he was a guy. And he delivered flowers."

"Big help," I said, pointing at the stool. "Read the card that came with the flowers, and then see if you can remember anything else."

She opened the card and read it. The color drained from her face.

"Oh God, Tory," she said, a little shaky. "Do you know what this means?"

"I know what I think it means," I said, flipping the pancakes and pulling a pitcher of syrup out of the microwave.

"Well, he was just a guy, you know. Old like you," she said, and then backtracked. "Well, you know what I mean, not old like Norman Oberle, but sorta older than you. Well, come to think of it, I think he was lots older than you . . ."

"Don't worry about his specific age," I said. When I was twenty, there hadn't seemed to be much quantitative difference between mid-forties and mid-sixties either. "Did you notice what he drove?"

"I think it was just a regular delivery truck. You know, one of those big van things."

The microwave beeped. I slid Rhonda the plate of pancakes and the pitcher of syrup. She went through the door into the cafe.

I thought of something. "Rhonda."

She paused mid-stride, holding the plates.

"Did the truck say anything? I mean, advertising on the sides—signs or anything?"

"Jeez, I didn't see it except for a glimpse through the door."

"Well, try to remember," I said. "Ask the people sitting in the window booths when the flowers came. See if anyone remembers anything about the guy or his van. I think we'll want to know that before we call the police."

"Call the police about what?" a voice said in my ear.

I jumped and dropped the spatula. And the egg I was flipping.

"Jesus Christ, Alanna," I said, heart pounding. "Don't do that!"

"What?" she asked innocently. "Can't I come in the back door of the cafe of which I own *exactly* 50 percent?" Her drawl was Oklahoma-perfect this morning.

"That's not what I meant. Come in any door you want," I said, calming down. "Just don't sneak up on me like that."

Like Del, Alanna was awfully spiffed up for a morning shift at a small-town cafe. She wore a skirt and jacket that would probably have served as conventional office garb if she had bothered to put on a blouse. Her hair was piled atop her head in a mass of blond swirls and curves. Diamonds, or something very like, sparkled from her earlobes, and a flowery sweet perfume drifted from her in waves.

"My my, we're jumpy, aren't we?" she asked with a smile.

"Yeah, well, I got an interesting message this morning," I said shortly, not looking at her as I read another ticket. "It's on the stool over there. Tell me what you think."

Knitting her brows, she read the card.

"What exactly does this mean?" she demanded.

"That's what I'd like to know," I said, continuing to cook, putting breakfasts together with less trouble than before. "It came with those flowers." I pointed at the vase now standing on the counter in the cafe.

"Well, I'll tell you what I think. I think someone in this town is sick," Alanna said loudly. "Sick enough to make a joke at a time like this."

"You think it's a joke?"

"Well, what else could it be?" Alanna demanded.

"It doesn't take a genius to figure that one out," Del said quietly through the opening as she clipped another order up. "How many explosions do you need before the word *BOOM* means anything to you?"

We both looked at her. Del shot an entirely phony smile at us, and then turned away.

"You think this is some kind of threat?" Alanna asked. "Against *you*?"

"Well, the flowers came to me," I said, taking down the order and beginning to assemble the breakfast. "I assume the message was meant for me."

I seemed to be on automatic pilot. The less I thought about the process of cooking, the easier it became.

Which, come to think of it, had been Del's point.

Being the food, I continued, "Personally, *I* don't know anyone who would send something like this."

"What exactly are you saying?" Alanna asked, voice flat, accent barely noticeable.

"The whole point of an anonymous threat, whether it's a joke or not, is that it can come from anyone. People we know. People we don't know. People we just met."

It wasn't a nice thing to say. But I wasn't in a nice mood.

Alanna inhaled sharply and clamped her lips together in a straight line. She looked at the card again, tapping her foot, getting obviously angrier by the second. Then she noticed the envelope that was still on the stool. "What's this?"

"It came with the flowers," I said, lowering the wire basket into bubbling oil for the doofus who wanted French fries for breakfast.

"Well, this says 'To the Owner of the Delphi Cafe,' " Alanna said, looking up at me, brandishing the small envelope.

No sleep compounded by new routines and unsettling messages were more than enough to upset my equilibrium without non sequiturs fired in variable accents while I was trying to cook. "I believe we covered that already," I said.

"So *those* flowers"—Alanna pointed into the cafe, drawl miraculously restored—"came with *this* envelope, and you automatically assumed that they were meant for *you*?"

That was so patently obvious that I didn't respond. I just ladled sausage gravy over a plateful of biscuits.

"Who's seen this?" she demanded.

"Del, Rhonda, and I," I said. "But I'm calling the police as soon as things calm down here. If someone is threatening me, even as a joke, I think they should know."

"Well," she said furiously, "did it ever occur to you that you aren't the only owner of the Delphi Cafe?" Her hand, the one holding the card and envelope, contracted into a fist. "Did it even once cross your self-centered mind that *I* am also an owner of the Delphi Cafe? That this"—she brandished the note and envelope—"*this* might be meant for *me*?"

For the last two days, I had mostly tried to put Alanna's existence out of my brain. She was an intrusion, a nuisance, an obstacle to be overcome—not a fellow human being. That the note might have been meant for her had not even occurred to me.

I shot a glance at Del, who had been eavesdropping. Alanna's point had obviously not occurred to her either.

"You people make me sick," Alanna shouted loud enough for all to hear. "Every last one of you with your smug airs and your snotty little cliques."

She pushed through the half-doors into the cafe, still shouting. "Well, you're gonna have to get used to me because I am staying right here!" She stood glaring at the crowded cafe.

The locals who had at least a notion of the internal power play that had taken place over the last couple of days seemed startled by the sudden attack on them. The out-of-towners, who were truly confused by Alanna's outburst, stared with openmouthed surprise.

"This is what I think of your jokes," she said, suddenly pulling the flowers out of the vase. She threw them on the floor and stomped on them. Petals, leaves, ferns, and water droplets spattered everywhere.

"And this is what I think of your threats!" she said, striding across the cafe, wadded card and envelope in her raised fist.

I had an inkling of what was going to happen next. "Del, stop her," I shouted, unfortunately just a fraction too late.

I pushed through the door into the cafe just in time to see Alanna barge into the bathroom, and to hear the flushing of the toilet.

Alanna reemerged with empty hands and a triumphant smile.

25

....

A Little Light on the Subject

You know before you even open a mystery novel that you are going to be fed a red herring or two, and that you're going to miss a clue here and there. Most importantly, you know that the most obvious suspect couldn't possibly have done it because fictional murderers are just too clever for everyone but intrepid protagonists to uncover.

That's the way it works in books.

Real-life murder is a little different. Most murderers are incredibly stupid, and most murders are impromptu messes. By the time the deed is done it's usually too late to hide the trail. If it seems obvious that the husband did it, then you can be pretty damn sure that the husband did it. Or the angry girlfriend. Or the cheating business partner.

And though the wheels of justice revolve pretty slowly at times, the bad guys are almost always caught, even here in the Midwest where the crimes are few and the investigators even fewer.

But there are some similarities between the real and the fictional, the kind of commonsense rules that shouldn't have to be spelled out, even to the most amateur observers:

Don't go into the basement alone.

Don't confront the suspected murderer unless you've told everyone where you're going, and why.

And it goes without saying that you never, ever, destroy the evidence.

"Do you know what you just did?" Del demanded furiously, closing in on Alanna by the bathroom door. "Do you have the slightest fucking notion?"

Alanna didn't back off. In fact, she stepped closer to Del, towering menacingly over her by half a foot, to the intense delight of the cafe onlookers.

"Yes indeed," Alanna said in a careful drawl. "I showed whoever sent those flowers that I will not be intimidated. If the joker isn't here right now, and I personally think that he, or *she*"—Alanna emphasized that word—"is, then word will get around soon enough. I know how the rumor mill works in these hick towns."

"You dumb bitch," Del snarled. "This isn't about you. It's about Aphrodite and the cafe." Del leaned in and whispered, "It's about murder."

I doubted that Del was nearly as worried about Alanna's destruction of possible evidence as she was about one-upping her in the undeclared Sex Queen War. And I thought that Alanna wasn't nearly as worried about stemming a tide of tasteless practical jokes as she was about drawing attention to herself.

"Ladies, ladies," Brian said from behind me. I had no idea how long he'd been standing in the kitchen, or whether he'd witnessed that whole sorry scene.

Del and Alanna both turned toward him. Del's snarl stayed in place, but Alanna's tight expression relaxed into a small smile for her son, and she moved back a half-step. The cafe's rapt attention was transferred from the near duel to the handsome young man.

Including Rhonda, whose face lit up.

The tension between Del and Alanna didn't dissipate entirely, though the interruption diffused the threat of immediate combat. Unspoken messages seemed to shuttle back and forth between mother and son during the brief pause. Realizing that the community focus was off her, Del stepped back and scowled.

Personally, I was relieved not to have to get in between them again. This argument had had the potential to sink very quickly into the physical. And I already had as many reminders as I needed of their ability to mix it up.

"Let's take this into the kitchen, shall we?" Brian said quietly to his mother. "I'm sure that these fine people would like to get back to their meals," he said more loudly.

It suddenly occurred to me that Brian didn't have an accent. Or at least not one discernible to my ear, and certainly nothing like the drawl affected by his theatrical mother.

With a great deal of put-on dignity, Alanna took her son's arm and reentered the kitchen.

"I have work to do," Del said shortly, and turned to refill the coffee pots.

Rhonda shot a puzzled glance at me. I shrugged and went back into the kitchen to confront the remains of the last few hardening breakfasts.

Scraping the grill, I said, "It really would have been better if you hadn't flushed that card, Alanna. It could have been evidence, but you destroyed it."

Actually we had already violated one of the unspoken rules by handling the card in the first place. If there had been any usable prints, our own had probably smeared them anyway.

"What card?" Brian asked, watching me fumble at the grill. My short-lived cooking competence was gone as inexplicably as it had arrived. "Here," he said, taking the spatula from me, "it works easier if you do it like this."

He deftly arranged the eggs and popped a couple of slices into the toaster. He picked up a ticket that was lying on the counter and read it. "Do you mind if I take over for a while? You look like you could use a rest."

"Thanks," I said gratefully, leaning back against the butcher block in the center of the kitchen. Except for the few moments of watching Del and Alanna prepare to exchange blows, I hadn't had a break all morning. "Evidently you've done this before," I said to Brian.

"Hey, I'm a jack of all trades," he said, smiling, as he peeled the paper off of a couple of hamburger patties and placed them on the grill.

The cafe had been so busy, and the orders so demanding, that I hadn't had a chance to look at the clock. It was verging on noon, and I'd been cooking nonstop for nearly six hours. No wonder I was worn out.

I watched amazed, and Alanna watched proudly, as Brian quickly and competently assembled a couple of Delphi Burgers.

"So," he said quietly, not looking up, "what's all the ruckus about?"

"A bouquet of flowers was delivered to the cafe this morning containing a tasteless joke about poor Mama's death," Alanna said quickly.

"I'm not so sure it was a joke," I said. Since Brian was manning the grill, I busied myself slicing tomatoes and chopping lettuce in preparation for the onslaught of the dinner crowd. "The flowers came addressed to the owner. And naturally—"

"And naturally, she thought they were intended for her," Alanna interrupted.

"And *naturally*," I interrupted back, "when I saw what was written on the card, I assumed that there was a connection between it and the explosion. It seemed pretty obvious to all of us that there was at least an implied threat."

"And what was written on this threatening card?" Brian asked his mother.

When she told him, he set the spatula down and stared at her. She held his gaze a moment, then flicked her eyes to me, saying, "It will do no good to speculate about what the message meant now. It's gone."

And because of that, there was no point in calling the police to report the bouquet and its disquieting message. But the message had been received, at least by me. And it had been duly noted.

Brian looked at his mother, and then said to me, "You've had a long day. Why don't you take off? Mom and I can finish out the afternoon. We talked it over and decided that we weren't ready to stay open for supper anyway. We'll just stick around until later this afternoon, and then close up shop."

Alanna nodded.

"If that's all right with you," Brian added.

"It's fine with me. Things are too jumbled to try to keep to a full schedule yet. We're going to need to hire another waitress, and a cook—I can't keep the kind of hours that Aphrodite used to," I said wearily. "Unless you want to take over the honors," I said to Brian.

"I thought you'd never ask. I love working the grill," he said, pausing to light a cigarette.

A sense of déjà vu washed over me as I watched him smoke as he flipped burgers. Also a sense of missing something, something important.

"What do you think about not opening at all tomorrow?" Brian asked me as he lowered more fries into the oil. "Out of respect. So that we can all go to the memorial service. The whole town will be there anyway."

Though Aphrodite's death was never far from my mind, the practical aspects seemed to get lost in the shuffle. I'd already forgotten about the memorial service in the morning. "That would be fine. Maybe tonight we can get together and talk. Neil and I can come over to Aphrodite's, uh, your house and he can pick up those books. And then we can sit down and iron out a few details about running the cafe. Together."

Mother and son exchanged another glance. "Tonight won't work for us. We still have to arrange a service for Daddy. And there are tons of paperwork involved with settling his estate."

"I'm sorry," I said, abashed. "It had slipped my mind that you had another funeral to deal with."

In fact, I'd bet that everyone had forgotten that Alanna and Brian were closely connected to both of the recent deaths.

"What about tomorrow night, after the service?" I suggested. "Neil and I can still drop by and pick up the books, that way you won't have to haul them around."

"How about if we meet here?" Brian said without turning around. "We can leave the *Closed* sign up. It'll be easier to discuss business matters here in the cafe. We'll bring the books with us then."

"Okay," I said. It didn't matter to me where we met, just so that we were able to talk without resorting to a street brawl.

Brian slid a couple of plates across the counter for Rhonda, whose adoring smile lit her whole face.

Hers was the first genuine smile I'd seen in days. I was glad it was back. Never again did I want to see her sobbing and miserable, in shock and grief the way she had been on the night of the explosion, standing in the back parking lot of the cafe with Brian's arm around her shoulder.

Something about that memory stopped me in my tracks. Something about Brian's arm around poor weeping Rhonda.

He hummed at the grill, flipping burgers like a pro as I peered at his back, trying to bring the fragment into focus.

I realized that it wasn't the arm around Rhonda that I needed to see. As I concentrated a little harder, the memory of that evening popped into full view.

There was Brian, watching flames shoot from Aphrodite's van with an unreadable expression on his face.

Brian with one arm around Rhonda's shoulders, and the other down at his side.

And clutched in that free hand had been a large green flashlight.

The large green flashlight that Rhonda had used to complete her Statue of Liberty costume on Halloween night. The one Brian had taken from her in the bar because she couldn't juggle it, a book, and a beer mug all at once.

The flashlight that Aphrodite had picked up from the parking lot and handed to me. Just before she opened the van door and turned the key.

26

....

Paper Chase

I remember hearing about Japanese soldiers stranded on Pacific islands in the years after World War II, who on being rescued, had been willing and eager to carry on with a war that they didn't know had long been settled.

Even in more recent times, word of events happening on the East Coast sometimes didn't reach the West Coast for hours, and the Midwest not for days, if at all. I personally don't remember hearing anything about Woodstock until the whole peace, love, and music festival was over.

News just didn't travel very fast back then.

But things have changed in the Information Age. Now you can find out anything about any subject or any person, anywhere, with just a few finger strokes and a couple of mouse clicks.

Problem is, there doesn't seem to be any quality control on the glut of info available to the gadget-happy and the computer-literate. If you seek, you shall certainly find. Whether you can actually use is another question entirely.

To work without being disturbed, Neil had posted a sign on the library door saying that he was preparing for Aphrodite's memorial service in the morning. He asked that patrons either serve themselves or come back tomorrow afternoon, when the library would be open as usual.

In truth we were as ready for Aphrodite's memorial service as we would ever be. What we were really doing upstairs in Neil's living quarters was searching out the cyberworld for traces of Aphrodite's life, and if we were lucky, clues to her death.

"Another batch is coming in," I said as the fax machine in the office off the kitchen beeped and started spitting sheets out.

Neil had contacted the Rockville, Oklahoma, newspaper again, and the owner/manager/searcher of archives had found a pile of articles to forward to him.

"Most of that stuff will be useless," Neil said, looking over his glasses at me from behind his computer monitor, and munching orange and black M&Ms. Between us, we'd managed to eat most of his leftover Halloween treats. "I had him send on any article with the name Ferguson, Hunt, or Luna in it, from as far back as the archives would go. We're bound to get a lot of junk."

"Which years did he search?" I asked, stacking and glancing through the first few sheets. Mostly they were routine articles and police reports. There were also quite a few ads for the Moonstone Cafe.

"All of them in the archive. Though anything from longer than forty years ago will take more time to locate because those papers are stored in a different place. But I'm also running a check of other newspapers in the area, and the courthouse in Boise City, which is the county seat. I might be able to get copies of things like birth and marriage certificates, and liquor licenses in the morning," Neil said tapping away on the keyboard furiously.

"Will we get any *real* information this way?" I asked, leaning my head against the window trim. The sugar rush from all the goodies had not given me any additional energy. I was worn out, exhausted, weary, headachy, tired, and near collapse.

Though it was still daylight, dusk was settling in quickly. I'd been sitting in the office window seat as we worked and speculated. Occasionally during the afternoon, I'd peeked through the blinds down to Delphi's main drag. Kitty-corner across the street from Neil's house, Del's and my trailer sat empty. I don't think Del had returned from the cafe during the afternoon. Presley had been home for a while, but he'd emerged deep in conversation with Mardelle Jackson a half-hour ago, and they'd both walked up the street toward her parents' bar.

If you craned your neck a little, you could see as far as the cafe, which was now also dark. Neil and I had both watched Alanna and Brian drive off in her Lexus in the general direction of Aphrodite's house.

Correction, Alanna's house.

"Well," Neil continued after he finished typing the request he'd been working on. "If we're lucky, the archive search might give us a bare-bones timeline of the years Aphrodite lived with Gus and his daughter. And it definitely should help us put together an outline of the more recent years, since Alanna's activities were so publicly recorded." He grinned and stretched, leaning back in his office chair.

"Are we doing the right thing?" I asked, still watching the shadows fall outside. "Isn't this invading privacy on a pretty large scale?"

"Given the circumstances, and the fact that two of the principals are dead, one not from natural causes, I think the ends justify the means. Especially after what you told me about this afternoon."

Over miniboxes of Milk Duds and Junior Mints, we had attacked Alanna's reaction to the bouquet enclosure from every angle, and no matter how we looked at it, what Alanna had done was highly suspicious. Whether she had actually been frightened or angry, flushing the note had been a tidy way of disposing of a piece of paper that might have yielded at least some forensic evidence—

whether it be fingerprints or ink used, or even a hand-writing sample.

All by itself, the green flashlight that had been in Brian's hand both before and after the explosion was ample reason to suspect the interlopers from Oklahoma.

At best, they were Okie oddballs. At worst, we were harboring one or a pair, of murderers in our midst.

"This'll take a while," Neil said, standing. "I have both lines tied up right now, so no one can call in. You feel like something to eat? I mean real food, not junk."

"Only if I don't have to cook it," I said wearily as he went into the kitchen, opened the refrigerator, and rattled a few pans.

Out the window, I saw a burgundy pickup truck pull into the trailer driveway and park. A figure sat inside the dark cab for a few moments before getting out.

Standing beside his truck, Stu McKee paused, looking at the unoccupied trailer. Then he turned around and scanned Neil's house. I pulled back, even though I knew he couldn't see me through the blinds or around the curtain.

I had not spared much thought for him, or us, in the last couple of days. Partly because circumstances had not allowed any time for entirely personal traumas, but mostly because I had deliberately put it out of my mind. I knew without making a formal and final decision (and therefore did not want to know) that our relationship had to end.

Carried away by the giddiness of wanting and being wanted, I'd fooled myself into ignoring Renee's existence while she'd lived in Delphi, and forced her out of my mind when she'd left. But she was back now, at least temporarily. And she was pregnant.

However much I'd fooled myself into thinking that a wife was irrelevant, I could not trick my errant morality into dismissing an impending child.

I watched Stu down below. His expression, visible in the dusk, seemed to be reflecting exactly what I'd just being thinking. I was startled by the sudden flush of desire that washed over me. Too tired to put up a wall,

I closed my eyes, no longer fighting the memory of his arms and his eyes and his laugh, the warmth of his body and the sheer joy of our times together. What we had done had been wrong, wrong from the very beginning. But it had been good, and wrong or not, it had been what I had needed.

Caught completely off-guard by an intense yearning for a man I could no longer have, I was horrified at the sudden tears that threatened to spill.

I had not been able to cry for Aphrodite. But evidently I was able to cry for myself, and my empty bed.

Finally Stu got back into his truck and drove off. Thoroughly ashamed, I turned to find Neil watching me from the kitchen doorway, brown eyes somber behind his glasses.

I could swear that he knew what I had been thinking and feeling. That he knew and he accepted. And forgave.

"How's stir-fry sound?" he asked softly. "I happen to have a couple of thawed chicken breasts and some Szechuan sauce packets. It won't be like restaurant food, but it'll be edible. I'll open a bottle of Chardonnay."

I shook off my self-pity. Or at least I forced it back a bit, and smiled. "Sounds wonderful. Can I help chop veggies?"

"Not on your life. You sit and look through these papers. I'll do the cooking."

He disappeared back into the kitchen, humming along to the sweet harmonies of CSN and sometimes Y, which were blaring from the speakers.

I raised an eyebrow. " 'Suite Judy Blue Eyes'?" I asked. I had long ago passed the point where I was no fun anymore.

"The sugar overload gave me a munchie flashback." Neil laughed.

"You aren't old enough to have a munchie flashback," I said, laughing back at him. Neil could always make me laugh. "That's the cross my generation has to bear."

"Hey, I'm a Boomer too. I'm on the tail end, but still part of the crowd," he protested, expertly slicing carrots on the diagonal.

My life currently seemed full of men who are more competent in the kitchen than me.

"Too bad you didn't inherit the cafe," I said wistfully. "At least then we'd serve good food there. I can't even cook as well as Aphrodite, and her food didn't win any awards."

He chopped the ends off a couple of green onions. "Well, I'm glad you inherited. I think you'll do wonderfully. And speaking of inheriting, I wish we had those other papers, the ones Aphrodite dropped in the cafe. I bet we'd find some interesting stuff in them."

"You know, I can't figure out what happened," I said twisting a corkscrew into a bottle of Chateau Ste. Michelle, 1991. "They seemed to have disappeared between the trailer and the cafe on Halloween night. I assume that if someone had found them, they would have called by now."

"Which means," Neil said, pouring oil into a wok, then expertly peeling and smashing a clove of garlic under the cleaver and scraping it into the pan, "that someone took them. And do you know whom I suspect?"

I knew who he suspected.

"You really think so?" I poured two glasses three-quarters full and handed him one.

The room filled with the wonderful aroma of sizzling garlic. The kitchen at the cafe had never smelled so good, even when Aphrodite was cooking.

"Don't you?" he asked, adding cubed chicken to the wok. "Maybe that explains why they're so reluctant to let us come over to the house." We'd also discussed the Luna/Hunt disinclination to invite us to tea. "Maybe they're hiding something."

"And maybe they're truly in mourning, and just want to be left alone with their memories."

Neil turned around and looked at me.

"Yeah, yeah, I know," I said, waving him off. "The flashlight pretty well proves that Brian had something to do with it. What I want to know is, how did it get from his hand to the parking lot by the van?"

"And, more importantly, *when* did it get there?" Neil dumped the carrots into the steaming wok.

"Well, he was in the bar with Rhonda when we got there. And she had it then," I said, squinting and remembering. "A little later I saw him talking on the phone . . ." My voice trailed off.

Neil turned around and looked at me, and we both said at the same time, "Just before Alanna started her striptease."

"Do you remember seeing Brian during the performance?" I asked Neil.

"Well, I wasn't exactly looking for him at the time," Neil said sheepishly.

"Or looking *at* him," I said, a vision of Alanna Undressed popping into my head. "Neither was anyone else in the bar. No one paid a bit of attention to anything *but* Alanna." More specifically, no one had looked at anything but Alanna's attention-grabbing chest.

"My, what a handy coincidence," Neil said.

"You know, he got a call at the cafe too," I said, remembering back to that first afternoon. "Rhonda intercepted it, and hung up on the person. Whoever it was asked for Mike Hunt, and she thought it was a prank call."

"Maybe you should have a talk with Rhonda in the morning," Neil said.

"I think I'll do that."

In the office, the fax machine beeped again.

"Incoming," I said, setting my wineglass down. "I'll get 'em."

The cover sheet announced the arrival of three pages from the *Rockville Reporter*. Waiting for the promised sheets, I peeked out the window again. Del stood on the trailer step with Ron Adler. She leaned over and gave him a kiss on the lips.

I sighed. It didn't take a psychic to predict more complications, more sadness, more trouble in the future.

A copy of a handwritten page rolled out of the machine. It read:

Mr. Pascoe,

I've searched the archives, and here are the earliest mentions I could find. I'll be looking forward to knowing what you make of all this.

All best,
A. L.

Another page rolled out of the fax machine and drifted to the floor.

I picked it up, and all thoughts of Stu, Del, and Ron, of Brian, and even of the wonderful supper Neil was cooking, went out of my head.

The sheet had a copy of an old newspaper article, dated in the late fifties. The headline read: NEW BUSINESS OPENS IN ROCKVILLE. The caption named the smiling trio in the photo as the owners of Ferguson Demolition.

In the picture, standing between a much younger (and far less bald) Alfred Ferguson, and a very youthful though still recognizable Norman Oberle, was a short, pretty, stocky woman with a riotous mass of what I knew was red hair.

I looked at the picture, inhaled sharply, and caught an unlikely odor in the room. I sniffed the air experimentally, and was absolutely certain that I smelled cigarette smoke.

27

....

Just the Fax

There is a notion that we in small towns know everything there is to know about one another. It's easy to
assume that there aren't any secrets when you can boast
a long acquaintance with your next-door neighbor's
grandparents, and can correctly rattle off their political
and religious philosophies while having a fair notion of
their bank balance. Very little gets by us. We pride ourselves on noticing when the bank teller has a new hairdo
and the mailman spends too much time inside one particular house and the bankrupt farmer is suddenly driving a new pickup.

After decades of minute mutual observation, we've
memorized the surface and allowed ourselves to forget
about the rest of the iceberg.

Last week, I would have sworn that I knew, and I
mean really knew, Aphrodite Ferguson. And though the
acquaintance was a good deal more superficial, I would
have sworn that I also knew Norman Oberle. And I
would have bet everything I owned that neither one had

any secrets that would blow our collective socks off.

It's a good thing I'm not a betting woman.

"Very interesting," Neil said with his mouth full. "They were all together way back when in Oklahoma. Let's see what else we have." He spread and arranged fax sheets along the counter, pausing only long enough to take another bite.

The old newspaper article announcing the formation of Ferguson Demolition wasn't very long or informative. It only reported that longtime Rockville resident Alfred Ferguson and his wife, Aphrodite, had formed a partnership with newcomer Norman Oberle. The trio, with the men doing the labor and Aphrodite serving as receptionist and bookkeeper, would, for a reasonable fee, tear buildings down (or blow them up).

I sat on a stool on the other side of the counter balancing a plate on my leg, looking over the pages. "But I would have sworn that Norman was a Delphi native."

Neil took another bite of stir-fry. "He is. He went to school with my parents. I've seen his picture in old yearbooks." Neil had been the late and only child of parents who had died in a car accident shortly after he'd hit it big in the lottery. "They were all around the same age. Gus and Norman were both World War II vets."

"I figured as much," I said, my own mouth full. Norman always wore his cap tilted jauntily to the side, a dead giveaway. "You suppose that's how they met?"

"Beats me," Neil said, in between bites. "I'm more curious about this demolition business of theirs."

"We already know that the partnership didn't last long," I said, reading the final fax sheet, a short newspaper article about the closing of Ferguson Demolition only a year after it had opened due to a poor business climate and the fact that one of the partners was moving. "And we know that both Aphrodite and Norman ended up in Delphi, so we know who moved. Or at least who didn't."

"It isn't the ending of the partnership that interests me. It's the day-to-day operation I want to know about."

"What do you mean?"

"Well, who did the tearing down, and who did the blowing up, for one thing."

"The article with the picture of young Brian said that he was learning everything there was to know about the demolition gig from his loving grandpa," I reminded Neil. "But I imagine that you can pick up most of the finer points just by working around the stuff."

"And there were probably quite a few 'munitions experts' floating around by the time the war was over," Neil said.

"We have to assume that they both knew what they were doing," I said, pouring the last of the wine into our glasses. "Which throws a whole new slant on the situation."

"Not really," Neil said. "Norman didn't go into the demolition business here. He's run that bread route here for as long as I can remember. And I certainly don't recall any suspicious explosions connected to him over the years."

"Or any explosions at all," I said, which jiggled a thought that wouldn't quite surface. "At least not until Saturday."

"So where do our esteemed Ms. Luna and son fit into this scenario? Did she give any indication that she knew Norman in a previous life? And did she pick up the tricks of the trade from dear old dad too?"

I thought back to the only times I'd seen Alanna and Norman together. He'd come back to the cafe with Aphrodite on Saturday and sat in the booth with Alanna and Brian while I scrambled to pick up legal papers off the floor behind the counter. I hadn't seen either one of them clearly before sneaking out the back door, though nothing in their voices had hinted at an earlier friendship.

Both Norman and Alanna had been at the school disco party in the gym, but Alanna had been and gone before Norman appeared. And I don't think Norman saw anyone or anything while the van burned.

"Young Cheryl probably wasn't even ten when they went into business together," I said. "So she might not have remembered Norman anyway. I'd be just as curious to know when the romantic relationship between Norman and Aphrodite began.''

Neil carried our plates to the sink and rinsed them off. ''Well, there's one way to find out.'' He sat the telephone in front of me.

''You're kidding,'' I said. ''You want me to call Norman and ask him about this stuff?''

''Well, you'll have to be subtle,'' he said, smiling, ''but it can be done. And it sure beats sitting here and speculating. There's got to be some sort of executor-type question you can ask him that will lead to the subject at hand.''

I scratched my head, concentrating, and finally came up with an idea. A lame idea, but at least it was a start. Neil slid the phone book over and I looked up Norman's number and dialed.

It rang three times before he answered.

''Hi, Norman? This is Tory Bauer. I'm sorry to bother you, but I wanted to ask you something.''

''Okay,'' he said, slowly.

''I'm here at Neil Pascoe's and we're going over the music selections for the memorial service tomorrow, and wondered if you knew what Aphrodite's favorite hymn was so we could sing it.''

''Well, she didn't go for church music much,'' Norman said. ''I don't think that there was any hymn that you could say that she liked particularly. She liked lots of different kinds of music though. Listened to it all the time.''

That was a surprise to me. I don't remember hearing Aphrodite express any sort of musical preference except for turning the radio off completely.

''What were some of her favorites?'' I asked.

''Well,'' Norman said, drawing out the syllable, obviously thinking. ''She seemed to like that Morrison fella.''

I searched my mind for any Big Band Morrisons and came up blank.

''You know,'' Norman went on, ''that rock and roll fella.''

"Jim Morrison?" I asked dubiously. I could not for the life of me picture Aphrodite as an aficionado of the Doors.

"No it wasn't Jim. Lemmee think a second." Norman paused. "Van, that was it. Van Morrison."

"Aphrodite was a fan of *Van* Morrison?" I asked incredulously.

Neil, who was washing dishes at the sink as he listened in, turned around with a raised eyebrow and a smile.

"That's the fella who sang that 'Moondance' song, isn't it?"

"Yep, that's Van Morrison all right. Okay," I said, shaking my head, wondering what Aphrodite's collective mourners would think if we played "Crazy Love" tomorrow morning. "Did she have any other favorites?"

I was expecting something a little more mainstream, like Percy Faith or Perry Como. Or Glen Miller.

"Well, now, I didn't know that much about her musical tastes," Norman said.

This was my opening. "Oh. Neil and I just thought that since you knew Aphrodite from back in Oklahoma when she was still with her husband, that you'd have known her well enough to help us tailor the music to what she would have liked."

It was awkward, and not too subtle, but it did the trick. Norman was silent for a long moment.

"How did you know about that?" he asked quietly.

"Um, ah, well," I thought furiously. I didn't want to let on that we'd been deliberately searching out information. "There were some references to your business partnership in with the legal papers that Darla Hoffart and I went over."

"Oh," Norman said.

Neil had finished doing dishes and was now going through the rest of the fax sheets, reading and arranging them in chronological order along the counter. He gave me a thumbs-up sign.

I plowed ahead. "We were pretty amazed to find that you all knew each other even before Aphrodite moved to Delphi."

"I didn't know her real well back then. She was awful busy with the new marriage and with Gus's daughter. We were partners, but not really friends."

"So how did you meet anyway?"

"Gus and I were overseas together, and he had this idea to start up a business after the war. He asked me to invest a little, and promised we'd make lots of money." Norman snorted. "Some big business. We both lost nearly everything. I think Gus met Aphrodite at a USO or something back East. They hadn't been married very long when we all got together."

"I know this is personal, but can you tell me what happened with Aphrodite and Gus? I mean, why she left him. You're probably the only person in Delphi that even knew that she was still married. And you're certainly the only one who knew her husband."

The phone was silent for a long time. I was just about to ask if he was still there when he finally answered.

"She really loved him. Gus, I mean. And she tried to make it work, but she just couldn't compete."

"With the first wife?" I asked. There didn't seem to be much info on Alanna's real mother.

"No, not with her. She was long gone by the time Gus married again. No, I mean with Cheryl herself. Gus thought the sun about rose and set on that kid's head. Nothing was too good for her, and she got every damn thing she ever wanted. Aphrodite tried to be a mother to her, to raise her up right and make her behave, but Gus got in the way all the time."

"There was some conflict, huh?"

"Conflict?" Norman chuckled. "There was outright war. Nothing she ever did was good enough for that kid. And Cheryl hated her. I mean *really* hated Aphrodite. She'd tell tales and Gus would believe every one of them. Finally Aphrodite just gave up."

"That was after the partnership broke up?"

"Not really. That was why the partnership broke up. Aphrodite was going to leave Gus and I couldn't watch him spoil that kid anymore. We just sorta dissolved everything."

"So you came back to Delphi, and Aphrodite followed you?"

"Not quite like that. I came back and married my Claire. I think Aphrodite stuck it out a little longer with Gus just for the kid's sake, and then she knocked around for a year or so trying to find work. Finally she called me and asked if I knew of any business for sale. It happened that the cafe here in town was up for grabs."

"So you helped Aphrodite move here?" I asked, surprised.

"Well I told her about it. But she came on her own. I didn't bring her here," Norman said quickly.

Almost too quickly. I wondered if "his" Claire had asked the same question before she died, about five years ago.

I glanced over at Neil to see what he thought of the conversation, but he was engrossed in one of the articles.

"Well, that's about all . . ." I said, but Norman interrupted me.

"And I'll tell you something else," he said. "I don't know why *she's* here, but she's up to no good."

"She who?" I knew who he meant, but I wanted him to tell me why.

"Cheryl, or Alanna or whatever she calls herself these days. And her good-for-nothing kid."

"I don't know why they came here either, Norman," I said tiredly. "But they're here now, and I guess we'll have to learn how to live with that."

"Yeah, well, maybe it won't last as long as we all think," Norman said.

"What do you mean?"

"Well, without Daddy to pave the way for her, I doubt that little Cheryl will be able to make it on her own. She never did before, and she's a bit old to start learning now."

There wasn't much I could say to that. Alanna had been a spoiled daddy's girl. Now she was half-owner of a cafe. Life takes strange turns for everyone.

Neil was still engrossed in a fax, and I was floundering, trying to finish the conversation gracefully.

"Well, I know you're tired," I said awkwardly, "so I'll let you go for now. Thanks for your help. With the music I mean. I imagine I'll see you tomorrow at the church."

"She was a wonderful woman," Norman said, voice breaking. "The town is never going to be the same."

"I know," I said quietly, and hung up.

To Neil I said, "Well, we learned a couple of things about Aphrodite and Gus, but nothing earth-shaking."

"All that is pretty well moot now," Neil said, handing me the page he'd been reading. "What do you think of this?"

It was another fax, of course. Of another newspaper article. This one had no pictures, but it detailed a series of mysterious explosions that had occurred over a period of several months in Rockville. Though causing mostly minor damage, the explosions had got more and more malicious in nature. Certain businesses, as well as certain individuals, had been targeted in what, at first, had seemed to be random vandalism.

Eventually the explosions had been irrefutably linked to an unnamed juvenile male who had been recently expelled from high school. Though the newspaper was forbidden to name the juvenile, in the tradition of small-town newspapers everywhere, the reporter managed to mention that the unnamed juvenile was the grandson of a longtime Rockville resident who owned a small explosives supply company.

The final explosion in the spree, the one that finally provided enough evidence to link to the others, was the complete and utter destruction of a brand-new Cadillac DeVille owned by the very married high school principal, who had been rumored to have been dating the young man's mother.

"He hurt my mom," the unnamed, and unrepentant juvenile was quoted as saying. "I'm just sorry he wasn't in the car when it blew up."

28

....

Making Scents

Not since the heyday of the Vietnam War has Delphi had a memorial service rather than a full-blown funeral. We lost relatively few of our own boys to the mess in Southeast Asia, and most of those deaths were straightforward in the sense that the bodies were found, identified, shipped home, and properly buried according to our tradition.

The MIA and presumed dead were few and far between, and most of those grieving families preferred to wait until they had concrete evidence before conducting services.

It throws us off-balance to be holding abbreviated ceremonies with less than the full complement of rituals. Without a body, there can be no viewing, no vigil, no trek to the cemetery, and no burial. And without those concrete reminders of death, it's easy to make believe that the dear departed hasn't quite gone yet.

"You know, it's weird, but it doesn't feel like she's really gone," Rhonda said.

We were standing in the vestibule of St. John's about a half-hour before Aphrodite's memorial service was scheduled to begin. People were arriving and milling about, unsure of the proper protocol since there was no coffin to pay respects to and no next of kin to console. Instead they made small talk with one another, waiting for the unspoken signal to go inside and sit.

"I know what you mean," I said quietly. I suddenly had the feeling that Aphrodite was there, in person, standing behind me. I looked over my shoulder, mostly to dispel the notion, and saw only Del and Presley coming up the stairs together, behind a man delivering yet more flowers.

"All the flowers are so beautiful," Rhonda said, voice wavering. "And they smell so good. Aphrodite should be here, she'd have been so pleased." Her blue eyes filled with tears. She sniffed and dug in the pocket of her good coat for a hankie.

"Oh hon," I said, patting Rhonda on the shoulder. "Shhh, it'll be all right. I'm sure she is here. And besides, you know how much Aphrodite hated funerals."

"Yeah," Del said sourly, "it made her crabby when people filled up on free bad food, rather than paying for it at the cafe."

That got a weak chuckle out of Rhonda, who sniffed again, squared her shoulders, and pretended to be in control. "How you doing, kiddo?" she asked Presley.

Pale and drawn, Pres shrugged without answering or smiling. Though I didn't doubt that he would miss Aphrodite in his own way, I thought that her sudden death might have triggered a realization that the mortality rate on this planet is 100 percent, a large concept to process even when you're not thirteen years old.

"Well you're lookin' good anyway," Rhonda said, joshing him.

We all looked good. Pres was wearing a button-down long-sleeved white shirt with a Jerry Garcia tie. Though he was still very much a boy, hints and traces of the

handsome man he will someday become were starting
to peek through.

His mother was dressed demurely in a long flowered
skirt and sweater that was only just a little too tight.
Rhonda wore her college uniform of a shirt and denim
jumper. I wore my only dress, and my only pair of
pantyhose, and, unfortunately, my only pair of good
shoes, which pinched my toes terribly and always left
blisters on my heels.

Pres smiled weakly at Rhonda, and then spotted something over her shoulder. His smile wilted.

Alanna and Brian walked through the door, deep in
conversation. Brian had on pretty much what he'd worn
when he and his mother had arrived in Delphi, including
the scowl. Del's lips tightened in a bloodless line when
she realized that Alanna had dressed in a long floral skirt
and a tight sweater.

"If she starts taking her clothes off, I'll shoot her, I
swear," Del whispered furiously, grabbing a couple of
memorial flyers that had been stacked by the guest book.
"Come on," she said loudly to Pres, who followed her
into the church with a worried glance behind him.

Brian's scowl transformed into a smile when he spotted Rhonda, who beamed in return. He nodded pleasantly at me though I could just barely make myself
return the courtesy.

After examining the damning newspaper articles, Neil
and I had come to the conclusion that Brian had had the
knowledge, and perhaps access to the materials necessary, to prepare and execute an explosion big enough to
destroy a vehicle. We, of course, didn't know if he'd
been plying that particular trade in Delphi, but it seemed
at least possible, and therefore wise to be wary in his
company. And to be careful when starting any cars.

On the other hand, we'd also decided that broadcast-
ing our conclusions could be equally unwise. From
something that the police had said at the trailer the other
night, I was certain that they were investigating the pasts
of all the individuals involved (which, I suppose, also
meant me). It also meant that they were probably fa-

miliar with the newspaper articles, which let us off the hook as informants.

I've come to stupid, and erroneous, conclusions before, and I had no guarantee that it wouldn't happen again. Keeping quiet and being observant seemed to be the best course of action.

And since I'd observed Stu and Renee McKee walking silently up the sidewalk, I deduced that my best course of action would be to get out of the vestibule immediately.

"I'd better go in and see if Neil needs my help," I said to Rhonda, giving her a swift hug. "You hang in there, okay?"

"All right," she said, sniffing again. "I'm going to sit with Brian and his mom if that's all right with you."

"That's fine," I said hurriedly, since Stu was rapidly approaching the door.

Ducking into the crowd, I walked swiftly down the aisle toward the altar, cursing my tight shoes with every step. The pews were filling rapidly. Nearly all of Delphi had turned out to say good-bye to Aphrodite Ferguson.

Willard Hausvik was openly wiping his red eyes. In the middle of the row, next to him, was his wife, Iva, who sat ramrod-stiff, face frozen. A couple of rows in front of them, not very far from Del and Presley, were Ron Adler and his wife. Ron fidgeted and blinked and fussed. Gina sat glassy-eyed in obvious mourning, though whether she mourned her husband's inability to stay away from Del or Aphrodite's death was probably a toss-up.

On the other side of the aisle, Alanna, Brian, and Rhonda carefully worked their way into the middle of a row and sat down next to a rather surprised, and not very pleased, Norman Oberle. Del, who was observing them closely, shot a murderous glance in their direction, which Alanna ignored. Gina Adler shot a murderous glance at Del, which she ignored.

The man delivering the flowers had brought in another armload of baskets and vases and potted plants to arrange around the podium. The intoxicating smell of roses and mums and carnations, and exotic flowers I couldn't identify, filled the air.

Neil, who was setting up his stereo system nearby, and who had seen me watching the guy, flashed a small "go ahead" signal. We'd already discussed quizzing the delivery man if we got the chance.

I took a deep breath. "Excuse me," I said softly, tapping him on the shoulder. "But did you deliver a bouquet to the cafe across the street yesterday?"

"Huh?" he said, straightening the foil that wrapped a yellow potted mum. He stood up, wiped his hands on his blue pants, and peered at me suspiciously. His blue-and-white-striped shirt had "Steve" embroidered over one pocket. "Uh, yeah," he said, squinting in the effort to remember. "I think I did. Roses, right? Something wrong with them?"

"No, no," I said quickly. "They were lovely. I was just wondering if you knew who sent them." I peeked quickly to see if anyone was watching my conversation with Steve, anyone who could read lips. But no one paid the slightest attention to us except for Norman Oberle, who nodded weakly before turning away from Alanna and attending to the pamphlet that had been handed to everyone at the door.

"Wasn't there a card with the flowers?" Steve asked shortly.

"Well, yeah, but it wasn't signed," I said. "And I was just wondering if you might know who sent it."

Steve smiled. "I gotcha now. You got a secret admirer and you want to know who he is." He bent down to pinch off a gladiolus bud that had been crushed. "Sorry, I got too many deliveries to make on Mondays to worry about who is sending what to who. I don't fix 'em up or write the cards, I just deliver 'em."

"Mondays are tough, huh?"

"Every day is tough, but Mondays especially because we don't do out-of-town deliveries on weekends, so there's always a backlog. I'm doing good just delivering the stuff, without worrying about anything else. If you want to call the office, maybe they can help you." He dug a card out of his pocket and handed it to me. It had the name and phone number of an Aberdeen florist. "But if I can give you some advice, honey, just let it go. Someone likes you enough to send anonymous roses, you should sit back and enjoy the mystery and smell the flowers." He looked at his watch and then at the door. "I got a few more to bring in, and it's almost time to start here, so if you don't mind . . ." His voice trailed off.

There was no point in disabusing him of the notion that I had a secret admirer. "Of course, I'm sorry for holding you up," I said. "Thanks for your help."

I put the card in my pocket and turned to see what Neil had thought of the conversation, but he was busy going through his backpack with a frown.

"What's up?" I asked him quietly.

"I can't find the Van Morrison CD," he said, still rooting around. "I thought for sure I put it in with the rest."

We'd chosen mostly conventional selections from Neil's vast CD collection rather than using a local soloist for the memorial. And thanks to Norman's lead, we'd also decided to honor Aphrodite with one of her favorite musicians. Personally, I was looking forward to the minor congregational confusion when he played "Brown-Eyed Girl" to people who were expecting "The Lord's Prayer."

"Damn," he said under his breath, annoyed enough to swear in church. "I really wanted to do this for her, and I'm not done setting up here yet. There isn't time for me to go back home and get the CD."

"I can get it for you, if you like," I said. "I'm done with everything I have to do, and I can be back with it before the service starts."

"Would you?" Neil asked, relieved. "That'd be great. It's gotta be on the desk in the library."

"No problem. I'll be right back," I said, hurrying down the aisle, carefully avoiding the glances of both Stu McKee *and* his wife, again cursing my tight shoes. I also avoided the glances of those who had taken in the fact that Stu McKee was sitting with his wife. And those who noticed that I wasn't. Tight shoes or not, I sped up even more.

Once safely in the vestibule, out of everyone's sight, I stopped for a moment to rub my sore, red, and raw heel, disgusted to note that someone had recently been smoking inside the church. Either that or someone had been right outside the door and the smell had floated in each time the door opened.

I pushed through the door, and sure enough a cigarette with red lipstick on the end lay still burning on the step. I stepped on it, twisting my shoe furiously even though that made my foot hurt even more, and then headed down the stairs and toward Neil's house, which was three blocks away.

A devious thought crossed my mind before I'd limped even a block, cursing not only the shoes but my impulsive offer to go and fetch the CD for Neil on foot. I was more than pleased to honor whatever was left of Aphrodite's spirit with her favorite music, but less than willing to do real damage to my Achilles tendon to accomplish that mission.

Especially when Aphrodite's house was much closer than Neil's.

If Van Morrison was one of her favorite musicians, then surely she'd owned a tape or CD of the music herself. And since Alanna probably hadn't had time to box up or give away any of Aphrodite's surplus possessions, it seemed safe to assume that her personal Van Morrison collection must still be in the house.

I paused in the street, thinking through this new plan of action.

A few stragglers were still going into the church, but no one was coming out. The high windows that faced this direction were of stained glass, which did not give a clear view of Aphrodite's house. Alanna and Brian were safely seated inside, in the middle of a row.

Popping into a friend's house unannounced on an emergency errand, even when the owners were not in residence, was a perfectly legitimate Midwest tradition.

If Alanna and Brian were going to become honest-to-God Midwesterners, then it was time they got used to the local eccentricities.

Besides, I was in a hurry. And it was cold and gray and the clouds threatened snow, and I'd forgotten to put on a coat.

But more than anything else, my feet hurt.

29

....

Free Spirit

I suppose it's like being a little pregnant. Or being a little indicted by a federal grand jury. Or being only mostly dead.

I guess there's no such thing as a little breaking and entering, though I honestly didn't define going into the late Aphrodite Ferguson's house in those terms. I was merely doing my live friend Neil, and my dead friend Aphrodite, a favor in the quickest and least painful manner.

That it would also get me into a house that had been, at least lately, vehemently off-limits, didn't even occur to me until I was standing on her dilapidated back porch.

I'd been in Aphrodite's little house before, though not often, and I knew that the back door would either be unlocked or the key would be under the mat. I'd taken the precaution of knocking, and then rattling the knob. Just to make sure, I'd hollered before going inside even though I knew full well that the occupants were up the street at the church.

Determined not to dawdle, or to snoop overtly, or to wonder why most of the books were stacked haphazardly on the floor, or the drawers and cupboards were askew, their contents strewn on the countertops, I strode purposefully and painfully, directly to Aphrodite's old stereo system, or at least to the place where Aphrodite's old stereo system used to be. In its place was a shining new state-of-the-art system, with row upon row of new jewel-case compact discs shelved more or less neatly behind it.

I stood admiring the setup for a moment, almost hearing Aphrodite's chuckle at my surprise. Stepping around the stereo, I scanned the shelves for Van Morrison, amazed at the scope and breadth of her alphabetized music collection. Though I didn't see any James Taylor, I grinned spotting Fats Waller and Pete Seeger and Leon Redbone neatly shelved.

I briefly considered suggesting to Neil that we play "I Want to Be Seduced" instead of Van Morrison during the service, but decided that sticking to the original program would be wiser. And faster. I needed to hurry.

I found "Moondance" with the M's (after first mistakenly checking the V's, Van Cliburn and Van Halen) and pulled it out, marveling at the new, and heretofore unsuspected, musical bent in my boss.

I could almost hear her say "Thought you knew all about the old gal, huh?"

"I apologize, Aphrodite," I said out loud in the empty house. "You were always one step ahead of me."

"Damn right," she said.

The CD flew from my hand and landed near the bedroom door as I twirled around, heart pounding, eyes wide, panting and listening like I've never listened before, doing everything in my power to convince myself that I had not just heard Aphrodite's voice. Not a flashback, not a hallucination, but her actual voice, as though she had been there and alive and standing in the same room.

The house was silent and empty except for the haze of cigarette smoke that wisped and curled in front of me.

Or maybe it was just dust swirling in a sunbeam.

I sniffed experimentally, telling myself that a permanent aura of smoke was not unexpected in a house where
both the former and present occupants indulged in a taste
for cheap cigarettes.

I stood perfectly still, looking as far around me as I
could without moving my head. Slowly I turned around,
breathing raggedly, listening, waiting for something to
happen.

Nothing did. At least nothing on the outside. Inside I
was in turmoil, too old to be saddled with a sudden case
of the heebie-jeebies. I have never been afraid of the
dark. I've never believed in horoscopes. Or spirit guides.
Or channeling.

But, my brain reminded me, *you saw her. You actually
saw Aphrodite and Nick right after the explosion.*

That was nothing but a hallucination induced by a
near concussion, I answered myself.

My brain continued, *Ah but what about the laugh you
heard in the cafe when you were cooking yesterday
morning? And the smoke you smelled in the library. And
the smoke in the vestibule.*

*And the still-burning cigarette on the church steps.
The one smeared with the red lipstick just like all of
Aphrodite's were.*

"Nonsense," I said out loud, waiting for a response,
breathing almost normally again. "I refuse to be haunted
by a lipstick-wearing, cigarette-smoking ghost."

There was no reply. No laughter, no rebuttal, no mysteriously lit cigarettes burning in ashtrays nearby.

Still, Aphrodite's spirit filled the house and it filled
me. She wasn't there, and yet I knew without a doubt
that she was.

"I'm just going to pick up the CD and take it back
to Neil," I said aloud, purely as a precautionary measure.

I walked stiffly over to the bedroom doorway and bent
down to pick up the compact disc and then nearly
dropped it again because I heard sounds coming from
the kitchen.

"Now this is ridiculous . . ." I started to say.

"Hide!" the voice interrupted suddenly.

Whether the voice actually came from somewhere else, or from inside my own addled head, was beside the point since an actual living, breathing, whistling human had just entered the kitchen. And judging by the heavy footsteps, he was a male. And he was heading for the living room.

I scrambled around the doorway. With no time to choose a better hiding place, I scrunched back as far as I could between the bed and the dresser.

Deciding that I'd much rather deal with ghostly apparitions than live intruders, I huddled on the hard and cold bedroom floor, clutching Van Morrison to my chest with my eyes tightly closed, terrified that I'd be accidentally discovered.

An infinitely more horrible thought surfaced. Perhaps he'd seen me leave the church and followed, knowing that I was in the house without permission, and was just toying with me for his own amusement.

But the steps and the whistling stopped near the stereo. I heard him pick up the phone and punch in a series of numbers.

"Yeah," Brian Hunt said into the phone, "gimme extension number two-thirty-one."

He was silent while the call was being transferred and then he spoke again. "Yeah, hi. It's me." There was a pause while he evidently listened to the person on the other end. "Well, what do you expect? I've tried calling several times but you're always out of the office, or she's always here. This is the first time I've been able to get through to you, and I had to sneak out of the fucking funeral to do it."

He listened again for a moment and then continued. "I think we have it tied up pretty well here. And no one's made the connection. As far as I can tell, they don't know a thing."

He listened some more. "Well, I'll keep an eye out, and let you know any developments. No, I'd rather not go that far unless we really have to. Yes," he said, exasperated, "I know where our priorities lie. And I know what I have to do if it comes down to it."

There was a short silence again before Brian continued. "Okay. You keep track of your end. I'll be in touch as soon as I know something. I better get back before anyone misses me."

He hung up and made a detour to the bathroom. I heard the back door close.

I sat another five minutes, unable to move, afraid that Brian had only pretended to leave, that he was still standing in the living room, waiting for me to poke my head around the doorway.

"Where are you when I need you?" I silently asked Aphrodite's ghost. "At least you could let me know when the coast is clear."

There was no answer.

Very carefully, and as quietly as I could, I stood up, leaning on the dresser for support.

Unfortunately, the dresser was on wheels, and it was sitting on bare wood. As I leaned, it rolled a few inches, squeaking alarmingly.

I froze for a long minute, but the house remained silent.

Silent except for a small rustle of paper behind the dresser when I tried to push it back into position. Oh so carefully, I pulled the dresser out again, and saw an envelope that either had accidentally fallen behind and gotten caught in the slats, or had been deliberately pushed into a crack to keep it hidden.

I didn't wait for any disembodied voices to tell me to grab the envelope and get the hell out of there.

I had already been gone more than fifteen minutes. Neil was probably worried. Soon others would notice my absence.

With the envelope stuffed into a dress pocket and the "Moondance" CD in hand, I carefully picked my way back through the living room, intending to run back to the church just as fast as my aching feet would carry me.

Instead I stopped and stared at the phone. With my free hand covered by the skirt of my dress I picked up the receiver and punched the redial button.

I listened to the series of beeps, heart pounding. A Southern female answered. "Consolidated Florists of Tulsa," she said in a singsong voice. "To whom may I direct your call?"

I swallowed and then said, "Extension number two-thirty-one, please."

"Sure thing, sweetie," she said, and then punched a couple of numbers.

The phone on the other end rang three times and was finally picked up by an answering machine. A deep male recorded voice answered, "You have reached the office of Robert Hunt. I'm not in at the moment, but you can leave a message after the tone."

30

....

The Woo-Woo Factor

As a kid, I delighted in letting hokey movies scare the bejabbers out of me. I'd scrunch down in a shabby front-row theater seat, happily munching popcorn and Junior Mints, spooked to the gills by *13 Ghosts* and *The House on Haunted Hill*. On TV, *The Twilight Zone* and *One Step Beyond* kept me awake all night in the delicious fear of nightmares.

My all-time favorite *Dick Van Dyke* episode featured Buddy, Mel, and Laura being replaced by walnut-eating space aliens with twenty-twenty-twenty-twenty vision. And I loved the time that Barney Miller and the boys from the Twelfth Precinct may or may not have arrested an actual werewolf.

The Woo-Woo Factor, as mystery buffs call the inclusion of supernatural elements into an otherwise mainstream story, can be a most entertaining fictional ploy. A mental diversion. An escape from the mundane.

But however intriguing the notion is on screen or paper, I had no desire to encounter any woo-woo stuff in real life.

And the further I got from Aphrodite's house, the less certain I was that I had just survived my own close encounter of the weird kind.

I mean, what had actually happened anyway? I thought I heard a familiar voice, and I smelled cigarette smoke in a place where not smelling stale smoke would have been a whole lot more unusual.

My Interior Believer, the part of me that had looked askance at walnuts for a good long time, and still sometimes thought there were monsters under the bed, tried to remind me that no one was ever allowed to smoke in Neil's house or in the vestibule of the Lutheran church, but I unceremoniously shut her up.

Purposely ignoring both the blisters on my feet and the remains of a recently crushed cigarette butt on the church stairs, I hurried inside as quickly and quietly as I could.

Neil, who had been anxiously watching for my return, shot me a relieved glance from the front of the church, where he sat on the carpeted steps by the stereo system, which was at the moment playing a lovely guitar version of "Ave Maria." We would have chosen "Amazing Grace," but after Saturday night, it just didn't seem proper.

Tiptoeing through the standing-room-only crowd at the back of the church, I was only mildly surprised at the number of unfamiliar faces gathered to send Aphrodite into the Great Beyond.

I wondered what most of them would think if I announced that Aphrodite might be just a bit closer than they realized.

Shaking off that notion, I walked up the side aisle and held out Aphrodite's Van Morrison CD to Neil, which he took with a puzzled expression. Since he carefully cataloged and labeled all his music, he'd known immediately that this particular album hadn't come from his collection.

I'll tell you later, I mouthed at him, as the last notes of "Ave Maria" faded, wondering exactly how much I would tell him about my experience at Aphrodite's house.

Just the facts, I decided, nothing even bordering on woo-woo.

Neil nodded, wrinkling his glasses up on his nose. He raised an eyebrow and tilted his head toward the mourners. As surreptitiously as I could, I scanned the crowd, noting a weeping Rhonda next to Brian and his mother, who were in turn sitting next to a stone-faced Norman Oberle. On the other side of the aisle were Del and Presley, and not far away sat a pair of very unhappy Adlers. Behind them was red-eyed Darla Hoffart.

Across the aisle again were the McKees. Renee was solemnly listening to Clay, who had returned to the podium and begun to speak. Stu's unreadable eyes caught mine in a gaze that lasted an eternity.

I swallowed, and looked away to find Junior watching me with an expression that was no more readable than Stu's. I would have expected to see contempt written large on her face, for surely she'd realized who I'd been looking at. But her look was almost kind.

With the exception of Junior's uncharacteristic neutrality, there were no surprises in the crowd. I looked back at Neil in confusion.

He tilted his head a little more and signaled again. I searched further back in the crowd, and finally saw what had caught his eye.

Standing near the big double doorway was Agent John Ingstad, the local Department of Criminal Investigations officer. Our own personal G-man.

I looked back at Neil, raising a weary eyebrow. Though a veteran of hundreds of hours of mystery television, not to mention thousands of novels, and, unfortunately, a couple of nonfictional dead bodies, I'd forgotten that investigators often attended the funerals of murder victims. And it had certainly slipped my mind that they might keep a watchful eye on the attendees for any suspicious activities.

Like, for instance, sneaking out of a funeral to enter the home of the deceased.

There was no point in lamenting what could not be changed. I carefully picked my way up the stairs to sit on the step below Neil's, extremely glad to be off my feet. I tried to attend to what Clay was saying, feeling guilty that I'd missed most of the service.

The Interior Believer supplied an immediate rejoinder that Aphrodite probably wouldn't care since she'd spent most of the service following me around anyway.

I squashed that thought firmly, lifted my chin, and pasted an expression of rapt attention on my face as Clay said, "In a last loving tribute to our friend Aphrodite, knowing that as long as she is in our hearts, she will never truly be gone, we'll play one more of her favorite musical selections."

Clay smiled at Neil, who smiled at me, and then punched the play button.

I sat back, prepared for the soft jazz intro to "Moondance," and ready to enjoy the confusion on the faces of those who were expecting another hymn, or at least something more suited to the Lawrence Welk oeuvre. Surprised to hear the gentle strumming of a guitar, I listened to a few bars before I realized that Neil had, at the last moment, chosen to play "Into the Mystic," a selection far more appropriate than he'd ever dreamed.

I flashed a quick nod of appreciation at Neil. The consternation in the audience was nearly universal, they fidgeted uncomfortably, disconcerted by the odd and unexpected music in an already unusual service. Here and there, though, faces registered both recognition and enjoyment.

Norman's face relaxed just a bit as he closed his eyes and swayed a little with the music. Stu's gaze softened.

At the podium, a small smile twitched at the corners of Clay's mouth. He caught my eye and glanced upward and all around. He'd already told me that he thought that Aphrodite's spirit was still in residence, so I knew he was saying that "the mystic" is everywhere, even in staid and respectable St. John's Lutheran Church.

That Clay Deibert himself was a slightly nonmainstream reverend for a thoroughly mainstream South Da-

kota town was evidently going to remain our secret. He
ended the service with a traditional prayer and an announcement that the church ladies had prepared a lunch,
and that all attendees were invited to partake in the dining room located in the church annex.

Making his way over to the stairs as people began to
shuffle out, Clay shook Neil's hand. "Good choice," he
said. "I love Van Morrison."

"It wouldn't have occurred to me on my own. You'll
have to thank Aphrodite," Neil said with a small grin.

Clay turned to me and said, "I might just do that.
What do you think?"

"I think you've lost your mind," I said, lying.

"No you don't," said Clay, who, regardless of his
vocation, was just a woo-woo kind of guy.

Involuntarily, I sniffed the air and smelled nothing but
Neil's wonderful after-shave.

"She's here, can't you feel it?" Clay asked before
turning away. People were beginning to gather around,
wanting to congratulate him for the lovely service.

"What was that all about?" Neil asked as Clay
walked down the stairs toward the door that led from
the church to the annex, accepting thanks and consoling
several of the weeping congregants on the way. He
paused to shake Norman's hand and to give a swift hug
to Darla. Before I could answer Neil, or even decide how
to answer him, Clay turned once again toward me.

"I forgot," he said, "Junior told me to be sure to tell
you to stop by the dining room. She has some papers
that you might need. A big envelope of legal stuff that
used to be Aphrodite's, I think."

"What?" I called after him, but by then he was
through the door, followed immediately by those who
have been programmed by long years of tradition to
crave large servings of free food immediately after funerals.

"What did he just say?" I repeated to Neil, who
looked as confused as I felt.

My mind raced. *Junior* had the papers? Aphrodite's
papers? The ones I had accidentally carried out of the

cafe with me on the day she was killed? The ones we had been certain were stolen? By Alanna and Brian, no less?

And if so, how the hell did she get them?

"What papers?" Del, who'd materialized at my side, asked. "Nice music," she said sarcastically to Neil.

"Dorky music, you mean," Presley corrected. "Too bad Aphrodite didn't like someone good. Smashing Pumpkins or Nine Inch Nails would have kicked."

"How would *she* have got the papers?" I asked Neil, ignoring both Del and Presley, who continued to argue mildly about what exactly did, and did not, constitute good music. I also ignored the faint whiff of cigarette smoke wafting on the air.

"And when? And another thing," Neil continued, "*where* did you get that CD?"

Before I could answer him, we were interrupted.

"Excuse me, Ms. Bauer. I'd like to extend my sympathy for your loss," said Agent Ingstad, DCI. "I know this is a hard time for you, but if it wouldn't be too much trouble, could you come with me? I'd like to talk to you privately."

"Ah, uh," I said, thinking furiously but making no sense, even to myself. "Now?"

"Yes," Agent Ingstad said softly. "If you can get away."

Though he had phrased it as a request, there was no doubt that it was an order.

"Um, well," I said, sending a desperate glance at Neil, who, not having been informed of my recent history of breaking and entering, was completely mystified. "Okay."

To the others, who stood openmouthed, except for Presley, who was now tight-lipped and ghostly pale, I said, "Go on ahead. I'll be along in a few minutes."

I hoped I was right.

31

....

G-Whiz

Show me the most anal-retentive, law-abiding, buckle-your-seatbelt, never-exceed-the-speed-limit, may-lightning-strike-if-I'm-lying American citizens, and I'll show you people who still quake in their boots at a summons from a federal law enforcement official.

I don't care if you haven't taken so much as a paper clip from the office at work, you're still going to feel guilty when the long finger of the law beckons. The hypnotic stare of the inquisitor brings out the urge to babble, and worse yet, confess, in even the most innocent of bystanders.

When you're not all that innocent, the primal need to unburden yourself to authority is damn near irresistible.

That Agent Ingstad knew that I'd been inside Aphrodite's house was a given. That he wanted to know what I had been doing there was obvious. That I should at least try to tread carefully, and volunteer no more than absolutely necessary, went without saying.

I followed him out of the church and down the stairs. I grabbed my coat and slipped it on, ignoring the curious stares of the few stragglers who had not yet made it into the annex. The temperature had dropped a couple degrees in the last hour, and the humidity had risen. It was damp and cold and windy.

Agent Ingstad tightened the belt of his standard-issue trenchcoat and peered suspiciously at the sky. "You think it's going to snow?" he asked.

He might have been a G-man, but he was also a South Dakotan, and a South Dakotan is always concerned about the weather.

"Probably," I said, practicing terseness. It doesn't come naturally to me.

I didn't have to practice being nervous.

Agent Ingstad nodded as we passed a young agent who had taken up position near the door to the church annex. We came to a stop beside another standard issue, the nondescript dark car identifiable only by its government license plates. He was parked in a diagonal spot in front of the post office, which was next door to the church. On the other side of the post office was McKee's Feed and Seed, and across the street was the Delphi Cafe.

We were in full view of the whole town, though most of the town was at that moment gorging on tater-tot casserole, marshmallow and green Jell-O, and salad, for which I was very grateful.

"Are you too cold to stand outside?" he asked me. "Should we sit in the car?"

"Nah," I said, looking up at him, watching the wind ruffle the fringe of dark brown hair that circled his bald head. "I have to go in pretty quick anyway. They're expecting me. This won't take long, will it?"

"That depends," he said, taking out a small notebook and flipping the pages. He leaned back against his car and waited for me to say something.

I tried to play his game and wait for him to break the silence. In the ensuing moments, Norman Oberle pushed through the annex door, and then held it open for the McKees. Norman said something to them, and then walked off. Stu and Renee stood several feet apart, speaking briefly before she walked away too.

Cutting across the brown grass with his head down, Stu was nearly to the sidewalk before he noticed us. Slightly startled, he nodded politely at the agent and then greeted me in a monotone. "Tory."

"Stu," I said back, equally monotonal. He turned down the sidewalk and went into the Feed and Seed with only a momentary, somber glance over his shoulder before disappearing inside.

I stared at that closed door for a long unguarded moment during which my firmly repressed loneliness rose to surface. And with that came an unsurprising longing for my old life, to have back what I had taken for granted.

I would have been more than happy to give back an inheritance I never wanted, for the privilege of turning back the clock a few days.

Agent Ingstad stood silently watching me.

Embarrassed, I ran my hand through my hair and tried to rearrange my face into something slightly less naked and yearning. "I know why you want to talk to me," I said, my voice a little shaky, forgetting that I wasn't going to volunteer information.

"Ah," he said noncommittally.

Oh well, I'd already started the conversation, I figured I might as well keep it going. It was going to come out anyway. "You want to know what I was doing inside Aphrodite Ferguson's house at the beginning of the memorial service." I tried a weak chuckle. "It's all perfectly understandable."

"You have a good explanation for why you left the funeral service of your good friend to meet Brian Michael Hunt in her house?" he asked evenly.

"What?" For a second I didn't think I'd heard him correctly.

I was prepared for the feds to think I'd broken and entered (though there had been no breaking involved). But I was flabbergasted to realize that he thought I'd set out to meet Brian deliberately.

"No, no, no, no." I shook my head with each word. "You don't understand. Meet Brian? *In* the house? *Dur-*

ing the funeral?'' My mouth opened and closed, but nothing came out except another round of ''no's.''

''Well, you were seen entering said dwelling at''— he flipped the pages of his notebook until he found the one he wanted—''at eleven A.M.'' He flipped to another page. ''Mr. Hunt entered the same house approximately four minutes later.'' He looked up from his notes. ''You were both inside the house for another, let's see''—he flipped the pages again—''six minutes, at which time Mr. Hunt exited the building. You left about five minutes after him, and then rejoined the memorial service.''

''I was in the house, yes,'' I said, realizing that the truth was going to sound much less believable than his interpretation of events. ''And Brian came in while I was there. But we didn't meet. We didn't even talk.''

''Did Mr. Hunt know you were going to be inside the house when he entered?''

''No.''

''I see.'' He wrote something down. ''And did Mr. Hunt express surprise upon finding you inside the house?''

I swallowed. Might as well get it over with. ''No.''

''And why not, Mrs. Bauer?'' Agent Ingstad tilted his head slightly, waiting for me to enlighten him.

I inhaled deeply, looking up and down the street, hoping, I guess, for some sort of diversion so I wouldn't have to tell the nice G-man what a doofus I am.

No such diversion appeared.

I plunged my cold hands deeply into my coat pockets and continued. ''He wasn't surprised to find me in the house because he didn't find me in the house.''

''Hmm.''

''I wasn't in there snooping or anything, but I needed to get a Van Morrison CD for Neil Pascoe to play at the service because he'd forgotten his at home. And I'm wearing these really tight shoes, see.'' I kicked one off in order to show him the incontrovertible evidence of my raw and blistered heel. ''And my feet hurt, and at the last second I decided not to walk all the way back to the library when I could just get the album from Aphrodite's collection. I was in a hurry.''

''And that's all you were doing inside the house?''

''Yes,'' I said, trying to keep my face neutral. Wild horses could not have dragged from me an admission that I might have heard and smelled Aphrodite Ferguson's ghost.

''Then can you explain why Mr. Hunt entered the house so soon after you did? And why he wasn't surprised to find you.''

I squinted into the wind, dreading having to say what I was plainly going to have to say. ''He wasn't surprised to see me because he didn't see me.''

''And why is that, Mrs. Bauer?''

''Because I was hiding.''

A pained look crossed the good agent's face, but he said nothing as I repeated what I'd overheard from Brian's telephone conversation. And what I'd discovered when I punched the redial button on the phone.

''Do you think there is some significance to the fact that Mr. Hunt's father works in the company of florists?'' Agent Ingstad asked, taking notes.

''Well of course,'' I said, exasperated. ''Since Alanna destroyed the bouquet and flushed the note that came with them. It's got to be significant.''

He looked up from the notebook. ''What bouquet?''

''Oh,'' I said.

I'd forgotten that we had not reported receiving the flowers. Or the note that came with them. Or their ultimate fate.

I reluctantly remedied that situation.

''Mrs. Bauer,'' he said wearily, ''in the past we have harbored differing opinions as to the nature of some of the deaths that have occurred in Delphi. But I think we're in agreement this time—Mrs. Aphrodite Ferguson died as a result of foul play. And we are conducting a murder investigation. It is your *obligation* to report any information that may have a bearing on this case.''

It was obvious that he was sadly disappointed in me.

"Do you possess any other information that might be germane to this investigation?"

"Well . . ." I said, my voice trailing off. "Have you checked the newspaper archives from Rockville, Oklahoma?"

"We have indeed," he said. "The question is, why have you?"

I countered his question with one of my own. "And do you know that several years ago, an unidentified juvenile male was suspected of blowing up an automobile belonging to an alleged boyfriend of his mother?"

"Yes we know that. Juvenile records are sealed by the courts of course, but I can tell you that that particular unidentified juvenile male spent several years in a youth correctional facility after confessing to that particular bout of vandalism. Do you have some additional information that might pertain to this case?"

We were dancing around Brian's name, but we both knew whom we were talking about.

"Perhaps. That's why Neil searched the newspaper archives." I was fairly certain that this info would not get Neil in trouble—newspaper archives were part of the public record, available to anyone who took the time to look.

"Would you care to share your information?" However nicely it was phrased, it was not actually a request.

I took a deep breath and told Agent Ingstad about the flashlight. How Brian had taken it from Rhonda at the bar, and how it had appeared beside the van just before the explosion. And most tellingly, that it had been in his hand again in the parking lot as the van burned.

It was damning information. And I knew that if it did not already, the focus of the investigation would now center on Brian Michael Hunt.

"I wish you had told us about this earlier," Agent Ingstad said, annoyed. He signaled to the agent I'd seen lurking earlier around the annex door.

"We only realized it last night," I said, whining in my own defense. "Late last night."

Agent Ingstad said something quietly to the other
agent, who nodded in reply. Then he turned to me. "I
will want to talk with you further, Mrs. Bauer. We'll
need to get a complete statement from you. We'll also
want to talk to Mr. Pascoe."

Neil would be so very happy to be an integral part of
this investigation, I thought.

But before I had time to say anything, he continued.
"We'll be in touch."

Then he and the younger agent strode across the street
to the cafe, where, I presumed, another questioning was
taking place, or would very soon take place.

The fat was in the fire now. I sniffed the cold air,
sorta hoping for the reassuring odor of Aphrodite's cigarettes, and then chastised myself for being silly when
none appeared.

Standing in the cold, I ran both of my hands through
my hair, wishing I could just go home. Unfortunately
there were still plenty of people inside the annex, and it
was time for me to join the other mourners.

And to see Junior about some papers.

I headed across the grass toward the door but heard a
voice call behind me. This time it was not a disembodied
voice.

"Tory," Stu called, trotting over to me. "Tory, will
you come over to the store a minute. We *have* to talk."

I looked into his lovely green eyes, knowing that however unpleasant the day had been so far, it was about to
become even more so. And I also knew that the conversation we were going to have was truly inevitable.

I glanced back at the annex. Those festivities would
go on for a while longer. And then I turned to Stu, with
whom the festivities were probably over forever.

"Please," he said quietly.

I nodded.

32

....

Breaking Up Is Hard to Do

Okay, so maybe Neil Sedaka isn't the first singer/song-writer that comes to your mind at the end of a relationship. If I were composing a list of wallowing music for the brokenhearted, he'd be way behind James Taylor, Paul Simon, and Carole King. He probably wouldn't even make the top ten.

On the other hand, Mr. Sedaka had a point. And that particular song, at least the slow seventies version, is soft and sweet. And inexpressibly sad.

And, unfortunately, true.

Breaking up is goddamn hard to do.

Which is why I'd avoided thinking about it.

But from the moment I'd seen Renee I'd known our relationship was over. One way or another.

I just didn't realize it was going to play out its last moments in the middle of a retail establishment. At least a feed and seed store doesn't do much business in November, there being no field work going on at the moment. And with most of the town still attending

Aphrodite's memorial luncheon, there was little chance
of being interrupted.

Stu leaned back against the old dark wooden counter,
facing the door. A couple of feet away, I propped my
elbows on the counter and examined a dilapidated box
of Kleenex.

The unlit room was made even darker by the noon-
time overcast. Assorted veterinary medications and un-
guents and livestock-handling equipment lined the old
wooden shelves down the center aisle. Bags of calf and
lamb feed were stacked along one wall. A barrel of alfalfa pellets sat next to the counter. The store smelled
like a musty barn filled with grain and hay.

"Maybe we should skip this whole thing," I said,
realizing that I liked that smell. It was somehow essen-
tially South Dakotan, homey and comforting. I mentally
added it to the long list of things I would miss about
Stuart McKee. "We know what's what. There's no real
point in saying it out loud."

In his office back behind the counter, an old radio
played a static-filled rendition of "The Best of My
Love," which I supposed would now and forever remind
me of this moment.

Add the Eagles to the list.

"I didn't intend for any of this to happen, you know,"
he said softly.

"What?" I asked, still not looking at him. "You and
me? Or Renee leaving? Or Renee coming back? Or the
baby?"

He was silent a moment. "All of it. Or maybe none
of it." He turned and picked up a pencil and began to
draw aimless circles on an invoice pad. "We just kind
of fell in together. You and me, I mean."

I knew what he meant. My own surprise and delight
in being desired had fueled the attraction. The years
without Nicky had been years without any companion-
ship. I would probably have been easy game for any
male who'd taken the time for a little seduction.

I had been lucky that Stu McKee had picked up on
my signals. He was a good man. A little sloppy about

that whole forsaking-all-others thing, but otherwise decent and honorable.

Honorable enough to be as miserable as I was. Honorable enough to know that this was as necessary as it had been inevitable.

"And now it's time to fall apart," I said, sighing.

I suppose some small corner of my heart wanted him to deny it. But he looked down and doodled some more. Then he said, "I didn't know Renee was coming back until she got here." The penciled circles got larger and darker, indenting the pages of the pad. "I was going to meet her at the Minnesota border and pick up Walton like always. But she drove the whole way here early. She got to town even before I was scheduled to leave, breezing in with some story about picking up a hitchhiker, and what the weather was like, and how Delphi hadn't changed at all.

"I just stood with my mouth open while she poured herself a cup of coffee and rummaged in the refrigerator. And brought in an armload of suitcases."

I'm not sure which was more shocking to him, that fastidious Renee had picked up a hitchhiker, or that she had made a complete about-face and was again in his house.

"I didn't know about the baby until Saturday, either. I want you to know that."

Avidly interested in the tag on a calf feeder, I asked without looking up, "Does she love you?"

I didn't ask the even more important question: Do *you* love her? Or tell him that she'd cornered me in the library, asking me the same kind of question.

The lead on his pencil broke. "I don't know. I don't know if she's back because she's treating our marriage like some kind of personal growth experiment. Or because she *loves* me." He put a bitter emphasis on the word. "Or because we're having another child and she wants us to stay together for them."

Inside, a small corner crumbled. The calculator in my brain had immediately worked out that Renee had become pregnant while still living in Delphi. Though there had been no rumor of an affair, I had cherished a minor hope that the child wasn't Stu's.

"I want to be a good father," he said softly. "That's the most important consideration."

"You're right. Your children"—the word was hard to say—"need you."

Cupping my chin in my hand, I decided to get to the heart of the matter. "You know we can't go on like before. I mean before Renee left. I can't sneak around anymore. I won't."

"No," he said. "We can't. And I won't ask you to. If this is going to work, then I have to put all of my effort into it."

The part of me that honored Stu for being a good man applauded his dedication to his children and his determination to do right by his wife this time.

The part of me that had reveled in the physical, that had yearned for the warmth and the laughs and the stolen afternoons, the part that wanted this man to share my body, cried in anguish.

"Tory," he said softly. "Tory, look at me."

I couldn't. I didn't want him to see the tears that had gathered. The tears that were already falling.

For something to do, I pulled a handful of Kleenex from the box on the counter and stuffed them into my dress pockets. And then I grabbed a few more and wadded them up.

Stu reached out and placed a warm hand on my cheek and gently turned my face to him. For probably the last time, he locked his astonishing green eyes on mine in a look that was so naked and private, a look that echoed everything I had just been thinking, that I tucked it away in my heart, afraid to see what was really there.

"You know that I—" he said, but I placed my fingers on his lips and shook my head.

I could not allow myself to hear what he had been about to say. It would sorely test my untested resolve to leave, to allow him to find his way with his family. For his children. For himself. And finally for me.

I gazed one last time at the man with the sandy-brown receding hair, the one who was handsome but no one's definition of gorgeous, with the beginnings of a paunch and a wonderful laugh and those beautiful green eyes, who had haunted my dreams and slept in my arms.

He leaned down and planted a soft, warm, perfect kiss on my forehead.

And then while I still could, I turned and left the store.

33

....

Call Waiting

I realized, with grim amusement, that I was headed back to one of the few gatherings where surplus tears wouldn't be questioned, though on the whole I'd rather have been inconspicuous at a wedding or a sad movie. Even a high school graduation.

Red noses and swollen eyes were evident, though by the time the mourners had made their way through the lunch line a couple of times, and juiced up on several cups of high-octane coffee, the edge had worn off their sorrow. An urge to remember the good times, and perhaps take a nap, were foremost in the minds of most of the attendees.

Though not all.

"I'm gonna kill him," Del said to me as I came in the door. In one hand she held a platter piled high with servings of bar cookies and several kinds of cake that had been baked by the church ladies. In the other was a stack of paper napkins.

"Who, Ron?" I asked absentmindedly, searching the crowd for Junior and Neil.

I guess married men were on my mind at the moment.

Del narrowed her eyes and said with some aspersion, "No, *not* Ron. Presley."

"What'd he do?" I asked, still scanning the room.

"It's what he didn't do that pisses me off," Del said. "No one wants to haul leftovers home, so he was supposed to take this stuff around and see if anyone wanted seconds. Or thirds. Or even fourths, just to get rid of it. But he disappeared without saying anything, and now *I* have to do it. So here, want a piece of cake?"

"Not now, thanks," I said. "Have you seen Junior?"

"You just missed her," Del said with a smirk. "The poor pregnant dear had a cramp in her leg or something. She had to go home and lie down."

"Damn," I said, under my breath since we were in a church annex. I'd have to drive out to their farm later to collect Aphrodite's papers. And hear the story of how they'd come into Junior's possession.

"Damn?" Del repeated, surprised. "You're sorry you missed her?"

"No, she just had something of mine. You know, those do look good," I said, inspecting the platter. "Is Neil around?" I asked, choosing a piece of carrot cake.

"You're outta luck there too," Del said, grinning. "The feds came and got him a while ago. It was all very mysterious."

I grimaced. I had wanted to warn him of the impending interview. And to fill him in on the recent developments. At least those concerning Aphrodite's death. I wasn't quite ready to announce to all and sundry that my afternoons would no longer be spent at area motels with the Feed and Seed dealer.

They'd all have to figure that one out for themselves. I had every confidence that they'd catch on soon enough.

"So did the dirty coppers beat you with a rubber hose?" Del asked.

"Huh?" I said, my mouth full of cake. I'd already forgotten about my interview with Agent Ingstad. "Oh, no," I said, swallowing. "But I did tell him about the flowers and the note that we got at the cafe. And how Alanna disposed of both of them.''

"Good," Del said harshly. "If I'd known it would cause her trouble, I'd have turned her in myself."

"I don't think it's Alanna they're looking for," I said quietly. Behind us, Presley came through the door and then held it open for Mardelle Jackson. I tilted my head toward them and said to Del, "Doesn't look like chivalry's completely dead, anyway."

"I'll show him chivalry," Del said darkly, motioning her son over. "So who are they looking for anyway?" she asked me.

Del handed the platter over to Pres just as I said, "It seems that the officers are interested in a young man with a history of blowing things up."

The platter slipped out of Presley's hand, splattering seven-layer bars and devil's food cake over a goodly portion of the indoor-outdoor carpeting that covered the annex dining room floor.

"Oh for chrissakes," Del said, disgusted. "I should have just taken them around myself and been done with it. I'll go get a garbage bag." She stalked off, muttering.

I squatted down to help Pres and Mardelle pick up the smooshed goodies. They worked wordlessly, exchanging worried glances. Glances that were far too agitated to have been caused by making an accidental mess at a funeral reception.

Something that Pres had said earlier at the trailer popped into my head. Something about explosions.

Plural.

"Agent Ingstad, who works for the Department of Criminal Investigation, was talking to me a little while ago," I said innocently. "He's especially anxious to chat with anyone who might know anything about what happened behind the cafe on Saturday night."

Pres swallowed. "Well, of course he's interested in that. A person died, for crying out loud. He'd want to know whatever there is to know about that explosion."

"But there were two explosions, remember? The one that blew up in the Dumpster, and the other that killed Aphrodite."

I was not playing fair, but I'd belatedly realized that Presley knew something that he wasn't especially willing to divulge, something that might have a real bearing on the case. Besides, the feds were asking around. They'd come to the same conclusion sooner or later anyway.

"The DCI guys are starting to wonder if there were a connection between the two explosions," I said slowly, trying to clean up butter cream icing without grinding it into the carpet.

"Oh, jeez," Pres said weakly.

"Presley," Mardelle said. It was a warning.

"I already know," I said. "So you might as well admit that the two of you set off the M-80 in the Dumpster. Right?"

At the trailer with Darla, Presley had said that he and Mardelle had been driving around. That they had been in a car, across town, when Aphrodite's van exploded. That they had only come upon the scene after the fire was already roaring.

Twice on Sunday morning he'd denied being anywhere near the "explosions."

His mistake was that he would not, on Sunday morning, have known that there was more than one explosion without having been on the scene a lot closer and earlier than he'd previously admitted. And since he and Mardelle had already been involved in several smaller blowups at the school gym, there was no reason to think they'd ended their fun at the dance.

Neither one looked at me.

"Listen," I said seriously. "No one is worried about damage to the Dumpster. And the officers will know right away that you had nothing to do with the explosion that killed Aphrodite. What I want to know is if you saw anything strange behind the cafe. Or if anyone with you saw anything strange."

"We weren't with anyone," Mardelle said, with a sidelong glance at Presley, who blushed furiously. "We'd been out, um, driving around, and we had this M-80 that we were saving for something big."

"And we figured since firecrackers had been going off all day, that we'd celebrate with a real bang."

He blushed again, and I shook my head.

Why couldn't humans reproduce asexually? Our way was too damn complicated.

Not that I thought that Presley and Mardelle were actually having sex (he was only thirteen, after all), but as I'd just rediscovered myself, not having sex can be every bit as complicating as getting some.

Pres shot another look at Mardelle before continuing. "We parked the car down the block a little, so no one would see us. And then we walked around the far end of the cafe to the Dumpster."

They were both silent.

"And you saw someone, didn't you?" I prompted.

They nodded.

"It was dark, but we could see that it was a guy. We could see that he was carrying something, but we couldn't tell what," Mardelle said.

"And he was prowling around Aphrodite's van," Pres said miserably. "But he heard us coming and he took off."

"We didn't pay that much attention to him. There were lots of people out running around that night," Mardelle said. "And afterward, well, we didn't know how to tell anyone what we saw. We thought they'd think we had something to do with the big explosion."

"Did you see who it was?" I asked, trying not to get my hopes up too much. "The guy by the van?"

"Nah, it was too dark," Pres said. Mardelle nodded in confirmation.

"I think you need to tell Agent Ingstad what you saw," I said, standing up with the platter. My knees protested loudly.

"You think *he* did it, don't you?" Pres asked, standing up and brushing cake crumbs off his pants. "That guy Rhonda has the hots for."

As if on cue, Rhonda came through the annex door, sparing my answer, which was an unequivocal *I don't know.*

She'd been crying recently, and was in a definite funk.

"Hi guys," she said with a halfhearted wave. "Are you hanging in all right?"

"We're fine," I said, handing the platter and remains of the cake back to Pres. He and Mardelle escaped without a backward look. "How're you doing?"

"This is just so awful," she said, tears spilling over her big blue eyes. "I mean, Aphrodite's gone. And the police are here, and they've been asking me all these questions."

"Oh," I said. "You too, huh?"

"They're talking to everyone," Rhonda said, sniffling, "which I can understand. But they kept asking me about Halloween night, and when I noticed that Brian was gone from the bar. And when I saw him again. And about that stupid flashlight."

She dissolved completely into tears.

I herded her over to one of the tables and we sat down.

"Oh Tory, I think they think Brian did it." She looked at me, the saddest twenty-year-old in the history of the world. "They think Brian killed Aphrodite."

"What do you think?" I fished in my pocket and handed her one of the crumpled tissues.

She blew her nose. "I don't know. I mean I did lose track of him at the bar. And I'm sure I didn't see him again until we were all behind the cafe. But, Tory, it was late and we'd all been drinking, and I don't know for sure what happened. If I tell the officers that I didn't see him, they're going to think that he did it."

A thought occurred to me. "You all left the bar after the first explosion, but before the van blew up, didn't you?"

"What do you mean?" She wiped her eyes and tucked the damp Kleenex into her jumper pocket.

"Well, Aphrodite and I were inside the cafe when the M-80 went off in the Dumpster. We heard it loud enough because we were right there. But did you hear it across the street in the bar? With all the noise and music and all?"

Rhonda thought back. "Well, there wasn't any music going on right then. Alanna had just finished taking her clothes off, and everyone was still pretty well surprised by that. No one much was talking."

"So you heard the explosion then?"

Rhonda tucked her hair behind an ear and stared into the middle distance. "No, I didn't hear anything. Or at least not anything loud. There'd been firecrackers and stuff going off all day. I might have heard something, but I wouldn't have paid attention to it on my own."

I thought about that. Aphrodite and I had been talking. She'd handed the green flashlight to me, but her decision to get into the van and leave had been triggered by the bar patrons coming around the corner of the cafe en masse.

They had all poured across the street *before* the van exploded.

"Rhonda, think back. What made everyone in the bar rush across the street to check out an explosion that no one actually heard?"

"Well someone heard it. It might even have been Junior," Rhonda said. "Yeah, that's right, Junior was standing at the door getting ready to leave, and she must have heard it, because she turned around and said something like 'Oh my God, there's been an explosion at the cafe!' "

"And everyone ran across the street to see what was going on?" I asked.

"Well, not at first. Alanna tried to say that it was probably nothing and that we were all pretty silly to get so excited over a little Halloween prank. But Junior insisted. She said that Neil had heard an explosion too."

I'd forgotten that Neil had arrived before the van exploded. He'd been walking home and he'd heard the Dumpster blow, a sound that had been magnified greatly by the metal enclosure. Though the bar patrons might not have heard it clearly, anyone on the street would have. And Neil had run back, frightened for our safety.

I remember seeing Alanna at the forefront of the bar crowd. I'd just assumed that she'd led the whole crew over. That she'd tried to dissuade the others from coming was a surprise.

A new thought surfaced.

"Did you lose track of Brian before or after Alanna started her striptease?" I asked. If Brian had been the shadowy man with the flashlight behind the cafe (and it seemed obvious that he was), then he would have had to leave the bar. Which he'd evidently done unnoticed.

"Well, he was on the phone for a little while, I remember," Rhonda said, calmer now. "But I don't remember seeing him at all during the, uh, strip."

Had Alanna's impromptu display in honor of her father's death really been a distraction so that Brian could leave the cafe and plant a bomb in Aphrodite's van?

The striptease couldn't have been all that impromptu, since she'd been wearing pasties and pull-away panties under her tartan.

Were Brian and Alanna, mother and son, in this together? Did Alanna, who at the time thought she was to inherit 100 percent of the Delphi Cafe, create a diversion so her son could facilitate that inheritance?

And what about the father, Robert Hunt of Consolidated Florists of Tulsa—was he in on it too? Brian had left the funeral service to call him. And he'd certainly called someone on the bar pay phone.

And he'd received a call at the cafe on Saturday afternoon.

"Rhonda," I said, excited. "That call for Mike Hunt, the one you hung up on in the cafe . . ." Rhonda blushed for an old blunder. "Tell me about the voice. What did it sound like?"

"Well, it was a guy," she said.

Good.

"And it was deep, a really nice deep voice," she said.

Even better.

"And he had some kind of Southern accent," Rhonda finished.

Bingo.

34

....

Untimely Arrivals

I am continually amazed by fictional detectives. Besides being drop-dead gorgeous and having glamorous and fulfilling jobs in exotic and exciting locales, most seem to possess the innate skill to amass a group of unrelated facts and immediately sort out the ones that are, and aren't, relevant to the case at hand.

I envy their near-psychic ability to know which questions to ask, and which answers matter. Which clues to remember and which to ignore. And the difference between the suspects who merit suspicion and those who are only bit players in the larger drama.

I, on the other hand, with no delusions of congenital detecting abilities, seem always to follow the wrong leads, make the wrong assumptions, and ask the wrong questions.

There's no doubt that we were getting plenty of answers. Unfortunately, every single answer posed new questions.

Not long after Rhonda's entrance, we were shooed out of the annex by the Lutheran Ladies League, who were eager to clean up and get back home or to work. Since there were no blood relatives to do the honors, I'd made it a point to thank each one for the time and effort expended on behalf of a woman who, after all, was not even a member of their church.

With every intention of going straight home to massage my poor aching feet (and perhaps to destroy the torture shoes), I slowly limped down Delphi's mostly deserted main drag.

The DCI cars were still parked in front of both the cafe and post office, so the interrogations had not yet been completed. Though it was fascinating, what I'd learned from Rhonda was purely speculation that did not seem to warrant an immediate repetition to Agent Ingstad. It would keep until he came to call.

The north wind whipped around the buildings and through me, damp and sharp. I pulled my coat even tighter and ducked my head into the collar, lost in my own morose thoughts.

I don't know how many times Neil called my name before I finally heard him.

"Tory." He trotted up from behind me, slightly out of breath, face red with the exertion, glasses steamed over. "Wait up."

"Oh, hi," I said. "Sorry, I didn't hear you." I remembered what he'd just been through, and said guiltily, "I guess I have some explaining to do."

"Nah," he said, throwing a companionable arm around my shoulders. "I got the distinct impression that the DCI was more than ready to check out the actions of young Master Hunt without our encouragement."

"You figured that out too?"

"Yeah, though I think something specific triggered the new focus. You wouldn't happen to know anything about that, would you?"

"Maybe," I said, grinning for the first time all day. I told Neil about the nonencounter with Brian and his phone call in Aphrodite's house, leaving out any mention of the lady herself. That segued into Presley and Mardelle's confession, and Rhonda's revelation.

"My, you have been busy," Neil said admiringly. "Are you ready for some more investigating?"

"No, I want to go home and throw these shoes away and take a nap," I said. I didn't add that what I wanted most was to wallow in self-pity.

"Too bad, we need to pay a condolence call," he said cheerfully, steering me back toward town, "on the bereaved fiancé."

"Norman?" I asked, confused. "Why bother Norman?"

"Because he's the only one who knew all the principals personally. Maybe he can give us some real insight on Brian and his mother. And because the spirit of Aphrodite is leading us in that direction."

I peered at him sharply, but he was making a joke. There was no hint that he'd been visited by voices, or the physical manifestation of Lucky Strikes long gone.

"Besides," Neil said, grinning, "he's expecting us. I called him."

Norman ushered us into his bungalow, a house that was much nicer and cleaner, and decorated far more tastefully, than I'd had any reason to expect from a widower of several years whose bread route was possibly slated for cancellation.

"Your house is really nice," I said, looking around the tidy kitchen, which had been recently repainted. The countertops gleamed and clean dishes were neatly stacked in a drainer beside the sink. The living room was decorated with furniture and drapes of a style and vintage that postdated the death of Norman's first wife, Claire. The house was small, but homey and comfortable.

He indicated the couch for us, and then sat in a matching recliner rocker. "Yeah, well, Claire and me, we scrimped all our lives so we could enjoy our retirement. Never bought a thing new if we could get it used, saved every penny. And then she died." Norman ran his hands through his thinning hair before continuing. "For a while after that, there didn't seem much point in saving or spending. I just kind of marked time. Until I met Aphrodite.''

The grief on his face was evident. I squirmed, feeling like an intruder. If we had not been there on a legitimate errand, I would have made my apologies and left immediately.

"But once *we* got together, we figured there was no point in scrimping any more," Norman went on. "We figured we'd better enjoy it while we could. We fixed up this house together. Spent money like neither of us has ever done before. She was going to bring some of her stuff like that new stereo, and move in here after we was married. And now—" He stopped, closing his eyes for a long moment, unable to continue.

"That's one of the reasons we're here," I said softly. "We're trying to put together a clear picture of everyone. You knew Gus. And you knew Alanna when she was a child. And from something you said on the phone, I think you knew, or knew something about, Brian."

"Can you tell us about Gus and Aphrodite? I mean back when they first got married?" Neil asked, sitting forward with his hands clasped on his knees.

Norman leaned back in his chair. He looked like a tired man, battered by circumstances beyond his control. "Gus was always pretty intense. He took himself seriously, and by God everyone else had to too. Sometimes those short guys are like that—always having to prove something to the rest of the world. Anyway, he and Aphrodite were happy at first. Or at least they seemed to be.''

"What happened to his first wife? Alanna's real mother?" I asked.

"I never knew, she was long gone before I hooked up with Gus. I know that it was just he and Cheryl for a long time. And he took real good care of that little girl. Wasn't nothing too good for her.''

"And that caused trouble in the marriage?" Neil asked.

"You might say that," Norman answered. "Aphrodite, she was excited to be a mom, and she tried to take

care of Cheryl. She was such a pretty little blond thing.
But it was like Gus wanted to make everything easy for
Cheryl, from buying her stuff to making sure that no
one ever got her upset. And I think he passed everything
he knew down to her kid.''

That had been one of our questions. Neil looked at
me, waiting for me to proceed. ''So Gus did teach Brian
about the explosives business?''

''Gus said he taught him everything. From the business to taking care of his mom. Especially after her marriage ended. He was always real proud of Brian and he
wanted him to make sure life was smooth for Cheryl.
Gus thought she was too delicate to be bothered with
everyday worries.''

Delicate was not a word that anyone who had seen
her nearly naked would associate with Cheryl/Alanna.
But like most parents, I suppose Gus saw the child rather
than the woman.

''Did you have much contact with her over the years?
Did you know Brian as he was growing up?''

''No, but I kept in touch with Gus. He wrote letters
a lot. He lived with Cheryl and her husband until that
marriage broke up. And then he lived just with her and
the kid for a while after that. But I guess business was
good, because not too much later, he moved into some
kind of retirement village and he's lived there ever
since.''

''How long ago?''

''Oh, geez, a long time. Real long time. At least
twenty years, or maybe even more.''

''Wasn't he kind of young for retirement? He couldn't
have been too much more than forty or fifty,'' I said,
doing some mental math.

''Sometimes people get lucky with investments and
stuff, and they get to retire early,'' Norman said ruefully.
''Didn't work that way with me.''

''Or for most of us,'' I said, figuring I'd never get to
retire.

''Well it worked out all right for Gus,'' Norman said.
''He got to enjoy *his* retirement. Years ago he told us

both that he had a bad heart. He always said he expected to go any time, though I mostly thought he was exaggerating to get Aphrodite's sympathy. I guess I was wrong."

"She told me that he wanted her to come back," I said, remembering our last conversation inside the cafe.

"Yeah, well she did feel sorry for him. I don't think she ever considered taking him back, but she never got around to divorcing him either. There was some kind of business arrangement between them that I never really understood, and she always said it was just easier to leave things as they were."

"Until she fell in love with you," I said, softly.

"Yeah well, I tried to talk her into divorcing him long time ago. But Aphrodite still felt guilty for leaving him, and only just lately agreed to file the papers." Norman thought a minute and then continued. "I figured that was why they all three of 'em showed up in Delphi together. To try to talk her out of the divorce. It guess it was just bad luck that his ticker kicked out on him here."

"Wait a second," I interrupted. "You thought that Gus, Alanna, and Brian arrived in Delphi together?"

"Well they must have. It would have been some kinda odd coincidence for all of them to show up separately on the same day, dontcha think?"

"I suppose," I said slowly, sorting out a chronology of last Saturday morning.

In all the sadness and attendant hoopla surrounding the death of Aphrodite Ferguson, we'd mostly managed to forget that there had been another death on the same day, which was indeed very odd.

But whether it had been a coincidence was another question entirely.

Though we hadn't known his identity at the time, Gus Ferguson had been seated in the cafe by noon. He'd ordered one of Aphrodite's Halloween lunch specials before expiring unceremoniously on the bathroom floor.

His body had been transported by silent ambulance at least an hour before Alanna and Brian had driven up alone in the silver Lexus and subsequently described the gentleman they'd expected to meet at the Delphi Cafe.

A gentleman whose death had gone largely unmarked. And whose arrival had been completely overlooked.

Gus had arrived in Delphi long before his daughter and grandson.

The question was how.

35

....

A New Policy

We're pretty good at seeing what's in front of us. After finally realizing the connection between Brian and the green flashlight, we had established to our satisfaction a creditable link from Alanna's striptease in the bar to the explosion of Aphrodite's van.

We had no proof, no corroborating evidence beyond that of our own eyes and memories and ample suspicions, but the assumption seemed solid and logical. Considering that the DCI vehicles were still parked in front of the cafe.

But like Sherlock Holmes and the dog that didn't bark in the nighttime, it took us a little longer to see what hadn't been there all along.

"It never once occurred to me," Neil marveled as we walked back toward his house after leaving poor Norman. "I'd assumed that Gus arrived with Alanna and Brian."

"Don't feel bad," I said, hands thrust deep into my coat pockets, wishing I'd brought along some gloves. "I sat there in the cafe and watched them drive up alone in their fancy silver car. They even told us that they were looking for Gus, for crying out loud.''

A few dry leaves blew across the road.

"Some detective team we'd make." Neil laughed.

"No shit," I said, sniffing the air. No whiff of smoke this time, just the cold and damp wind. It smelled like snow.

"Did he drive himself then?" Neil asked, squinting at the uniformly gray sky, rewinding his wool scarf around his neck.

"If he did, where's the car?" I asked. There had been no unclaimed cars left in front of the cafe. And an abandoned vehicle anywhere else in town, especially one with out-of-state plates, would have been noticed by now.

"A taxi then?"

"Yeah, right."

A taxi would have been even more conspicuous than a pink Cadillac. Or a silver Lexus. We just don't get many fare-paying passengers in these parts.

"On the bus."

"If it had been any day but Saturday, maybe," I said. "But buses don't stop here on the weekends. Nobody delivers anything to Delphi on weekends. Besides, if he'd been in town any earlier than Saturday morning, Aphrodite certainly would have seen him."

"You're sure she didn't know he was here in Delphi?"

We'd stopped at the sidewalk in front of Neil's house. "Pretty sure. She didn't say anything about seeing him alive. And she sure as hell was surprised to see him dead."

Surprise was hardly the word. The lit cigarette had dropped from her mouth in shock.

"I find it hard to believe that she didn't notice him sitting in the cafe when she was just inside the kitchen." Neil removed his glasses and polished them on a scarf end.

"I don't," I said, remembering my disastrous morning as chief cook. "The President of the United States could come into the cafe and no one in the kitchen would notice. And things were a mess on Saturday anyway. It was Halloween, remember?"

We'd been inundated with trick-or-treaters all morning, not to mention the Ghoul Scout Singers. "I'd say she was completely flabbergasted to discover Gus in the bathroom, dead or alive."

"Well, there's always the chance that Alanna and Brian brought him in early and dropped him off, and then staged the grand entrance later."

"But why?"

"Who knows what evil lurks in the hearts of men? And big-busted strippers?" Neil asked, laughing. "Listen, I have a ton of paperwork to do inside." He nodded at the library. "Do you want to come in and keep me company?"

"Sounds lovely," I said, "but I have to call Junior about Aphrodite's papers, and I'll probably end up driving out to her place to pick them up." I yawned. "But what I really want more than anything is a nap."

Neil gave my shoulder a squeeze. "Go and do what you have to. And then sleep awhile. We can go over those papers later, if you want me to help."

"That'd be great," I said over my shoulder, heading up the stairs into the trailer.

The first thing I wanted to do was take my shoes off and dump them in the garbage can.

The second thing I wanted was to plug in some music. J. T. could be my handyman anytime.

The third thing I wanted was to avoid calling Junior. Two out of three ain't bad.

As the phone rang at Junior's I realized that I was famished. I'd only eaten one piece of carrot cake all day.

With music playing softly in the background, and the receiver cradled between my shoulder and ear, I dug the strawberry-rhubarb jam out of the fridge, opened the silverware drawer and extracted a knife, untwisted the bread sack and dug back for a couple of only marginally

stale pieces, and rooted in the cupboard for the peanut
butter.

"Hello," Junior answered sleepily.

"Hi, it's Tory," I said, unscrewing the lid to the Jif.

"I recognized your voice," Junior said shortly, making me feel silly for mentioning my own name.

"Well, you sounded sleepy," I said, annoyed that
Junior could aggravate me in four words or less. "I
thought introducing myself was the polite thing to do."
I spread peanut butter furiously on a slice of bread.

"Well we've established your identity and your innate
courtesy," Junior said. "Did you just call for positive
feedback on your personal growth or did you need something?"

"Damn, you're crabby today. Are you still without
running water?"

There was a small pause. Junior continued in a more
contrite tone. "Sorry, I'm just so tired all the time. And
I haven't felt well for several days now. I didn't mean
to snap."

The apology sounded genuine, and life was too short
to keep a running total of how many times Junior annoyed the living shit out of me.

"Well, I'll leave you be in a minute. But Clay mentioned that you had some stuff of Aphrodite's to give
me. I missed you after the memorial service, and thought
I'd run out to your place now and pick it up." I finished
making my sandwich and took a bite.

"Well, ah . . ."

Junior wasn't the only one who practiced rudeness in
our family. With my mouth full, I interrupted her. "And
I'd really like to know how *you* got those legal papers
and documents to begin with. The last time *I* saw them
was early Saturday evening and they were in an envelope in *my* coat pocket. I've been looking for them ever
since."

"Oh really? Well, if you'll let me finish a sentence,
I'll tell you. But first, I'd like to know why *you* had
those papers."

"What do you mean?" I wondered why every conversation with Junior immediately turned adversarial.

"Well, they obviously weren't yours but they were in your possession before Aphrodite died. Why?"

"I accidentally walked out of the cafe with them," I said, not intending to explain further. "And I meant to give the whole bunch back to Aphrodite at the disco party on Saturday, but things got a little wild, remember?" I wanted Junior to remember that we'd had at least one civil conversation. I took another bite of sandwich. "I'm assuming that you didn't take them out of my coat pocket."

"Of course not. On Sunday morning I let myself back into the school to make sure that the cleanup had been adequate. I found the manila envelope on the floor of the cloakroom. It must have fallen to the floor the night before."

So much for the scenario Neil and I had concocted where someone had purposely stolen the papers for nefarious purposes. I had simply lost them. And Junior, of all people, had found them.

"And of course you looked inside," I said.

"Well, there wasn't any name on the outside of the envelope, so there wasn't any other way to discover the owner," she said defensively. "I barely glanced at them, but since most of the documents mentioned Aphrodite, I figured she'd dropped them. I did see that you were named executor. That's why I told Clay this morning that the papers should be turned over to you."

I'll bet she barely glanced at the will. So that was how Clay, and probably the rest of Delphi, had known I was handling Aphrodite's estate. And inheriting half of the cafe.

"Well, you were right. Can I come over and pick them up now? There may be some important documents among those papers that Darla Hoffart and I have to go over."

Not to mention Neil.

"I can't give them to you," Junior said.

"Why in the hell not?" I was beginning to get a head-ache.

"Because I already gave them to Norman Oberle."

"You already gave them to Norman Oberle," I repeated.

"Do we have a bad connection?"

"Why," I said slowly and clearly, "did you give Aphrodite's papers to Norman Oberle?"

"Because he said that they were his," Junior said simply. "He overheard Clay tell you that I had the papers. So he asked me for them."

"And you *gave* them to him? Just like that?"

The rest of my sandwich lay forgotten on the countertop. J. T. sang unnoticed in the background.

"Well, he told me that they were his," Junior said.

"With a copy of Aphrodite Ferguson's will in the stack," I said, "not to mention her divorce papers, you still thought that they belonged to Norman?"

"He said that those were copies she'd given him for safekeeping. You evidently didn't look through the papers thoroughly," Junior said with no small amount of triumph in her voice.

"Well, evidently you did."

"Well, I didn't right away. But this morning I read them through. So yes, and after talking to Norman, I decided that he might be the rightful owner after all."

"Want to tell me about it?"

"I really think that's too personal for us to get into," Junior said primly.

"Arrrrgh," I growled dangerously.

The line fell silent for a moment. Finally Junior continued, "Oh all right, if you must know." I think she'd been dying for an opportunity to tell, she just had to pretend that I'd wrangled it out of her. "Among other things, there were some insurance papers. A large life insurance policy had been recently issued on Aphrodite. It had a double indemnity clause. That means the payoff doubles in the case of death by foul play."

"I know what double indemnity means," I said, stunned. "Do I have to ask who the beneficiary is?"

"Not unless you think it was someone other than Norman."

"What else?"

"Well, there were some court papers too. I'm sure that there hasn't been a ruling on it yet because we'd have seen it in the paper, or heard it somewhere already, but Norman Oberle had just filed for bankruptcy."

36

....

Smoke Gets in Your Nose

It was a natural assumption, after all. Aphrodite had been carrying the papers when she and Norman entered the cafe on Saturday afternoon. And it had been Aphrodite who had dropped them upon sighting the good ship Luna.

It's not my fault that I read the situation wrong.

Under those circumstances, I think anyone would have.

As I cleaned up the sandwich mess, I reassessed the entire scenario, factoring in all the new bits and pieces, like the fact that Norman was scheduled to receive a very large settlement from a soon-to-be unhappy insurance company.

Before hanging up, I'd asked Junior the magic number and had been mildly astonished at the total, even before the indemnity clause.

I wondered how all of Norman's new and tasteful furniture and drapery fit in with an anticipated bankruptcy hearing. Especially considering that his livelihood was in jeopardy.

And how Aphrodite fit in with all of these new facts. She had happily announced to me that she intended to marry Norman. I did not think I was jumping to an unreasonable conclusion in assuming that she knew of Norman's financial difficulties since she had been carrying the very papers that stated that fact. She had evidently been willing to accept him regardless.

I wondered how their marriage would have affected his bankruptcy proceedings.

I wondered how he'd managed to end up in the kind of debt that necessitated bankruptcy proceedings, since he and Claire had scrimped and saved for their unrealized retirement.

I wondered why, after many months (or even years) of resistance, Aphrodite suddenly decided to divorce Gus and marry Norman.

And for the first time I wondered just exactly how much Norman knew about the nuts and bolts end of the demolition business.

I wanted badly to hash this all over with Neil, to hear him chide me for suspecting poor lovelorn Norman. But his phone was busy.

I sat at the Formica kitchen table and dialed another number on the avocado wall phone, taking a chance that she'd maintain her regular office hours after the memorial service.

"Hi Darla," I said. Darla could not afford a receptionist for her Delphi office so she answered her own phone. "This is Tory Bauer."

"Hi Tory," Darla said happily. "I recognized your voice."

"There's been a lot of that going around," I said dryly.

"Huh?"

"Never mind," I said. "Listen, I found out some things this afternoon that are pretty interesting. Can I ask you a couple of questions?"

"Go ahead, shoot," Darla said.

"Okay, would it be possible for Aphrodite to have taken out a large insurance policy on herself without you knowing about it?"

"Sure. I'm her lawyer, not her accountant," Darla said. "Or her mother. She could spend her money any way she wanted."

"But wouldn't you have seen a large premium check go through her bank account?"

"I might have, if it cleared before the last statements were sent out. But if the check cleared after that, it won't show up until the next statement. And up until the day of her death, it would have been business as usual. And that's if she used one of the accounts that she told me about."

"What do you mean?" I asked.

"Well, people don't always tell their lawyers the whole truth and nothing but the truth," Darla said. "Some people like to keep secrets. Sometimes they even fudge on court-ordered financial statements. A general client is under no legal compulsion to reveal anything, and there's no way to enforce a full disclosure. They squirrel money away in secret accounts. They bury it in tin cans. They keep it stashed . . ."

We said at the same time, ". . . in their vehicles."

Darla said, "Damn, I forgot to check into that. As soon as I hang up, I'll call the police and see if they found any traces of cash in the ashes of Aphrodite's van."

"I have another question," I said. "If it had proceeded normally, how long would Aphrodite's divorce have taken?"

"Without complications, several months. With complications like their business agreement, it could be a year. Or more."

"And how long would a normal bankruptcy proceeding take from beginning to end?"

"I presume there is a specific reason for these questions?" Darla asked.

I told her about Norman, and the information in the other papers.

I didn't have to tell her about my suspicions. She figured them out all by herself.

"Whoa," she said. "This puts a new slant on things, doesn't it?"

"What sort of effect would marrying Aphrodite"—I didn't add *and her money*—"have had on Norman's bankruptcy?"

"That would depend entirely on the flavor of bankruptcy. In some cases, without a prenuptial agreement, the wife's assets can be used to offset debts incurred previously by the husband."

"And did Aphrodite ask you to draw up a prenup?" I asked.

"It would have been premature to work on an agreement before she'd finished ditching husband number one," Darla said matter-of-factly. "But the subject never even came up."

So Norman's financial difficulties would have been eased, if not alleviated completely, by a marriage to Aphrodite.

They were, however, absolutely eliminated by her death.

Darla said, "Why don't you stick close to the phone, and I'll call the police and find out about the evidence left in the van and get right back to you."

I agreed that was a good plan and hung up. I sat, drumming my fingers on the table, trying to sort out all the new complications. I was so wrapped up in my own speculations that at first whiff I thought the trailer was on fire.

Less than a second later I realized that it was cigarette smoke.

A lot of cigarette smoke.

"All right," I said out loud to the ceiling, exasperated. "What am I missing? What do you want me to see?"

The smell was so strong, and so pervasive, that it produced a very large sneeze.

Next time I'm haunted, I want a ghost who only speaks. None of this olfactory stuff.

"See what you're doing to me?" I asked the air, sneezing again. "Are you happy now?"

I reached deep into my dress pocket for a tissue, and felt something rustle.

Bewildered, I pulled an envelope from my pocket.

The one I'd taken from Aphrodite's house.

The one I'd forgotten about entirely.

I sniffed again, and the air was clear.

37

....

More of Gravy Than the Grave

It goes without saying that the whole notion of Aphrodite Ferguson's unquiet spirit hanging around staid and boring Delphi, South Dakota, just to point an even more staid and boring waitress toward her killer, was too silly for words.

I'd had little or no sleep for three days running and more than enough emotional trauma to produce several weeks of sleepless nights and months more of grief. No doubt the weird manifestations were hallucinations caused by exhaustion, or possibly a fragment of underdone potato. I could only be grateful that my overloaded system had not also dredged up confrontations with my dead husband.

I could not begin to imagine what Nicky would make of the current situation. And was delighted to keep it that way.

That said, I held in my hand an envelope containing a letter that had come from the house of the late-but-perhaps-not-quite-gone Aphrodite Ferguson. However it had come to be in my pocket, whether I would have found it on my own, or was led purposely by an avenging spirit, I didn't need a ghostly apparition to tell me to read the damn thing.

The envelope bore the return address of Prairie View Manor, of Tulsa, Oklahoma. The postmark date was October 10 of this year, and it was addressed to Mrs. A. Ferguson in a shaky hand.

Inside was a one-page, handwritten letter to Aphrodite.

My Dearest Dite, [the salutation read]

I am shocked and distressed beyond words that you want to end our long marriage. When Cheryl came to me with your letter, I was wracked with pain and I was afraid that my poor tired heart would not hold out. You know that my health has been dicey for a very long time and I think you are being very selfish to put this additional strain on me. Poor dear Cheryl sobbed and cried when you wrote and told her of your plans.

Since the laws of this country no longer support a wronged spouse, I will not be able to use the court system to stop you from making this terrible and final mistake. But as I told my lovely Cheryl, we will fight as long as we must to keep our working arrangement in effect. You signed that agreement in good faith many years ago, and Cheryl and Brian and I all agree that you cannot be allowed to renege now.

Cheryl has consulted an accountant and she says that I will not be able to continue to live here if our business arrangement is terminated. As you know, I have lived here for many years and I am very happy. The people are very good to me. I would not survive a move and Cheryl and Brian agree that it cannot be allowed to happen.

Please think again and stop this foolishness. I

warn you that we are prepared to take whatever
steps necessary to keep things as they are.

As ever, your husband,
Gus

I flopped back in the kitchen chair, rubbed my aching
head, and said sarcastically to the ceiling, "Gee thanks,
that explains everything."

I got no answer from the ceiling. Disgusted, I reread
the letter and found to my surprise that it had, after all,
answered a couple of questions.

According to statements written by his own hand, Gus
had not financed his retirement with investments lo these
many years, as Norman had supposed. Instead, Aphrodite had worked twelve-hour days and seven-day weeks
to support him via their unfair and outdated separation
agreement.

That Gus was distressed by the planned decamping of
his cash cow was obvious.

That poor dear Alanna and Brian had been equally
distressed by the impending dissolution was equally understandable. With Aphrodite's money out of the picture, they'd have to support Gus on their own. Or,
heaven forbid, he might even have had to go to work
and support himself, bad heart or no.

The fact that Gus was now dead, felled by that bad
heart, engendered absolutely no sympathy from me. He
and his family had shamelessly leeched off Aphrodite
for decades.

I was glad that she had survived him, even for only
a few hours.

And I was glad that Aphrodite had started to think of
herself and her own happiness, though in providing relief for Norman's financial woes, she'd proved that old
bad habits are hard to break.

Not that Norman was the only one who stood to profit
from Aphrodite's newly found sense of independence
and financial whimsy.

I stood to be on the receiving end of her largesse too,
once Alanna and I figured out how to run the cafe to-

gether without open warfare. And perhaps I'd already been on the receiving end and hadn't even noticed.

I went into my bedroom and shuffled through the stack of my unpaid hospital bills from last summer, searching for the latest statement. The most recent one I could find was dated mid-September.

Back in the kitchen, I called the accounting office at the hospital and found, to my absolute astonishment, that all my bills had recently been paid in full, in cash, by an anonymous donor.

I hung up, not only marveling at Aphrodite's amazing generosity, but grateful for the honesty of the poor drudges working in accounts receivable.

Though the totals paid on my behalf were large enough to have taken me several years to pay off on my own, they didn't come close to the full amount rumored to have been stashed in Aphrodite's van.

I wondered how much cash it took to buy a large life insurance policy on an elderly, overweight female smoker.

Even though Darla was planning to call soon, I chanced tying up the line to discuss these new speculations with Neil, but his phone was still busy.

I yawned, and laid my head down on the cold Formica table to wait either for Darla to call or for Neil to hang up, and was dreaming of flower delivery men who were swamped on Mondays and then suddenly startled awake by the jangling of the telephone before I even knew I was asleep.

"Hello," I said groggily, stretching to get rid of the crick in my neck.

Formica does not a good pillow make.

"Tory, I have some interesting news for you," Darla said.

"Me too, but you first."

"Well, I just got off the phone with the investigating officers, and there was absolutely no trace of cash found in the remains of Aphrodite's van."

"Could it have burned up completely?" I asked.

"Highly unlikely. Even scattered bills would leave identifiable ashes. Cash that is bundled together in stacks and then stored in a container like a leather pouch or lock box would barely burn at all, even in a fire as nasty and hot as that one. The oxygen wouldn't be able to get between the bills, so the outside ones would be charred and burned, but the inside stuff would be pretty much like new.''

Unsurprised by her news, I told Darla about the mysterious cash payment of my hospital bills, and my thoughts about the life insurance premium. And then I told her all about the letter from Gus, though I didn't mention exactly how, or why, I had it.

"Well, that explains it then," Darla said.

"Explains what?"

"After we talked earlier about stray accounts and client disclosure," Darla said, "I did a little checking around at area banks on a hunch. On my fourth call, I hit the jackpot and found an account in Aphrodite's name at a bank in Waubay.

"Deposits to that account were made regularly in cash, by mail. And the only checks ever written on it were issued once a month for a period of several years, to Cheryl Ferguson Hunt and Prairie View Manor, of Tulsa, Oklahoma. Jointly.''

We both agreed that things were getting curiouser and curiouser.

Darla hung up with the promise to do a little more account scouting.

I sat back to mull over Darla's additions to the canon, but couldn't focus on any single item.

Grandsons and insurance policies and bad hearts and inheritances and agreements and joint checks and fiancés and divorces and telephone calls and explosives and stripteases all jumbled together. And flowers and delivery men.

Flowers and delivery men.

I realized something. One of those in-plain-sight things that might even have slipped past a fictional detective.

I sat up straight, wide awake and thinking furiously, putting this new revelation into a proper perspective, easing it into the chronology.

It all fit.
I went over it again.
It still all fit.
I knew. Finally I knew.
And I swear that I heard Aphrodite chuckle and say,
" 'Bout damn time."

38

....

Afternoon of Atonement

I didn't have it all, of course.

There were still details that were fuzzy, timelines that didn't jive perfectly, and motivations that were a riddle inside a puzzle inside an enigma.

But I knew enough. And I knew what else I needed to know.

And I knew where to find the answers.

First I called directory assistance and got a number with a 918 area code. Then I called that number and asked for the managing superintendent. Her very existence answered my most important question. We chatted pleasantly for a little while and she was happy to answer my questions about rates and payments, staff, and most importantly, policies about personal leave.

Then I gathered up my courage and dialed a local number, one I knew by heart.

It was not yet four o'clock. Stu would be working at the Feed and Seed Store for another hour and a half, so I knew who would answer the phone.

"McKees' residence," Renee said tentatively, as though she should not be in that particular house, answering that particular phone.

"Uh, hello, Renee," I said tentatively, knowing that I would probably never dial that particular number again. "This is Tory Bauer."

The line was silent.

I plowed on. "I know this is awkward, but I need to ask you a question." So as not to let her think that I wanted to pry, I asked her what I needed to know about Saturday morning.

Her answer was the final confirmation of what I'd suspected.

I thanked her and hung up, profoundly embarrassed, and enormously relieved that this ordeal was nearly over.

I had harbored some pretty nasty suspicions about some fairly innocent people. Though I would much rather have taken a nap, or drunk large quantities of alcohol, or spent an hour at the library hashing it all over with Neil, I put on my coat and a pair of comfortable shoes, dug out some gloves, and ventured back into the cold to get the final answers.

And to do a little penance.

39

....

Astrological Notions and Small-Town Murder

Somewhere toward the beginning of this tale I mentioned the relevance of the Big Bang theory. The popularly accepted notion states that all the ingredients needed for the big explosion that created the entire universe were in existence, all in one place, right from the start.

It's an interesting idea. And I have come to realize that as with the origin of the universe, so it is, or at least it can be, with the origin of murder.

So I went back to the beginning.

Or as far back as I could, since a couple of the main players had already been taken out of the game plan.

The parking places in front of the post office and cafe were empty, so I assumed that the agents of the federal government had called it an afternoon. I had no doubt that they would return. In fact we would probably summon them shortly.

But for the time being they were not in evidence, and that was just as well because I had some questions I wanted answered, and I thought I'd get the answers more easily and honestly without any sort of *official* presence.

That Alanna and Brian were surprised to see me standing on their doorstep is an understatement.

"I should think you would be afraid to show your face here," Alanna said with traces of what was probably her original Okie accent, not the exaggeration she'd displayed the last few days.

"You're right. Courage isn't my strong suit," I said, shrugging. "But sometimes you gotta do what you gotta do."

"Who is it?" I heard Brian ask from the living room. He stepped into the kitchen to peek out the back door. "Oh, her," he said to his mother disgustedly. "Tell her to go away. We're busy."

Both were wearing everyday workclothes, and both were slightly disheveled and sweaty, as though they had been working feverishly.

"I'm sorry," Alanna said, looking over her shoulder anxiously, "we're in the middle of something and would rather not be disturbed."

By craning my neck, I was able to peek around the corner to see into the living room, where books lay open all over the floor and compact discs were scattered on the carpet. Every shelf was empty.

"That's all right," I said. "I know what you're looking for. And it's no longer necessary."

Alanna narrowed her eyes at me, and then glanced back at Brian for reassurance. Brian opened a book, quickly rifled through the pages, shook it upside down, and tossed it aside, and said nothing.

"I *know*," I said.

Alanna turned and walked back into the living room, pretending nonchalance. "And what exactly do you know?"

I followed her, carefully stepping over Neil's inheritance.

"I know you're not going to find what you're looking for in any of the books or behind the shelves or anywhere else in the house. So you can stop making excuses and box this stuff up for Neil's library," I said.

Well, actually, it was possible that Aphrodite *had* stashed more letters from Gus around her house. But the point was moot because I'd already gleaned the damning information from the one in my possession.

I held it up.

They both stopped what they were doing and stared at me.

"Gimme that," Alanna said sharply, grabbing the letter from my hand. "How did you get this?"

I didn't fight her for the letter because it didn't matter anymore. And besides, I already knew that Alanna could mop the floor with me.

"It's a long story," I said, "and I'll apologize a little later. But first, I have some questions."

Brian sat down on the couch, crossed one leg over the other, pushed up the sleeves of his sweatshirt, and said, "How about we play a game. You answer a couple of our questions, and we'll think about answering some of yours."

This was a show of bravado. Over the last few days, I had forgotten that Brian was still a very young man.

"All right," I said, moving a pile of books from a chair to the floor.

"Okay, then. You say you know; we'll leave it at that. What I want to know is," Brian asked. "What was the *big clue*?"

This was a challenge, another show of youthful bravado. A display of attitude, an indication that he thought I was all wet.

"The flowers," I said simply, sitting down.

Mother and son shot sideways glances at each other.

I continued. "Goods and supplies aren't delivered to Delphi on weekends. Shipments that are supposed to arrive on Saturday or Sunday are always delayed until Monday. People from bigger cities or more populated states don't realize how isolated we are here, that we

really do live in the boonies. Overnight does not mean
overnight in South Dakota. FedEx cannot guarantee
next-day air for us. There just isn't a big enough population base to make weekend deliveries profitable, so
we wait and we bitch about the inconvenience. We're
so used to it that even *we* forget sometimes.''

It had been the flower delivery guy himself who'd
reminded me at Aphrodite's memorial service that he
always had a backlog on Mondays.

"So the flowers came a day or two late," Alanna said
nervously. "What does that prove?"

"They were addressed to 'The Owner of the Delphi
Cafe.' On Monday I thought that meant me. On Monday
you did a huge production number about how the flowers were actually meant for you. And then you destroyed
both the note and the bouquet," I said to Alanna.
"Though you of all people should have known that there
wouldn't have been any relevant fingerprints on either
the flowers or the card. You panicked and overreacted
and drew my attention to the very thing you were trying
to cover up."

"And what was that?"

"That the flowers had been scheduled for delivery on
Saturday, and the owner of the cafe on Saturday was
Aphrodite Ferguson. The card was intended for her, not
me. The threat, if that's what it really was, was not intended for me either. No one ever threatened you,
though you knew that immediately."

"And you got all that from an anonymous card and
a bouquet?" Alanna asked.

"Well, I made a couple of phone calls," I said. "And
Neil Pascoe and I read a lot of old newspaper articles
from Rockville."

"How the hell did you know about Rockville?" Brian
asked, mouth open in surprise.

"Your mom handed out business cards almost the
minute you two arrived at the cafe. She gave us the
pertinent info, and all we had to do was call the chamber
of commerce in Rockville for the name of the newspaper."

"Well, that was pretty stupid, don't you think?" Brian asked his mother.

"Go easy on her," I said. "At the time, she didn't know that your grandfather was dead. There was no reason to hide your origins, no notion that anyone's history of working with explosives would be crucial."

Mother and son exchanged worried glances.

"I was nearly fooled by the fact that *your* father," I said to Brian, "works for a florist, but I finally realized that that was a coincidence. And then I thought that Norman Oberle might have had something to do with engineering the explosion because he'd worked with Gus in the old days. And because the poor man had the bad luck to be in financial difficulties at the moment and stood to collect a substantial insurance settlement with a double indemnity clause. But those were coincidences too."

I would forever feel guilty that I had suspected poor bereaved Norman of having any part in arranging Aphrodite's death.

"The two of you did a pretty good job of redirecting everyone's attention. Including the DCI," I said. "Such a good job that you inadvertently focused attention on yourselves." I paused for a moment, and then asked Brian, "Or was that so inadvertent?"

"What do you mean?" he asked nervously.

"Well, from what I can gather, this isn't the first time you covered up for the real culprit."

"Now wait a minute," Alanna said, trying to interrupt.

"No you wait a minute," I said to her harshly, "or do you want your son to go to jail again for a crime he didn't commit? He already served three years in a juvenile facility for an explosion that he didn't cause. I don't suppose that was a pleasant experience, but it's nothing compared to what will happen if he goes to prison, a real prison, on a murder charge."

I turned to Brian again. "This is no time to be noble. And there is no reason whatsoever for you to go to jail again to protect your grandfather."

Mother and son slumped.

"I know that Gus killed Aphrodite, and I know how and I know why and I can't allow an innocent person to take the blame."

40

....

The Loose Ends

In mystery novels, this is where the hero, having foolishly risked life and limb to subdue the miscreants,
stands around gloating for pages and pages of exposition, explaining to the reader exactly how the improba-
ble truth was discovered.

In this case, no one risked much of anything, but there
was still a measure of exposition needed because a couple of the near-miscreants had no notion of how I'd
come to discover that a dapper and charming elderly
man who had the bad luck, and worse timing, to die in
the bathroom at the cafe, had succeeded in ensuring that
he would never be anyone's ex-husband.

And I needed a couple of answers myself. Like why
Alanna and Brian went to such extraordinary lengths to
protect the reputation of a dead man.

"I knew that stupid fucking flashlight would come
back to haunt me," Brian said ruefully.

"Well, it pointed me, and unfortunately the DCI, in
your direction, that's for sure. And it's not our fault that

we didn't realize what you were really doing back there by Aphrodite's van," I said, with a small smile.

"I tried," Brian said sadly, looking at his mother. "Both of us tried to prevent what happened."

"It was your dad who called at the cafe, wasn't it?" I asked.

"Yeah, and Rhonda hung up on him because she thought it was a prank call. The story of my life," Brian/Michael Hunt said. "I was named after Robert Michael Hunt, whom my grandfather hated and refused to mention by name. So he called me Brian, and it was just easier if Mom called me Brian. But my dad refused to. To him I was always Mike."

I turned to Alanna. "Was your father's dislike the reason the marriage failed?"

She shrugged. "One of the many. But Bob was a good father, and he kept in contact with Brian, and with me."

"So even though you didn't get to take the call at the cafe, you knew who had called. And you knew that it was important," I said to Brian.

"Dad knew we were coming to Delphi to intercept Grandpa, and he knew we were going to the cafe. He would only have called us there in an emergency. But once we realized that Grandpa was dead and nothing terrible had happened, we figured we were home free. I mean beyond the fact that he was dead, which was bad enough. So I didn't even think about calling my dad back until that night."

Alanna added, "We were always on good terms, and Bob always did what he could to look out for us."

"Up to and including checking up on Gus occasionally in Tulsa. In the Prairie View Manor, right?"

"Right. He'd go over to the home and check in with the nurses and attendants, and let us know if he needed anything. Of course, he didn't visit Daddy personally, because just seeing Bob would set off one of his rages."

I told them that Norman Oberle had said that Gus Ferguson always was a "little intense." Norman had only known him during the early stages of his obsession, when his need to arrange and control his dear Cheryl's life had been odd but not frightening. Before it drove Aphrodite, and everyone except Cheryl and her son, away.

Before his own insanity forced his family to place a seemingly gentle and loving father in an upscale mental institution that bore the innocuous name of Prairie View Manor.

A private mental institution that charged a bundle for the care and restraint of the charming and outwardly docile Gus Ferguson.

Long-term care that had been financed by money from the Delphi Cafe. Of course, when Aphrodite signed that agreement guaranteeing Gus 50 percent of the profit from the cafe in exchange for his purchase of the business, she hadn't known that he was on a permanent downward spiral. She'd only known that his obsessions were more than he could handle, and that his daughter, even as young as she was, seemed to be a calming influence on him.

By the time his illness was readily apparent, Cheryl was almost grown and most of Aphrodite's money went toward medications and private nurses. By the time Cheryl's marriage had ended, and Brian had learned more than he ever needed about explosives and his grandfather's tendency to use them to make a point, his illness had necessitated institutionalization.

"You don't know what it is like living in a small town with a crazy relative," Alanna said.

I thought I could beg to differ on that point, but kept quiet.

"It was hard to keep him under control in the old days, and to put a good face on things. He'd already driven Bob away." Alanna looked at the ceiling, and then shot an embarrassed glance at her son. "I was seeing a man."

The high school principal, if I remembered correctly.

"And Daddy took an immediate dislike to him just because he was married."

"Fathers tend to react that way," I said simply.

"Well, they don't usually try to kill the guy," Alanna said.

"I was already having a hard time in school because of Grandpa's peculiarities," Brian added. "And Mom's profession."

Being the adolescent son of a stripper, especially in a small town, could not have been easy.

Brian continued, "And I took out my frustration on a few mailboxes and things. I was young and pretty stupid, and I didn't cover my tracks very well. They warned me after the first few times. That's what sent them after me when the car exploded."

"And it didn't occur to either of you to tell the truth? To turn Gus in?"

"No," they said together, aghast. "We could never turn in our own family."

Well, maybe I did understand their point.

"So you went into the juvenile home to protect your grandfather," I said to Brian.

He shrugged. "They never thought I was trying to kill the guy, only make a mess, so I wasn't treated like an attempted murderer or anything. It wasn't so long, and it wasn't so bad. And I learned to cook while I was there, and I ditched the accent. By the time I got out, Grandpa was in a place where we thought he'd be safe, and where they'd keep him under control."

"So much for assumptions," I said.

They'd assumed that Prairie View Manor's residents were kept under lock and key at all times. They'd assumed that the residents would have their outgoing mail monitored. They'd assumed that the expenditure of personal funds, especially the ordering of long-distance bouquets with cryptic messages that would be perfectly understood by the intended recipient, would not have been allowed.

They'd been wrong.

"Yeah. By Saturday night, I knew we were going to stay here"—he hesitated a bit, unsure of what to call her—"at Aphrodite's house. Of course she knew about Grandpa's escape by then, but we still didn't want her to know about our other worries. Especially since we thought he'd died before he could do any damage. And I spent most of the day with Rhonda." He grinned shyly, and then continued. "So it wasn't until that night that I took a minute and called my dad. From the bar."

"And that was when all hell broke loose," I said.

Brian and Alanna had thought that the worst was over with the death of Gus Ferguson.

We now knew that he'd had plenty of time to set the whole disaster in motion because that had been the question I'd asked Reneé McKee: Was the hitchhiker you picked up on Saturday an elderly, balding, charming man? And did you arrive in Delphi with him before nine A.M.?

The answers to both of those questions was yes. Reneé had added on her own that it was an uncharacteristic thing for her even to consider picking up hitchhikers, but coming back to Delphi itself was uncharacteristic, and he'd looked so old and tired, and completely harmless, that she never worried at all. She'd let him off, carrying a fairly heavy satchel, across the street from the cafe. And what with everything else going on, the subject of who he was never came up between her and Stu.

I wasn't surprised.

Brian continued. "On the phone, Dad said that he'd had bad news from Rockville, that someone had broken into Grandpa's old dynamite warehouse."

"We knew what that meant," Alanna said.

"So you created a diversion," I said, "so Brian could do a little reconnaissance."

And what a diversion it had been, though considering the fact that Alanna had been dressed in her Highland best when she arrived at the bar, I thought that she might have been planning to divert us in any case.

No one had noticed Brian's exit from the bar carrying Rhonda's big green flashlight. And no one would have seen him trying to check the exterior of the cafe, and the interior of Aphrodite's van for explosive riggings, if not for Presley and Mardelle's decision to blow up the Dumpster.

"I knew I'd dropped that stupid flashlight, but I couldn't go back for it," Brian said.

"And when the first small explosion went off behind the cafe, the one that Junior announced to everyone in the bar, you thought the worst had already happened," I said.

Alanna shrugged. "I grew up around explosions, and I knew that one couldn't have been very big or have done much damage. I was relieved that Daddy'd only set a small charge just to scare Aphrodite. And I figured that we were off the hook. So when everyone poured over to see what was going on, I thought it would look odd if I didn't go too."

Alanna had arrived behind the cafe just in time to see the efficacy of the device her father had attached to the ignition switch of Aphrodite's van. A van that had, just by the purest of coincidences, not been started between early Saturday morning and after midnight that night.

"I have a question," I said. "Why didn't you want Brian to talk to his father after the explosion? Why did he have to sneak out of the funeral to call him?"

They exchanged glances, clearly wondering how I knew about that. I'd explain later.

"I knew that the police would get around to investigating us sooner or later. It just seemed wiser not to have any traceable calls to a florist when those damn flowers had arrived with Dad's note."

It was just another piece of the cover-up that had begun the moment after the explosion, with Brian unobtrusively picking up the flashlight after it had been flung from my hand by the force of the explosion.

"One last question," I said. "Why did Aphrodite slap you at the school party?"

Alanna looked down at the littered floor. "The money from that old agreement never was enough to keep Dad in the home. Brian and I had to make up the difference so they wouldn't kick him out. We were horrified when Mama let us know that she wanted out of the agreement.

"I would have come to Delphi even if this mess with Dad hadn't happened, just to try to talk her out of it.

There was no way that Brian and I could ever have raised enough money on our own to keep Dad in Prairie View once we got him back to Oklahoma. When we got here, we all put on a good face for the town, and didn't discuss private stuff until later when we were alone.''

I had thought that their show of family solidarity rang false from the beginning.

''But by Saturday night, there was no longer a need to worry about financing Gus's care,'' I said.

''I was still so angry that I accused Aphrodite of abandoning Dad. I'd already done some stupid things to supplement the money going into Prairie View.''

I assumed she referred to the missing funds from her Moonstone Cafe in Rockville.

''And by trying to dissolve the agreement, she would also cut you off from your inheritance,'' I said.

''What I thought was my inheritance,'' Alanna said ruefully. ''I said some terrible things about you and the rest of this town.''

And Aphrodite, our unlikely knight in shining apron, had defended our honor.

Alanna continued, ''Of course, I didn't know that everything was already set in motion. That the will had already been changed. It was too late right from the beginning.''

She shrugged at me.

That's what I meant about the Big Bang—everything was there at the start.

''I know that you did what you could to protect your dead father's reputation, but you can't allow Brian to take the blame again,'' I said.

''No, I suppose not. Though we hadn't really thought of it in those terms.''

''Someone better call the police then,'' I said.

Brian sighed, and then got up and dialed the phone.

As Brian talked quietly to Agent Ingstad, I realized that Alanna had performed at least one piece of creditable acting. ''I really and truly believed that you hated Del on sight,'' I said with some admiration.

''Oh,'' Alanna said with an evil grin, ''that wasn't playacting.''

Epilogue

It was still daylight when I left Alanna and Brian await-
ing the arrival of Agent Ingstad and his merry men.

Even though it was out of my way, and my feet hurt,
I walked over to the cafe and stared at my reflection in
the big front window.

They like to say that things never change in small
towns, but things change all the time. Problem is, the
more they change, the more they say the same.

I would miss Aphrodite terribly. But eventually her
loss will become the new normal and life will go on as
it always had. We'll eat and laugh and work. And we'll
forget what it was like to hear her low-pitched laugh and
smell her terrible cigarette smoke.

Did Aphrodite have a premonition of her own death?
Was that the reason for the abrupt change in her personal
status quo? For the divorce proceedings, Norman's insurance policy, the change in the will? For paying off
my hospital bills?

I'm afraid that question will remain a mystery.

The other puzzler seemed easier to answer.

Had Aphrodite's spirit actually been here, still in Delphi three days after her death, expressly to help me to solve her murder?

It didn't seem likely.

Not a single clue discovered with her dubious *help* would have gone unnoticed for long. Agent Ingstad would have uncovered Gus's mental illness and his escape from Prairie View Manor. He would eventually have come to the same conclusions I had.

It was far more logical to assume that my own exhaustion, combined with wishful thinking, had produced Aphrodite's ghost because I was unwilling to let her go.

I was still unwilling to let her go. But it was time to learn how.

"You don't make it easy," I said out loud to the sky, which was cold, flat, and gray. "What am I going to do?" The tears rolled freely down my cheeks, this time for Aphrodite and not myself. "I didn't even get to say good-bye."

"Yes you did," she said behind me. "Hang in there, you'll be all right."

I whirled around, but of course no one was there.

And the burned-out cigarette butt with the red lipstick smears lying on the roadway could well have been there for weeks.

The faint whiff of smoke dissipated as the first snowflakes began to fall.

It took author KATHLEEN TAYLOR thirty-seven years to write the first Tory Bauer mystery. With practice she narrowed that time-frame down considerably and expects to spend less than a year completing the fifth book in the series. She has lived for a very long time in rural northeastern South Dakota with her enormously patient husband.